25 *and Under/Fiction*

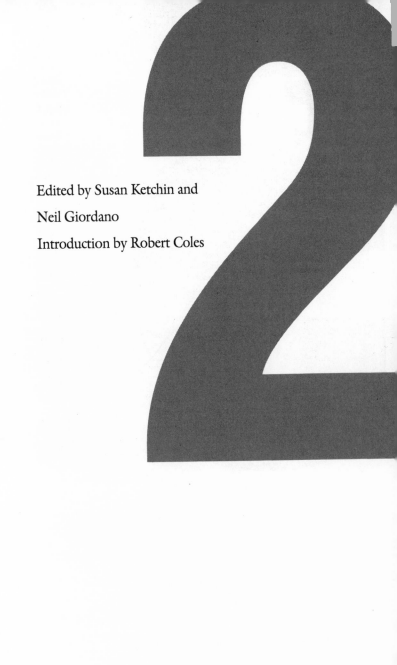

Edited by Susan Ketchin and

Neil Giordano

Introduction by Robert Coles

5

25 and Under/Fiction

969425

A DoubleTake Book

published by the Center for Documentary Studies

in association with

W. W. Norton & Company New York • London

The text of this book is composed in Carter & Cone Galliard with the display set in Helvetica Black Condensed. Manufacturing by Maple Vail. Book design by Richard Eckersley. Typesetting by Tseng Information Systems.

Library of Congress Cataloging-in-Publication Data appears at the back of this book.

W. W. Norton & Company, Inc., 500 Fifth Avenue, New York, New York 10110.

http://web.wwnorton.com

W. W. Norton & Company, Ltd., 10 Coptic Street, London WC1A 1PU

0 9 8 7 6 5 4 3 2 1

DoubleTake Books & Magazine publish the works of writers and photographers who seek to render the world as it is and as it might be, artists who recognize the power of narrative to communicate, reveal, and transform. These publications have been made possible by the generous support of the Lyndhurst Foundation.

DoubleTake, Center for Documentary Studies at Duke University, 1317 West Pettigrew Street, Durham, North Carolina 27705

http://www.duke.edu/doubletake/

To order books, call W. W. Norton at 1-800-233-4830.

To subscribe to *DoubleTake* magazine, call 1-800-234-0981, extension 5600.

This anthology is dedicated to the gift of story and to all storytellers who, for whatever untold reason, are unable to continue creating, and especially to the memory of Wade Edwards (1979–1996), a young writer.

ACKNOWLEDGMENTS

The editors would like to express our gratitude to the staff at the Center for Documentary Studies and *DoubleTake* magazine for
their invaluable contributions of time, insight, expertise, and encouragement during
the making of this book. In particular, we
would like to thank Liz Phillips, assistant to
the project as well as a manuscript reader, for
her boundless energy, skill, and good humor
in our search for new talent in fiction writing. The mailings and announcements she
developed and sent to an astonishing variety
of institutions and individuals enabled us to
gather and process hundreds of submissions
from writers of diverse cultural and educational backgrounds. ¶ We are especially in-
debted to the rest of our team of dedicated
and indefatigable readers—Ed Gerwig, Josh
Farrar, and Brad Kellam—for their careful
and thoughtful consideration of each sub-
mission. Our conferences were characterized
by lively, often impassioned discussions of
the stories and the writing process. Throughout the selection process it was clear that
these readers cared deeply about the stories,
and about the young writers, some of the
youngest of whom had submitted their first,
fledgling efforts. These individuals reviewed
submissions with clear judgment and an eye
toward the remarkable potential inherent in
each story. ¶ In addition, we would like to

acknowledge our gratitude to Robert Coles, Alex Harris, and Iris Tillman Hill for their ongoing interest in and enthusiasm for the project. Dr. Coles's belief in the nurturing of young talent has sustained and inspired the editors and readers on this project, just as it has the spirits of the many young writers he has worked with over the years. Alex Harris offered suggestions and ideas for this project, and sought out ideas from us for other books in the *DoubleTake* series; this kind of collaborative effort enhances each endeavor individually, we believe, and we are very grateful. Iris Tillman Hill's expert overseeing of this book and of the series as a whole has been encouraging and responsive and has made our jobs tremendously easier. ¶ We would like to thank Tabitha Griffin and W. W. Norton & Company for their commitment and belief in us, and in the value of young writers' contributions to literature and to society. We are grateful to them for the opportunity to bring the work of some of the nation's most talented young writers to the widest possible audience. ¶ Finally, we express our deepest gratitude to all the writers who bravely worked to create and submit their best efforts to scrutiny by strangers, and to all the writing teachers and friends who supported their efforts. We hope that they know, even if their work does not appear in these pages, that their voices and visions are important, not only to us, but to our future as a society.

CONTENTS

25 *and Under/Fiction*

INTRODUCTION

ROBERT COLES

The conventional wisdom about wisdom—the time of its arrival in our lives—has such a moral and psychological achievement coming toward the end of our time here: an earned introspective knowledge that is the weather of many years of trial and error. Young people are often called naive, if not callow; men and women in their thirties are frantically on the make, are fiercely competitive; those in their forties and early fifties struggle with shifting loyalties and obligations, and often enough are susceptible to nervous collapse—the notorious "change of life" syndrome, wherein hair dye and plastic surgery and clothes conspire to delude the middle-aged that they will succeed where Ponce de León failed. But by our sixth or seventh decade we are supposed to have settled into this life, figured out its rhythms, come to understand its inevitable ups and downs, earned a proper skepticism and humility, not to mention humor, an appreciation of the various ironies, complexities, paradoxes that hover over us, haunt us, and sometimes hound us to the very edge of distraction and worse. Therein the great virtue of wisdom—a spiritual kind of knowledge, an awareness of the fatefulness of things, the luck, good and bad, that awaits us, the contingencies that have a way of making a mockery of the smug, prideful side of ourselves, with its inclination to self-importance, to a sad kind of self-centeredness that is unmindful of history's lessons. Once older, we are supposed to take note of those lessons—to some extent, surely, because we have lived through a few of them, watched high hopes come crashing down, noted the difference between big-shot expectations and the hugely demanding cost, not rarely, even of small changes in our social or political order.

Of course, a certain kind of suddenly chastened youth can sometimes be granted a waiver—be dubbed precociously thoughtful and reflective, often a consequence of a tragedy in which he or she has participated, and from which big lessons have, alas, been learned. In that regard, I well remember the compliments extended some of the civil rights activists, as they came to realize, in the company of Dr. Martin Luther King, Jr., while in Cicero, Illinois, and elsewhere, the limits of a certain struggle—they had stumbled upon the inevitable obstacles, finally, that life has a way of presenting to us, and if they were now frustrated and saddened, they were also "newly educated," one finger-wagging journalist informed them. He went on to amplify, tell his readers and the people of whom he wrote that youth heretofore "stubbornly challenging to the status quo" had now become "sensitive" to the difficulties that block all sweeping efforts at reform—with the result that "wisdom" had befallen the "heretofore rash." For most of us, though, it is a matter of waiting long enough, living through enough trials, errors, impasses—so that time will bring the exquisite kind of awareness, the sense of proportion and balance, the wry detachment that comes with lots of experience, with disappointments encountered, losses sustained.

The above notion—that of a wisdom only gradually obtained in the course of a life—seemed increasingly dubious as I absorbed one, then another story in the collection that follows. Here, after all, are a group of quite young Americans, none of them older then twenty-five, who are just starting out as writers of fiction, and who surely have much to learn about a particular craft, not to mention the subject matter of that craft, which in the broadest sense of the word is "life," all that it has to tell us. Perhaps these are a specially gifted group—their stories have withstood the determined winnowing of many readers, who (no doubt) as they tossed aside one, then another effort, have thought about youth and its innocence, if not gullibility, even its capacity for self-indulgence, for the unearned emotion that is sentiment. Still, here are youths all right—and what they have to show us for their early struggles as writers of short fiction will have our close, grateful interest, entertain us, give us emotional and moral pause, and not least, prompt us to take another look at the assumptions about wisdom (who has it, and why) that I have just mentioned.

These are, in their sum, wisely knowing stories—some of them startlingly so. I have in mind "Manna Walking" or "Flamingo"—here are mothers who are bravely introspective enough, independently *themselves* enough, to stand apart from the respective "cultures" to which they belong: the Navajo one, and the medical one that so many of us don't even know to recognize for its demanding assumptions. I have in mind another mother, and her husband, who appear in "Naming the Baby"—again, the resourceful insistence of a writer that her characters be vulnerable, untutored (as any young pair of parents will inevitably be), yet wonderfully shrewd and sensitive about family life. Here is a young married couple who need none of our dreary instructional manuals, which are prepared to tell us anything and everything about—anything and everything. All they have is their creator's poignant, intelligent charm—in the non-superficial sense of that word: a delightfully determined engagement with their new life, whose importance they do not underestimate, even as they are loath to exaggerate their own worth, their particular situation. A quiet, amusing shrewdness, a poised perspective about what this life offers us as beginning parents, radiates through this story—makes us its grateful recipients no matter our age or experience. Yet another mother makes an appearance in this collection—but now, in "Waiting Game," we are at the edge of American surrealism: a parent in pursuit of a game show appearance, and with it, the kind of singular worth and renown millions of us have learned to covet.

Other stories also challenge so-called reality—and are no less beguiling and funny. "Borges Rides the Cyclone," for instance, which surely the great master himself, somewhere in this universe, is noting with some pleasurable interest. Our game shows, our roller coasters—they offer us a chance to shake our fists at this life's frustrating constraints: to spring free of gravity and poverty, to live it up as household gods of sorts for a few minutes before we return to the beaten paths of day work, the forgotten dreams that stir us to those anxious awakenings that finish off the night.

If Borges would smile at his New York visit, he'd smile even more at "The Dog Lover," recognize a morally energetic storyteller for the great promise that awaits him. This is a story that many readers will remember for years—the first one they've read of a writer whose work, surely, will command our intense, persistent interest. A similar moral energy courses through "Indian Summer Sunday"—yet another New England minister struggles mightily with his faith as he tries to prepare words meant to help others with their faith. Some of us, of course, may find a good deal of hope in this minister's Saturday-night trial—a boozy spell of doubt, despair evidence aplenty that a soul is not taking too much for granted. In a quiet but powerful way this story connects today's readers with those who heard the Puritan divines of an earlier New England—faith is nearest us when we are closest to throwing it aside. Surely a few theologians twice or three times twenty-five would marvel at the ease with which a mere youth, trying his hand at short fiction, can pose the riddle of God's grace as it presses upon us at the most unlikely times and places. But then, the Bible is hardly a repository of abstract argument, disquisition; rather, we move in Holy Scripture from tale to tale—and good readers that we try to be, those narrative moments stick fast to us, become signposts in our journey from late Saturday night to late Saturday night.

In "Geese" and in "Untitled" we leave the United States for Japan and Australia, glimpse in those countries no escape from life's various burdens, be they spiritual or material. In a way, Australia brings to mind one kind of American frontier, Japan another. The raw desperation of earlier years is more than matched by today's tenacious self-consciousness—fear is the constant presence, though: fear of being wasted, down and out, with no prospects, or fear of being left out of things, forsaken in the urgent rush of others for success, for social significance, acceptance.

Meanwhile, back at home the "park bench" continues to offer writers a place where they can help their characters begin their search for love—its public privacy part of our long populist legend. So, too, with the Mississippi River, which waters our heartland—we can't get much closer to ourselves, our history, than by recalling it, bringing it yet again to life, as happens in "This Is Not a Joke Like Vietnam." If Borges is with us in New York, Mark Twain is rubbing his eyes (apprehensively, maybe) in this startling evocation of "life along the river." Little did Huck and Jim know what would one day come to pass, a century down the line, on that river. We are reaching the point in this country that a future Conrad will find a trip to the Midwest as precisely the moral destination required for the toughest look possible at the West's "heart of darkness."

In that regard, three excursions worthy of the Anglo-Polish master take place here—efforts to render aspects of a late-twentieth-century American "social scene": "White Flight," with its reminder of the price our children pay for our various failures; "Like a Crossing Guard"—another evocation of race in all its provocative capacity to make us strangers to one another, whatever the reasons for us to link arms in understanding, forgiveness; and "Asylum," whose haunting, unnerving, powerfully compelling voice renders our hope for direction and purpose in life. The central paradox of an "asylum" as a place where someone's convincing pursuit of meaning, of articulated moral energy, can take place relatively unhindered is, naturally, a wry play on a word spacious in its possibilities.

Here, then, is young wisdom unashamedly at work—descending upon us with fictions that hint of, forecast, another century's, another millennium's, substantial achievement. These are assured, capable voices, able to achieve control over the mother tongue—but they are also voices of good sense, of humor, of moral seriousness, of high imagination, of great force, of commanding or suggestive authority. If this is what these men and women can give us when they have yet to turn twenty-five, we can only speculate on what will be forthcoming from them in twenty-five years or fifty—a great collective boost to American storytelling, a time of new heights for our imaginative writers as they eye us, tell of us, give their readers a chance to catch sight of themselves in the uniquely particular, probing manner a short story enables.

THE DOG LOVER

JASON BROWN

Give not that which is holy unto the dogs.

—Matthew 7:6

Today my father's playing golf. Not the kind of golf you play on grass but the kind of golf you play in the mind. A blind man's game. He tees off at 12:30, wanders around the house following the same path between tables and chairs, the number of steps between objects memorized, and finishes the eighteenth hole in the kitchen next to the refrigerator at seven over par. I hear his slippers scraping along the hardwood floors, pausing every few seconds for his mind to line up a drive or a putt. Longer pauses indicate rare trouble: the woods maybe or a sand bunker.

Waiting for him to finish his golf this morning, the one day I visit him each week, I reach down into my bag and pull out a small manual on raising dogs. In my spare time or in the moments before sleep, I think about dogs. One day I would like to raise them professionally. Lexi, the collie that my father gave to me several years ago, wanders into the living room from the kitchen, presses her nose against my thigh, and slowly lowers her hindquarters at my feet. She closes her eyes, but she does not sleep. The growth which originally caused pressure in her neck has spread pain throughout her entire body by now. Her breaths are more like gasps and her chest quivers in anticipation of a relief that does not come. I reach into my pocket and pull out the thermometer. Seven weeks since conception and her stomach has started to bald. She hasn't eaten much of her food the past few days. It's a race between the puppies growing in her stomach and the disease growing in her body. My father's right—if it were not for the puppies, we would have put her to sleep long ago.

When her temperature dips below one hundred degrees, it's time for the birth, but I should put the thermometer away, because we are far from that time. I go over the procedure in my head, just in case it does happen early. In the foyer outside my kitchen, the whelping box is readied with layered newspapers and an old blanket. The puppies should come in half-hour intervals. Lexi should do most of the work if she can handle it. Even if she lives to the birthing time, she may die before the pups come out. I'm there to cut the cords, clean up the mess, and make sure none of the puppies get jammed. Old-timers suggest evaporated milk, corn syrup, and egg yolks as a supplement to mother's milk. Watch for puppies scratching the mother. Feed them at three months. Wean at five. If she doesn't live or she is not strong enough, the vet can cut her open and free the puppies that way, but then they would not have their mother.

Lexi wanders away from my hand. I hear his slippers. Her toenails click down the hall and pause where she finds my father. The scraping stops almost immediately after the clicking stops. "Weight shifts to the inside foot," my father says as if he were making it happen. His body never moves during a swing. "Head still. The arms and hands roll over. Right elbow folds under and points to the ground. Shift weight left. Unwind. Swing through. Head still. Then look."

Sometimes on Sunday afternoons over tea, my father and I argue quietly about dogs—their function and how they should be raised. When I was young and since then, we have always had dogs. I am full of theory; he is full of experience. My father would say that a dog is a voucher for one human life, nothing more. If you're not careful when training a dog, he would say, he will grow to believe what you believe, fear what you fear. Then he is of no use to you. When properly trained, a dog will ignore what he knows to be true in order to please you. He will go where you are afraid to go. This is what my father would say.

When they found a tunnel, my father sent the tunnel dog down first. They were never allowed to blow the tunnels up until they first searched for prisoners, maps, battle plans, or caches of weapons. Using dogs was apparently my father's idea for saving men. The dog was trained to detect the presence of living humans and return through another entrance to the Vietcong's underground complex. It had to be a small dog in order to maneuver well in the narrow tunnels that were often too small for many to pass through. If the dog returned and barked twice, my father or someone else would go down through the tunnel with a flashlight and a .45. If the dog didn't return, sometimes they'd blow the tunnel up against orders, and sometimes my father would have to go down and see anyway. In 1968 he lost thirty-five dogs, but he saved thirty-five men.

My father's slippers scrape down the hall to the living room, where he pauses in the gray light. Lexi stops behind him, feebly raising her head to the back of his legs. He turns to me and sits down in the rocking chair. He purses his lips and hangs his hand off the end of the armrest. Lexi nestles her nose into his fingers, which run over her snout as she walks forward. She pauses where his hand sits on the back of her neck.

"I don't think we should wait any longer," he says.

"What do you mean?" I pretend not to know what he's talking about.

He reaches into his robe and pulls out the old, tarnished military-issue .45. He points it, butt first, at my hand. "Do you want to do it, or do you want me to do it?"

"I see no reason," I reply.

"Do you see this dog?" he raises his voice, the gun still held out in front of him. "It is already dead. Do you understand?"

"There are the puppies," I say.

He pulls the gun back into his lap and tilts his head toward the front window. "Don't make her suffer—she will not live to have those dogs."

"She might," I say.

"You know that's not true," he says. "And even if she were to, they would die without the mother."

"I will raise them myself," I say.

"Don't be ridiculous," he yells and stands up. "You're not a dog. You have no idea what you're doing." He pauses then, turns away from me and back once more. "It is God's will that life be taken away," he says.

"I've been reading about raising these dogs," I say weakly, thinking of the vet's prediction that Lexi would not live another three weeks, while there are at least six weeks until the puppies could be born.

My father turns his back to me and slips the gun back in his pocket. Lexi watches his every move. "It's your dog," he says and starts back down the hall. I lean forward to put my hand behind Lexi's ears, but she stands up and follows my father. She was his dog before she was mine.

In 1968 my father was the golf champion of Qua Trang Province, but now he works over in the basement of City Hall selling Mars bars to people overdue on their parking violations and what not. When I used to work down on Middle Street selling vacation packages to places I couldn't afford to visit, we would have lunch together twice a week at the Front Street Deli.

Things are different these days. I used to be a travel agent, then I worked in a lab and now I am looking for work. When I was very young my father and I would go fishing north of the paper mills, but I can hardly remember those times; he is hardly the person I would want to remember. We used to attend church twice a week. Over the years, even while my mother was alive, I stopped attending church, while he believed all the more. Since my mother's death he no longer believes but still goes to church two, sometimes three, times a week, while I will never set foot in church again.

We studied the Bible every night after he had returned from the war when I was seven. My mother, my father, and I would sit around a table. After the war, my father always read with his eyes shut, his thick, dark fingers dancing over the oversized Braille Bible he'd been given at the army hospital after he was wounded. We read it together, cover to cover, several times, but by the time I could even partially understand what was being said, my father had decided to keep us focused on Job. He cited the price of rent and groceries, the number of murders in our neighborhood, and what he called world economic downturn as examples of the inevitable return of Christ.

He cited Job's corruption as an example of why Christ would have to return. At night I lay awake in bed picturing Christ wearing a robe and sandals, the blood still pouring from his hands and feet, picking up my friends from the neighborhood and tearing off their limbs. When I finally did fall asleep I often had a dream about walking along a sidewalk in front of our house when suddenly the ground would give out beneath me and I would be plunged into a volcano of fire. I would wake screaming and would continue screaming until my mother came running down the hall and placed her cool hand across my forehead.

Every Sunday I kneeled and ate of the body of Christ, the man who would come for me, and then I drank of his blood for reasons I could not understand. With the wafer sitting under my tongue, I looked up at the cross and the sculpture of his naked, starved, and bleeding body. I could only assume that I had been somehow responsible for the suffering of this great man, and that someday he would make me pay. I did not understand then that it was God that made him pay.

One Sunday morning as I knelt with the wafer in my mouth waiting for the cracked and dried hands to pass with the silver chalice, I sealed my lips shut. When the chalice paused before me, I stared straight ahead at the pulpit and would not open my mouth. The chalice waited for a second, the wine poised on the edge, until the hands moved on. Without realizing it, I had decided that I would no longer kneel before a man to whom I had done nothing, who would punish me no matter what I did. The next week when my father woke me for church, I told him that I would not go.

"Are you sick?" he asked, staring directly at me even though he could not see. In Vietnam, he had once told me, they had learned on night patrol to see with their ears. I could hear my mother shuffling back and forth downstairs. "You don't sound sick."

"I'm not sick. I'm just not going anymore."

"You're going," he replied and left the room. He returned a few minutes later and grabbed my arm, pulling lightly. "Come on," he asked politely—something he had never, to my knowledge, done before. I dug my fingers into the side of the bed. He turned around and faced the door. Then he flipped suddenly around again, grabbed my leg, and hauled me off the bed. The back of my head crashed against the floor, but I would not stand.

"Stand up!" he screamed at me.

"I'm not going," I said.

"You're going!" he screamed, reaching down for my arm and yanking me to my feet.

"I'm not going—ever again!" I screamed at his face. Very suddenly and without warning, he squared off and slapped me in the face. He was accurate even without being able to see. I suppose the military had trained him for that. I fell to the floor and could not open my eyes or think straight. By the time I was able to walk downstairs, he and my mother had gone off to church. We never talked about it again, I never attended church again. We stopped the nightly readings from the Bible. Whatever thoughts he had about the end of the world were kept inside his head, which was fine with me.

Over the years I reread Job on my own dozens of times and carefully considered the pronouncements my father had made. At one point, sometime in my teens, long after my mother's death, I sat down with him and tried to present my case.

"First of all," I remember saying to my father that morning, "what is Job's sin?"

"What are you talking about?" my father asked, his breakfast half finished. I did not know that he no longer believed the things he had told me when I was seven.

"This is what God Himself says about Job in the beginning: 'Hast thou considered my servant Job, that there is none like him in the earth, a perfect and upright man, one that feareth God, and escheweth evil?' That there is none like him."

My father held his fork next to his plate of half-finished eggs.

"There is no one more innocent than Job, so what was his sin? That he questioned a God who was tricked by Satan into punishing him—that was his only crime."

My father stood up, put his plate in the sink, and returned to his bedroom. I heard the door click shut and the radio chatter. I sat at the table and continued my argument, sure, at the time, that his exit signaled defiance. It seemed important for me to finish.

"God's defense is no better than the ramblings of Job's friends. They all offer the same excuse, even though God claims that his answer is different. And I tell you what," I said, "Job knows this. He doesn't say so in the end, but he does. It's obvious." I had been waiting for more than seven years to possess the language and understanding to defend that morning I had refused to drink the wine from the chalice. When I finally finished my speech, I took up my Bible and returned to the living room, knowing full well that my defense had not been enough.

My father takes five steps down the hall, turns, and takes four steps into his bedroom. On days when he works, he takes fifty-seven strides to the bus stop (ten to the sidewalk, forty-seven straight to the left down the walk). Off the bus there are ninety-three steps to City Hall. Seventy-nine strides to the front entrance and then twenty-two stairs. He reverses this procedure to return home. Then on Saturdays and on certain days off he pauses at three o'clock to count his knives and also his spoons. On average he washes his face from four to six times a day. Groceries and supplies are delivered.

Sometimes before bed, I walk by my father's house and stand across the street. At 10:25 I can see him walking along the perimeter of each room, touching the table and chair my grandfather made in his shop. He turns the lights off, and on moonlit nights I can see his outline making steady headway down the hall into the windowless, pitch-dark center of the house.

At night when I am at my own home I think mostly about dogs. From books I know that the ideal collie stands twenty-two to twenty-six inches tall at the shoulder, weighs seventy-five pounds, and has a majestic air that borders on aloofness. To achieve this every collie should be on a regular feeding schedule and kept just a little bit hungry at all times. But there is much more, like frequent nail clipping and occasional bathing. Training ultimately depends on how intelligent you are and how intelligent your dog is. Think as your dog thinks, and he will understand you. The most important words in your dog's vocabulary: heel, sit, come, stay. When giving these commands use the shortest phrase and use the same word with the same meaning at all times.

Short, frequent lessons work better. Train before breakfast, then your dog assumes that the meal is a reward. You may teach him the lying-down maneuver, you may teach him the envied trick of staying parked outside a store for hours, only budging for you, but remember that collies have a natural tendency to chase anything that moves. Once the dog is allowed to practice this habit, it may be very difficult to break your collie of it. Any dog may run away, but a good dog will return home. If nobody's there, he will wait.

My father follows the wall to the foyer table, over to the counter, and back into the kitchen. After a few moments he starts down the hall toward me. Lexi follows right behind. "I got stuck in the rough on the eighth. Had to draw it out," he says. "People think they know how to play golf, but they have no idea." Lexi presses her nose against my leg, nudging me until I take her head in my hand and start stroking behind her ears.

"The first thing," he says, "once you have your clubs, is to choose your grip. The Vardon grip," he says, his hands wrapped around air. "Or the interlocking grip." The fingers mingle together. "Or the baseball grip, not used much anymore. If you don't know what club to use or what grip to take, wait and it will come to you. The other thing people don't know," he says, "is that you should never move your head. Keep your head steady at all times. If your head isn't steady, the ball will not know where you want it to go."

I nod my head.

Lexi jolts, her ears stand up, and she walks cautiously to the front door. She looks out the window. A dog senses out there what we can only guess at. I think back over what I've been reading about dogs and I look at my dog and think: What a dog stands on is more like a foot than a paw. The metatarsal bones may fall short in length, but, as with humans, the tibia falls into the tarsal bones, and the phalanges reach forward into the next step, curling into the earth for support. She turns her head back to look at me. Sometimes when I am too afraid, I remind myself of all the dogs' lives in her, and how they depend on what I do.

To raise happy dogs, in my opinion, it is important to be happy, and I have considered many forms of happiness. On certain days off, I take out an hour to sit on the edge of my roof looking down the hill toward where Broadway turns into Fort Williams Avenue. From there, I can see almost everything that people do. I think I have come to understand that most people's lives are no larger than my own.

My father reaches over to his left and pulls one of his pipes down from its cradle. He pulls a brown leather pouch out of his pants pocket and digs out some of the earthen material. He packs it in with his thumb, lights a match, holds it atop the pipe with his thumb and forefinger and takes quick puffs until the smoke bellows out of his mouth.

Before bed each night, he sits in his chair smoking his pipe and listening to 93.7 FM. He has one pipe for each day and a spare one in case of accidents. Only on days off does he smoke it during daylight hours. Today the pipe lights but then goes out. He takes it out of his mouth, holds it in front of his face, then places it back in the cradle.

After a long silence, my father picks up one of Lexi's paws and runs his hand along the bones, then along the front leg, then along the flank. I stare into his blank, circled eyes. A couple of years after he returned from Vietnam my father shot our family dog. I was nine at the time, the dog thirteen. One morning I found my father in the living room, his body wrapped around the dog's body. My father's chest heaved and his arms and legs seemed to tremble as he clenched his blind eyes shut and bared his teeth in the kind of grief that looks like rage. At nine I could not understand as he led the dog I had known for my entire life outside into the backyard, held a gun to the side of her head, and blew her brains all over the back lawn. Over time I have come to understand a part of what he knows, but at that moment I flew out the door into the yard screaming and throwing my fists at him, who thought he had been alone. He held my arms to the sides of my body until I calmed, and then he tried to explain that the dog had become old and ready to die. I did not know then and do not know now how he decided this. And looking at the circles under his eyes, I think there may be things I know about despair that even he does not understand. The nature of the blackness that creeps into the mind and body from some unknown source is that it stays precisely as long as you can take it and then leaves suddenly, but with a promise of return visits. Many people who can take the blackness itself are killed by the promise of its return. The smallest details, daylight and the pipe in its cradle, become intolerable in anticipation of that darkness returning. And when I say despair will stay just as long as you can take it, that threshold is only seen in retrospect. At the time, you ask yourself every minute how much longer you can go on, and some people are never able to find out.

From his letters to my mother I know that golf ended for my father on October 5, 1968, when he left the rear base of Da Nang and headed for a small firebase somewhere in Qua Trang Province, the northern tip of South Vietnam. No one played golf because everyone lived underground. He hid beneath sandbags in the one-square-mile base. He was ten days into an attack by the Vietcong, who had completely surrounded them. He would go for ten more days before seeing the sun, and each night as part of the recon-ranger team he would lead a patrol to locate the position of the enemy. Then on January 3, 1969, he lost one of his dogs down a tunnel. The dog went down, according to his letter to my mother, and they waited for ten minutes but nothing happened. He had the choice of sending someone down who had never been before or going down himself, so he went. He wore a T-shirt, pants, and boots, carried a .45, a knife, and a small flashlight. After dropping down, he crawled along a horizontal corridor, no more than three feet high, measuring the distance traveled in his mind, until he reached an intersection. He paused before it, shining the flashlight all around, checking for prints, human or canine, in the dirt, and then he just listened for a while. He heard nothing, so he moved forward. When he had reached the very edge of the intersection, there was a scuffle to his right. He aimed the .45, but it was too late. The man had his hand on the pistol and was pulling it toward him. My father pushed back the other way, but the other man was stronger, and the gun was pressed sideways against my father's face when it went off. It blinded him, but it killed the other man. If the other man had not been killed, my father would have been.

My father leans down again, running his hand along Lexi's flank. "What is it you would do with all these small dogs?"

"Give them away."

He nods. "I'm very tired," he says.

I nod. He rises, walks three steps to the edge of the room, fifteen down the hall, three into his bedroom, and then closes the door. In a few moments he will be asleep. It's dark now, Lexi's eyes closed at my feet, and the lights up and down the lane are starting to move from the first floors of people's houses to the upstairs bedrooms.

I was the kind of person who promised people anything and gave them what they got. It often occurs to me at night that I have not been a person in whom people have recognized a great deal of potential. I listen to classical music on the radio but don't remember the names of the composers. I wear nice shoes. Nine times out of ten, for me, happiness amounts to the interval between the absence of pain and the onset of boredom. In that sense I'm like everyone else, I suppose. I could say that today is the first day of the rest of my life and start anew, but I have said that countless times before.

These last three years since I have been clean, when I have gone out for coffee and a movie, sometimes I giggle, sometimes I'm morose. I laugh hysterically during the scenes when people's limbs are ripped off. When I dance to the radio in my bedroom my feet jut out and back, and my hands move over my thighs like crabs. I occasionally wear a cowboy hat in private and once every month or so smoke cigars. I worry that there might be someone like me out there thinking the things that I think.

I live alone in a one-story house at the end of a long street, and it has been the nature of my moodiness after work to walk through the empty bedrooms at night. It occurred to me in one of those rooms that I am not someone whose belief amounts to much. I have been able to see few miracles. I'm unemployed now, but in my last job I worked in a lab, and by and large miracles were not a part of my experience. With the little formal education that I have, I worked my way from the packing department, sending off test tubes, to a kind of low-grade, lab-coat-wearing technician with no real responsibility. After work I would rush home because Lexi would have been inside all day. I would feed the dog. After walking her at night I'd thank God and climb into bed.

I have been anxious and troubled, yet curious. As a former lab technician, I recognize in the world around me a certain degree of order that suggests an even greater degree of order that has not been explained and will never entirely be explained. Don't misunderstand me. I have not been a party to such burning bush experiences as eventually draw people out there to California. The job of the mystic and the job of the scientist are nearly the same. By scientist I don't mean people like myself, who are the clergy of numbers, but the scientist to whom nothing seems adequately explained, who tears down and rebuilds our concept of the universe.

Any fool can see that God is not just, or if He is, then we are talking about a kind of justice which would make it impossible for many of us to live in the world. If God is love, as I would like to believe, then God is blind, unthinking, and vengeful—untrustworthy and jealous. Maybe it is our responsibility to forgive God. We are the ones, it seems to me, who must act with grace, turn away from our enemies, bury lust in the pit of the stomach, carry hope to each other like salesmen, door to door, and in the end be grateful.

What if Christ lied to us up until the last moments of his life? "What manner of man is this, that even the wind and the sea obey him?" asked his disciples. Only someone who knew the ugly truth about God could have created a lie that humanity would believe. Knowing that he would be punished, Christ still called out, "My God, my God, why hast thou forsaken me?" The answer is unacceptable, which is why even Christ had to lie to himself in order to live his life. The cry, let out moments before his father had mercy and released him from the world, was itself a relinquishing of the lie. I do not deny that Christ's power comes from God's Love; the secret is that God became jealous of his son. For Christ practiced Love with the kind of grace, justice, and humility that God has been able to exhibit only sporadically and without resolve. As Christ found, the price of defying the father is always self-destruction.

At night when Lexi and I would walk before she became too weak, I would try to follow the path that her nose takes along the streets that wind downtown from my neighborhood. She seems to be led by the odors that other dogs have left behind and by the odors of other animals, cats and mice. Even though she is sick now, when she can hear their little feet in the bushes, every muscle yanks against the leash. City dogs live, by necessity, like prisoners. Because I feed her every day, the purpose of our walking ritual is the ritual itself, and it does not seem to bother her that the tugs against the leash are merely token protests. You cannot curb a millennium of instinctual behavior by explaining that plenty of dog food will be provided, that she does not need to catch her own food.

Every morning I ask for God's help and I wait but there is no answer. I listen throughout the day, but no answer comes. It has occurred to me that of the people who ask for God's help, most receive no answer that they can understand. I may not know how to listen. So I try harder, asking down on my knees that my life be blessed with the kind of love that does not destroy, and yet I have no faith in my ability to tell the difference between one kind of love and another. The most important thing I do each day is feed the dog and the dogs' lives lying in Lexi's stomach. When I rise in the morning and late at night, when I am trapped in my own thoughts, this is the only truth I know. I know that the kind of love that carries me home to my dog is the kind of love I hope for God. Love without desire.

When I was lying in detox in a New York hospital, my father sat by my side for the thirty hours it took me to regain consciousness; and when I woke he leaned over my ear and asked: "Are you awake?" I nodded my head. "Lay down your weapons," he told me, "and ask for God's help." I did. I asked for God's help, but I could not lay my weapons down because I did not know what that meant. From the moment, however, after I declared on my knees that I did not know the first thing about how to live, my life seemed to take on a certain clarity. For the six months in the hospital and for several years afterward, the path out of my previous life seemed clear. And for that I thanked God every night. I have no idea why my father was able to make that one trip on the bus to see me in New York, why he managed to do one day what he had not been able to do for the previous eight years and has not done in the years since. But I do understand that he could ask me to place my life in the hands of a God that he himself no longer trusted, because in the end it only mattered if I believed what he was saying, which I did.

More recently, before breakfast after I wake, during the day, in my sleep, and in the half-waking moments throughout the night, I obsess about the needles, the smell of the stuff and the places where I did it and the people I called my friends; but I can imagine, in my dreams, the feeling I always chased but never found. Almost all my ideas are bad ones.

When Lexi and I walk these days when she is feeling stronger, I find myself taking her along the western prom where I used to live before moving to New York, where I know some of my old friends are living the life I have been able to renounce. She walks more slowly every day. Last night we paused at the West End Park. Though a dog, in my opinion, has no sense of beauty, except insofar as her own actions are beautiful to us, Lexi sat staring out at the sunset which spread like a fire across the watery horizon. My eyes were trained down on the park where a group of people stood huddled around each other in the shadows of a hundred-year-old oak tree. When I rose this morning, rolled over on my knees, and spoke to God, my mind was still trained on those people down in the park. I can define myself by little else than the object of their desire. Though I try to spend my days thinking of nothing but walking Lexi, I become exhausted.

In August of my tenth year my mother took her own life with one of my father's guns. It seems that all the events of my life, both before and after, have been moving away from and back toward that August morning. Many years after her death, waking up in the hospital in New York, I realized I had traveled full circle and come to know the kind of isolation and confusion that my mother had known and could no longer bear. By way of explaining the outrage I felt in that hospital I could tell you about the months leading up to her death, the sitting with her at the kitchen table, listening to her delusional talk about the neighbors spying on her, people plotting to kill her. I watched her pull down the blinds and hide, sobbing, under the kitchen table. I have gone over my nine-year-old's arguments a countless number of times, but I have never decided what I could have said to contend with her false beliefs. I have since come to understand that delusions contain within them the kind of love that allows us to live, even if those delusions eventually kill us. By this I think I mean that it is necessary not only to lie but to believe the lie.

I'll tell you the kind of love story that I believe. I was five years old and I hated nursery school. My mother hated taking me there. On the playground and in the classroom I spoke to no one. I know these things from what has since been told to me about myself. What I do actually remember is walking along the edge of the playground, kicking stones near the mesh fence. I leaned down to pick up a stone—I can see it now, a mixture of vanilla white and crystal. At that moment the recess bell rang, and I started to run for the building with the stone in my pocket. I felt suddenly full of power. At the end of the day, lying in bed, I handed the stone to my mother. She turned it around, held it up to the bed light. She placed it in her pocket, shut the light off and vanished into the dark hallway.

Every day now I am running across the field, identical to all the other kids except for the secret I carry in my pocket, and I wait through the rest of school and arrive home but no one is there. If there were someone there, she would not understand. She would say, "What is this?" And I would have to say, "You're right. I am too late." I do not know whether I am eight or twenty-eight.

While I descended the stairs and walked to the day camp bus on that August morning, my mother turned into the empty house and my father paused at the curb, waiting for a ride to work from one of his friends. There were many days when I turned back from the bus and spent the day with her because I was afraid of what might happen. On that day I ignored my fear, not because I thought nothing would happen, but because I lost hope in my own ability to love my mother enough. So I climbed the stairs of the bus, thinking over all the things I had said to her, hoping she would remember them. It was a musty, humid morning. When the bus arrived at the reservoir we filed off and wandered slowly down into the lukewarm water. When the water reached my knees, I stopped and felt as though I could not breathe.

My father found her later that day, but no one from the neighborhood knew what had happened or cared to ask when the ambulance arrived to take the body away. Because the news did not reach beyond our house, it never left our house. And when I came home to discover what had happened, I rushed at my father as I had on the day he had killed our dog. I did not understand, and still do not, why he had not been able to prevent her death and why, in my own mind, it had become my responsibility and my fault. I ran into his stomach and started punching him as hard as I could. The distance between my father and me and the distance between us and the rest of the world grew larger with every year until I could not be sure if I had not actually been responsible for her death. I could no longer separate what actually had happened from my worst fear of what had happened.

When she grabbed my hand before I boarded the bus the morning that she died and squeezed the blood out of my palm, my mother was reaching across a distance that no amount of love could bridge. So when I walked sternly across the playground with that stone, the gift of love burning in my pocket, that in the end could not be received, it was swallowed by the distance that grew between my mother and the rest of the world.

When I think of my father and what he could have done to save my mother, as I always do sitting alone in his living room, I think of this story about a time before Vietnam when the future events of our lives lay just beneath our skin. I must have been five and my little cousin was eight when my father took us canoeing down the Allagash River. I fished all day and caught nothing. Toward the end of the first day, we paddled hard across Long Lake in order to reach the camp on the opposite shore before the orange horizon sank. On the second day it rained but we pushed downriver anyway. In the late afternoon I dropped the fishing rod overboard. My father stretched his long body out over the water but could not grab the rod before it sank. He succeeded instead in tipping the canoe over. My heavy rubber boots dragged me feet first right to the bottom. The surface of the water lay two feet above my head, but I could not move. I saw my cousin's flailing arms and my father's thick legs, his chest, shoulders, and head rising above the water into the air where I wanted to be. His hands closed around my cousin, lifting her out of the water, and then his legs moved away. In a few moments I stood alone underwater, and in my memory it seems that I accepted my situation absolutely. I accepted that my father would not return, as of course he would, and in those few moments I felt relieved to experience the kind of aloneness that my mother must have felt, that I would come to expect and that I would spend many years inflicting on myself.

Moments after a calm befell me, I saw my father's distorted outline above the rippling window of the water's surface, and then I saw the legs moving underwater toward me. Finally I saw the hand crash down from the sky and grab me by the collar. For many years I could not reconcile the force that drove his legs away from me, his love for his brother's daughter, and the force that drove his legs back to me, his love for me. It seemed impossible that two such forces, one evil, one good, could coexist. And if they did, how was I to anticipate which force would dominate my life? Only recently have I been able to see that the same love which drove my father away from me drove him back moments later. I knew, standing on the bottom of the river at five years old, when I saw my father's distorted image descending from above, that I was not forsaken, but I have never been able to understand, on some level, why his power to steal life back was extended to me but not my mother. I have always been in awe of the illusion of this power to give and take life at whim, and that I am alive because this love favored me.

I wish I could say with any degree of certainty that desire, the kind of love that crushes at the same time it empties, the kind of love that can never be fulfilled, is not the love of God. When I think back on those five or six years of my life that were consumed by a single obsession for a substance that nearly killed me, there is nothing that I like but everything that I want. When I feel this desire moving ferociously through me, as I do now and have for some time, I am most convinced that God loves me and is, at the same time, seemingly indifferent to my own destruction.

One night in New York I came to know about myself, God, and the world—just what I desperately wanted to avoid. I was in a bar with people I knew down the street from my apartment on 43rd Street. A woman one of our friends knew sat down at a table with us. She pressed her lips together and nodded at me, and I remember nodding back to her. I raised a glass to my mouth, watching her lower lip, and then closed my eyes. There my memory stops until the next morning when I raised myself out of someone else's bed and looked down at the dirty street. Even when I turned around to find the woman I had met the previous night, her face covered with bruises, lying unconscious on the floor, I still could not remember what had happened. My one broken knuckle explained enough. I found my sneakers under the bed and pulled them on my feet. At the sink I cleaned my hands with dish soap. Finally, I checked the woman's pulse with my pinkie, found a beat, and crept out of the apartment. Later I called an ambulance from halfway across town. I sat on the street corner outside my friend's apartment. I sat there until well past dark. I knew then, as I know now, that I am capable of anything and that everything proceeds from a kind of love that knows no boundaries or limits, that dwells in darkness as well as in light. There is no way of knowing, when I step into the world today, whether I will go back to that life. There is no way of knowing what kind of love the world will suffer at my hand, and sometimes there is not enough time in one life to understand the consequences of what I have done.

And what could I do when my friend with his glazed-over eyes came tumbling down the front steps and asked me to come inside where some people were sitting around a room in the dim light, their eyes half closed, smoke in the air? The knowledge of what I had just done should have guided me. Though I did not ask for help, I did pause and wait for the right answer, as if time would sort out the truth and save me from myself. What excuse can I give now except that I bowed my head and walked up into the apartment because it was the only thing I knew how to do.

Lexi, who has been lying toe over paws in front of the fire, suddenly raises her head, straightens her ears, and barks at the door. I stand up and pause behind her. There is a level of despair that cannot be communicated by words. I recognize in Lexi's bark the tenor of this despair. She turns and walks cautiously down the hall toward my father's room. I hear the swishing of his slippers slowly making their way toward me. Craning my head away from the front window, I wait for his face to emerge from around the corner. He stops so that half his face and body are concealed by the wall, tilts his head in my direction, and not finding me there, tilts it toward the other side of the room. Finally he turns and drags his slippers back down the hall. Lexi's toenails click after his heels to where, in the kitchen, I find him pulling dog biscuits out of the cupboard. He leans over, running his hand along the side of her face. She presses against him and opens her mouth to receive the present.

My father hears me pause by the sink and pour myself a glass of water. He straightens his back and leans against the cupboard, pulling the bathrobe across his old chest. "I couldn't sleep," he says. I nod. "Would you like some tea, or do you have to go?" he asks. And even though I am tired and have to rise early to look for work, I push away from the sink and, moving toward the stove, say, "Why don't you sit down while I make the tea," but he has already lifted the pot and laid it down on the stove.

On the kitchen counter sits his old military .45. I cradle the gun in my hand as Lexi nudges her nose against my leg and lies down, resting the uneaten biscuit by her face. She lets out a sigh that becomes a whine, her body shuddering with each breath. I run my hand along the top of her head. She has laid herself at my feet.

Lifting the teapot from the stove, my father hears me pulling the slide back on the .45 as I have seen him do dozens of times over the years, slipping the cartridge into the chamber. He turns the gas off and replaces the pot on the burner, his hands bracing against the stove front as I open the back door and lead Lexi out into the yard. When I stop walking, she collapses at my feet, closing her eyes.

In that tunnel with this gun, I believe I would have died. I have spent too many days in struggle against myself to think that I could win against another human being in a fight for my life. A man who has had a gun to his own head may not be able to turn it against someone else, possibly because he knows there is no such thing as killing the enemy. I am afraid that I am still a child and may never become the kind of man who is strong enough to relieve suffering by removing life.

I lean down, rub her ears, and ask myself what a dog could know about the predictions and explanations given by a vet. Though I have been lucky enough to live a life I can partially explain to myself, there seems little hope in the end of explaining the absence of life, even if it does mean a respite from pain. I rest my head against the back of Lexi's head, hoping that she will speak through her faltering breath, and guide me, but she cannot. Nor does my father, standing above the sink with his eyes closed, lift his head or utter a sound. I wait a moment longer, as I once waited when I was five on the bottom of the river for my father's hand to crash down through the water, and I wish I could ask him what kind of love grows out of a lie. Does it falter, will it rot any sooner? Lying to him is the only way I know how to live. Maybe if I were the kind of person who could find truth buried in his own chest, I would not need to lie in order to hide the kind of love he will never understand. Placing one hand on the back of Lexi's head, I raise the gun in the air and pull the trigger against the sky.

PARK BENCH

JUDY BUDNITZ

This is the park bench where I fell in love with Denise. It looks the same: wood slats, chipped green paint, somebody's initials (not ours) carved on the back. It was autumn when it happened, and the trees were like traffic lights, going from green to yellow and red. The air was crisp and smelled of burning leaves.

This is also the park bench where I saw Denise for the last time. It was autumn that time too, same details: chipped paint, initials, burning smell.

It happened like this. I was crossing through the park during lunch hour, scuffling through the leaves and holding a bag with a sandwich and a bottle of pop in one hand while trying to loosen my tie with the other, when I saw Denise sitting there. Only I didn't know her name was Denise then.

She was sitting there reading a book. It was a big thick book, I remember, with tiny print, and she was almost done with it. She sat with her ankles together and her knees together, kind of hunching forward like she wanted to dive in and blast through the last pages.

I sat down on the bench next to her, but not too close. Her hair was cut short, but it looked good on her, she had the right sort of head for it. I waited for her to look up. I rattled my bag around, cleared my throat. She turned the page and her eyes flew back and forth over it.

"Hi," I said.

She looked up and blinked. Her eyes were like swirled marbles, gray and green mixed. "Hi," she said.

"Jack," I said, introducing myself.

"Denise," she said, and that's when I knew, seeing her lips hissing out the end of her name; I knew she was a home run, a keeper, a real thing, a long-term plan, something worth hanging on to forever or for at least a month and a half. I can't explain how I knew. Call it intuition. Call it fate.

"So . . ." I said, trying to get started. I crossed one ankle over the other knee. I stretched my arms out along the back of the bench. "So, what's a nice girl like you doing in a place like this?"

She laughed a polite, mechanical little laugh and went back to her book. We sat there a few minutes. She read. I stretched out and stared at the sky. We were quite companionable, really. I mean, some people have to be talking all the time; it's rare to find someone you can just be quiet with, you know, not need to say anything because you already understand each other. She was quite comfortable with me already, like she'd known me a long time. I could tell this by the way she wasn't at all self-conscious in front of me, she even picked at her nose a little as she read, as if she knew I liked her enough not to care.

It was good like that. But we needed to move on. We were neither of us getting any younger. The leaves were turning, turning. "Denise," I said, and "Denise . . ." I said again, my voice choked with longing, and she turned to me, and we locked eyes, we looked deep into each other's souls and knew each other, truly, deeply, and in that split second we smashed down all the barriers of gender and class and politics and age and sex that people write books and advice columns about. One brilliant flash, I swear to God it can happen even in this shabby old world, brilliant flashes, true communion, that's what I felt as I sat on that park bench and squashed my sandwich under my thigh in my excitement.

She gazed long and longingly at me and didn't say anything. There was nothing left to say. I took her in my arms, I kissed her, a deep probing kiss that plumbed her very depths; deliciously delirious, I nudged the base of her brain and tickled the backs of her eyeballs with my tongue. I didn't stop until I knew her insides the way a blind man knows the face of a loved one beneath his fingertips.

She pulled away, blushing, suddenly shy. She drew back to her end of the bench. She crossed her legs and laid her book on her lap. But in spite of her demurrings I knew she was as inflamed as I. This thing that had sprouted between us was growing unchecked, we could not resist it, we could only follow along.

I took off my jacket and tossed it over the back of the bench. I took off my tie. I bent to unlace my shoes and pull them off. I took off my socks. She was watching me.

"So you're staying, then," she said. Her voice was cool.

I straightened up. "I thought you wanted me to," I said.

"It looks like you're planning to stay whether I want you to or not," she said, getting all defensive, like she was afraid to trust me.

"I'm only trying to do what you want—what we both want," I said. "I won't stay on your bench if you don't want me to." And I stood up.

"Yes, yes, I want you to. Please stay with me," she said after a moment, holding herself as if she were cold.

So I stayed and we made love on the bench as only two people who are truly in love can make love, and we leaped and swooped and flew in a fantastic oneness surrounded by fireworks in slow motion and Vivaldi violins, and with love like that, who notices the hardness of the boards, or the splinters?

Afterward she cried and said I would leave her like they always did. She held me fast by a belt loop and prepared for a struggle. But I had no intention of leaving.

We set up a home there, on the park bench, and we started out the way all good idealistic unions begin: with lots of love and hope and few material possessions. We had all we needed: the ventilation was good, the facilities adequate, the provisions only slightly squashed.

We thought our love would sustain us, but unforeseen difficulties arose. She adored me. She was attentive—too attentive. She hovered over me constantly, tending to my clothes and the maintenance of my body. I am self-sufficient by nature. She was suffocating me. And she was dissatisfied with the place, she wanted to move; she thought a higher elevation would be healthier for the children, when they arrived.

Our lovemaking was still a glorious tumbling union through space, but I began to feel the roughness of the bench where I had not before. Her short hair tickled my nose, making me sneeze.

"I wish you wouldn't throw your clothes around," she said. "You know I hate it when you do that." She folded up my jacket, rolled the tie into a neat ball.

"And I hate it when you nag," I growled. She leaned over and untied my shoelace so that she could retie it in a neater knot. "Quit it," I said, jerking my foot away.

She turned away and sulked and opened her book. I had to coax and plead with the back of her neck to get her to turn around.

Our lovemaking grew less and less like gymnastics in zero gravity; it was becoming slow and ponderous like sumo wrestling.

I liked to sit still and watch the world go by. But she could not sit still. I watched the leaves fall in slow spirals; she fidgeted and stroked the hair at my temple. "Oh, look," she said. "A gray hair." I felt a *ping* of pain in my scalp as she pulled it out. Her fingers moved again, stopped again. "Oooh, here's another."

I slapped her hand away. "Pick, pick, pick. Nag, nag, nag. That's all you ever do. You're worse than your mother."

"You've never even met my mother."

"But I know what she's like, and I bet you're even worse than she is."

"You leave my mother out of this!" she screamed.

"You know she's just an old bag, a lonely old bag who does nothing but nag and pick the clothes up off the floor, and—"

"Stop it, stop it, stop it!" she screamed.

"—and one day you'll be just like her!" I finished. She beat at me with her fists. Boy, I'd really struck a nerve with the mother thing. But I couldn't stop myself, it was like I could see her turning into her mother before my eyes, I could see her growing old long before I did, and suddenly I was terrified of our future together.

"You don't know anything about it! What do you know! Insensitive clod!" she cried. She snatched up my clothes and things and flung them off her bench. "Get out! Get out! Get out!"

I stood up. "Don't worry, I'm leaving, and I'm not coming back. You'll be the one to regret this one day, not me. One day when you're all lonely and old, dragging around, you'll remember Jack.

You'll remember the one that got down on his hands and knees and offered you true love and you just threw it away."

I was rather proud of that last part, about the hands and knees. I made it up on the spot. I stood there and tried to remember our happy times together, our immediate intimacy, but all that was gone, suddenly I didn't know her at all, and all I could think of was the way she'd nagged and smothered and held me down on that bench for so long. Resentment curdled the air between us.

That was that. I gathered up my clothes, and the sandwich in the paper bag, and the soda pop. I left her exactly the way I'd found her, with her legs tight together and her head bent. Only this time she was weeping with fury and (I'm sure) regret. She looked up and screamed: "Get out! Get *out*, I said!" So I did.

I was only a little late getting back to the office. I got right back to work on the accounts I'd begun earlier. I lost myself once again in the columns of numbers, and soon I felt like I had never left.

But I didn't forget Denise. I still haven't; she's stayed in my head all this time. I mean, here it is already Friday, and still I'm thinking about her. That's why I'm back at the park, looking at the same old bench, with this foolish kind of hope that maybe just maybe she'll still be here.

Of course she isn't. I sit on the bench gingerly and watch the leaves fall. I think of all the time I spent with her. Then I think of all the ways I might have used that time instead: golfing, learning Spanish, traveling the world, loving another woman.

But I think the time was well spent. These days it's hard to keep track of time once it's past and done and gone. Sure, some people take pictures, write it all down. But it's just paper, it doesn't mean anything. All you can do is try to hang on to those significant moments.

And that's what it was with Denise—the brilliant flash, the moment of communion. *That* moment I'll hang on to. And I can make it as long or as short as I want it. It is safe in the past just as I want it to be; no one can prove it is otherwise.

So this is how it will be: Denise and I sit on a park bench, eyes locked, lost in the brilliant flash, whirling in the celestial dance and squashed sandwiches, giving off sparks, knowing each other to the deepest and fullest, completely naked to each other, no, beyond naked, *skinned,* maybe, metaphorically of course, our inner workings exposed to each other, incredible intimacy, our insides dissected, centrifuged, laid out on microscope slides, numbered and labeled down to the last chromosome, *that's* how thoroughly we know and understand each other and ourselves and everything is clear and right in this one glorious melding moment that lasts a hundred thousand thousand years.

THIS IS NOT A JOKE LIKE VIETNAM

AARON COHEN

We've got extra tanks of JP-4 fuel, three cases of malt liquor, two fifths of Jack, a dime of weed, a dozen cans of Bumble Bee tuna, seven loaves of Wonder bread, a large bottle of green Tabasco sauce, Chunky Beef Alpo for Mr. Hooper, a four-string Vega banjo, and a coconut cream birthday cake. We've also got Tang for vitamin C, Folger's instant coffee crystals, Dinty Moore beef stew, a first-aid kit, and lots of crossed fingers. We've got everything but my boy and my smack. Just now, the chopper has stopped shaking and shuddering. I haven't. I'm worse. Coming off an eighty-dollar-a-day skag habit.

Three of us: Tubs, me, and Mr. Monkey, who has latched upon my back. I'm in the passenger seat wearing my lucky prosthetic leg, Tubs is flying, holding on to the reins so tight his old knuckles are white, like teeth are popping out of his fists. Tubs has a blurred, fading tattoo of a red, white, and blue bald USMC eagle, globe, and anchor covering his bald head. Tubs has just turned fifty; I'm ten years his junior. Since we buddied up in Nam, we haven't gone a week without getting seriously shitfaced together, although ethanol is his poison and, as I said, smack is my drug of choice. At least in my experience, once you mainline heroin, everything else just kind of falls away. Tubs is not wearing a shirt and I can see his beer belly and his sagging chest. We also have a mildewed hemp rope ladder with a case of gangrene and two life preservers; God let us hope it doesn't come to that. Our mission is to find my boy Ryan, to talk to him, to be calm to him, to say we love you, we miss you, and we are very sorry that we forgot your birthday.

Picture: we're in this bright orange half-homemade HU-1A dust-off chopper with a red cross perceptible beneath the paint designating "Medic, please don't fire," and we're buzzing over the middle part of the Mississippi with the vengeance of a seventeen-year cicada on growth hormones. It's a river the color of Nestlé milk chocolate, and it carries yesterday's mud, chic reconstructed gambling paddleboats, garbage barges, and river gossip nearly five thousand miles, from somewhere around Duluth, Minnesota, to Baton Rouge, Louisiana, before emptying its considerable brown effluent into the Gulf of Mexico. We wouldn't be doing this no matter how stoned we were, but our raft is missing from our pier, and I'm pretty sure my thirteen-year-old is on that raft.

Tubs has just explained that after three days Ryan could arguably be two thousand three hundred seventy-six miles down the stream. Tubs said there are only easy-to-pass-by levees—no spillways or waterfalls—from here to the mouth, so don't worry about Ryan falling ten thousand feet to his mad-ass flailing-armed death. Tubs's words are no big-league comfort to me: my son swims about as good as an anchor in the water. Ryan has no friends except for a fat kid named Randy, who is a bit of a revolutionary himself. Ryan has just turned thirteen. He wants more independence than his mother and father are willing to hand over to him, even though he is a very independent young guy. He's very headstrong, our Ryan, and extremely pissed off in my general direction. One consolation—he has taken Mr. Hooper with him, our brindle bull terrier, a very level-headed dog until he's kept indoors or on a leash for more than five minutes at a stretch.

Besides Ryan and Mr. Hooper, we must vigilantly search out bridges, Smokey copters, phone lines, and boats. Ryan's been gone pushing four days now. Lois said I didn't even bother to notice. Which naturally stunk. She had just gotten home from an emergency trip to New York City, visiting Lisa Anne, her sister, who'd had premature twins. Before she left, Lois underscored my two assignments: give Ryan a dynamite birthday party and feed Mr. Hooper once a day. When she returned from her trip she said I'd *promised* to take him and Randy to the Gateway to the West on my raft. She blamed his cutting out on me, called me a consistently despicable fuckhead, and slapped me three times across the face. At the time I felt a little physical pain, but later, coming off the smack, I felt it in the worst of ways.

Once airborne Tubs pushed the chopper full-bore. We're traveling at maximum speed now headed due south. Sometimes it seems
we are sliding straight into the open mouth of the great midwestern
sun. Depending on the course of the river, the sun moves slightly
to the left or right of us. I clapped on my shades and passed a pair
to Tubs. The bright sun and all this aircraft noise is beating me up.
I'm in one of those stages of heroin withdrawal that's not so easy to
shake off.

We started from home, in Hannibal, Missouri, and we're going
down the river's eroding banks hell bent for leather all the way to the
Mississippi Delta. Now we've just passed over the Missouri River
and view St. Louis to the right, where we can see steamers with
tourists packed in like sardines. We buzz the floating McDonald's
and can smell the river and famous french fries while everyone below
ducks down probably thinking we're Muslim terrorists on some sui-
cide mission. Farther down we can see farms with Chevy trucks, red
barns, and wide lolloping green fields where steers chew content-
edly, unaware of their impending fates: the gestapo train-trip up to
the bloody stockyards in Chi-Town. To the left, in Illinois, as we
rise up and over the hawks and crows, we can see roofers bustling
about new construction sites like worker ants. There are square plots
of rich farmland, lush forests, ranch-style homes, schools, turquoise
swimming pools, snaky roads, and graveyard after graveyard after
graveyard.

It's late afternoon. About two hundred forty miles to Memphis;
Tubs says we'll arrive there in another five hours. We're flying so
close to the river I could touch the water with the toe of my boot.

Tubs tells me to keep cool, says we will go all the way to the
Caribbean Sea if necessary.

See us fly: in the air, mosquitos and flies and water bugs, maybe an
occasional small bird, splashing onto our already filthy windshield.
Lunatic kayakers, who shouldn't be in this treacherous water anyhow, are presenting us with the occasional middle finger. The air is
making a lot of whistling and laughing noises through our cracked
windshield. Tubs and I are utterly exhausted but keep putting away

those beers, trying like hellfire to reduce the strangeness and cruelty of the day.

And we're breaking every air-traffic code in the book, flying this low, fast, and wobbly. Our exhaust is so black and full of noxious particles we've moved the doomsday clock fifty seconds closer to midnight. This is a mission with a passion, the most hazardous kind: either we bring Ryan home or we crash and we burn.

I'm a proud father and I must tell you that Ryan has a touch of genius. He's a fair boxer, the pepperpot on the baseball field, and the best speed chess player in all of Hannibal. But more than all that, he's a sweet kid—got a heart of gold—and is extremely industrious in his ways. I should spend more time with this boy. I *will* spend more time with this boy. Lois, a dedicated fifth-grade teacher, patiently coaches him through his homework every night while I sneak out to the garage and shoot dope and goof or work out my biceps. Phantom pain is actually a very silly thing, but that's only if you think about it. If you don't, it's quite serious. A foot that I haven't got, that's now a shattered skeleton somewhere back in Vietnam, throbs and itches and burns and screams and tells me to put a sock and a shoe on it and tells me to go jogging around the block. Went from aspirin to Tylenol #2, 3, and 4 to Percodan to Demerol and finally to street dope, which is easier to find in Hannibal than one would think. Down deep I love Ryan with all my being. But I can't convey this love, or convince anyone of it. My family is without a doubt the most important thing in my life. Without them, I am the symbol for everything you never want to be: a one-legged junkie whose human emotions are wrapped in plastic and locked in a deep freezer.

I will change all that when I find Ryan; I must wrap him in a beach towel and rock back and forth with him; I must play catch and hoops with him; teach him how to clean a rifle; to build a fire in a rainstorm; to find water in stone.

After checking the usual hideouts—Larry's Arcade and Theater, the handball courts, the marble-shooting alleyways, the shopping center, Sue's Diner—I went over to Randy's house, and searched over there. I took my hoodless Monte Carlo and checked in the fireplace, blackening my palms. Randy's mom, Tubs's second wife, was interrogating Randy in his room, which gave me an opportunity to spark up. After I took a couple hits, I grabbed a Mickey's bigmouth from the fridge, gulped the good-tasting brew down, and crammed it in the trash compactor, which was in a state of serious overflow. This was done before Randy and his mom found me looking under the sink. After looking through Randy's room, the dryer, the closets, the car port, and the lawn mower shed, I decided Ryan was officially on the loose again, and that's when Randy said, with a Ho-Ho in his mouth, "Do ya think he took the big old raft, Mister Carpenter?"

Without delay, without asking Randy why he hadn't said so in the first place, I raced home and hobbled down to the sun-bleached pier to see if *Huckleberry 1982* was still there. Almost everyone in Hannibal busts ass trying to outdo everyone else when it comes to these rafts. *1982* won us first place and a trip to Hong Kong before Ryan was even born. Just the other day, in fact, I warned Ryan all she was good for anyhow was poling out on calm days and laying a few catfish lines. No way was she tough enough for one of these long hauls.

Back in my bedroom I discovered Ryan's note in my wooden box of secrets: a quarter ounce of Mexican regs, a ten-pack of diabetes syringes, cotton balls, my cooking spoon, and a note that said in scraggly letters, "Fuck you! Fuck you! Forever and ever and ever." My hair nearly stood on end. He could have easily taken my James Brown. I proceeded directly to the bathroom, sat on the closed toilet seat, drug out my works, cooked up, tied a vein, and fired off. As that funk ran its glorious course, I began to nod. I hadn't realized Ryan knew about the wooden box of secrets. After the rush I went back out down to the dock. The river was running high and fast, and my head was in orbit.

I drove to the police station, where I spoke with a bluecoat at the reception desk, a dour man with a toothbrush mustache, sharp teeth, and wire rims. The guy says, "Could be he's not on the river at all. Could be he's hiding in the attic. Could be he's yanking your chain." My head hammering with fury, I maneuvered away from him, tried to remember what he looked like so I could club him later with my leg, and drove straight home.

Tubs was a commanding officer in Vietnam, where I earned a Bronze Star but was never promoted. Over the phone, he suggested we try *Zip,* his bass boat. I went out there, arm in arm with Lois, who was quiet, frightened, and red-faced. A big bucket of guilt had already slopped over me; I don't know what else she wanted me to do. The boat was missing its motor. Tubs came out there and said, "Fuck, man, he boosted my fucking eggbeater! And the two cans of high octane! And all of my pistachios!"

Tubs walked around, scratching his head and then his chins.

"Oh God!" Lois sobbed. "Christ no!"

We found Tubs suddenly staring at the giant tarped-over helicopter, which was planted dead in the center of his mighty backyard, in a clearing between a maple and a tipped-over jungle gym.

Tubs walked around the copter pulling the plastic tent stakes from the grass. "No way, Tubs," I said. All four of us were staring at Tubs from different angles when he yanked the tarp off with a *fwap!,* revealing an object of total insanity. Randy ran outside and pleaded that he might go with us.

Tubs had been supposedly flying her at nights.

Randy was wearing ripped-up parachute pants and a dented Army brain bucket, but we all pretended he was invisible. Jenette poked out of the open kitchen window with a cigarette in her face. "Tubs, you son of a bitch, you fly that thing again, you'll end up in . . . I don't know . . . the justice system!"

"Sugarbeet, this here's a bona fide emergency," Tubs said. He turned to me and unbuttoned his shirt. "I think she's our only way to go, to speak truthful. I just knew this thing would come in handy someday," Tubs whooped, heaving his beer into the river. "Hot damn!"

We fly over the wide brown muddiness where junked, mud-filled cars, washing machines, and orange bricks are piled up on the right side to stop flood-inspired erosion to a spot where Huckleberry

Finn is said to have lost his straw hat. So goes the rumor, I told Tubs, who paid no attention.

Damn, cold turkey! I feel like a wild horse trying to shiver off flies, but the flies won't budge. I feel paranoid but I've got good reason. I'm questioning things, making promises to myself I cannot keep for more than five minutes. At the same time I'm staring at the black tracks on my arms. The needles on the dashboard are fibrillating. I'm thinking about the sweet dope back on my bed in plain view, hoping Lois doesn't usher police investigators through our bedroom, and kicking myself for forgetting it. I'm also plain kicking, which is a real motherfucker. I mean, you just don't *forget* something like heroin in my situation!

Presently Tubs struggles to steady the monster, to dig into pockets of air, then to thrust out of them. Thank God there's no sign of rain. We move over the wild earth, trees and water and fishermen and boats going by in a great big blur beneath us, kids throwing rocks at us or skipping them or old fishermen looking up in awe and fear. Some of them duck, sheltering their heads with dirty elbows or holding on to their hats and newspapers. When we're that close to the water, the wind makes things in the river that look like whirlpools or ugly faces. The giant river catfish must be thinking it's the end of the world.

Another bridge up ahead, a low one.

Half-drunk, Tubs says he's going under it, but at the last minute he pulls the bird up. We lean forward, the cake slides back from its position under my bucket seat, the gasoline sloshes in the back cabin, and we fly up and over the bridge. Tubs is laughing, going, "Whew hoo! Come and get us now!"

"Crazy son of a concubine," I say, "don't ever *do* that again!" But he keeps laughing. I've crossed my arms and hunched over, waiting for the wave of cramps to pass through me, but they linger. I need a fix just about yesterday afternoon.

The air is playing games with us. At every swooping and veering and regaining of control we seem closer to death than the time before. We've grazed the water three times now. I've closed my eyes and braced for a collision more times than I can count. Impending doom forces them open again.

Somewhere in Tennessee, the sun finally goes down: It is dark, I work the spotlights scanning the river. It's a relief to have something to do. Tubs tells me to reach in his pack and what I pull out are infrared binoculars. I put them over my head and use these for a while, seeing everything green.

"Where'd you get these ugly things?"

"Uncle Sam's in St. Louis."

"What'd you, uh—"

"Fifty bucks, talked 'em down to twenty."

"They worked?"

"No, no. I fixed them. Watch this."

He presses a blue button and a hideous siren goes off.

"Jesus," I say, grabbing another beer.

"Stole it off a cop car. Hey, hit me with one of those ice-colds."

He turns it off, laughing. "Easy, Bud," he says, punching my knee. "We'll find your boy! Don't worry!"

Dawn. Tubs is flying close to the water. I'm still sick and stiff, and I am squirming in my seat like a boy in church. I kick the plastic leg out to a forty-five-degree angle. I wish I could tell you differently, but it was blown off in the war.

Weekly, Tubs tells Ryan war stories. All lies about seeing little Vietnamese children running around being chased by pigs, skinny raped children with mud on their lips and backs. He tells him about black bodies, split-apart helmets, shoes with feet tangled in hair, foxholes filled with purple remains, flashes of silver, burning bridges, twinkling dragon kites, on-fire leeches. Ryan transforms these scenes into cartoon drawings, turns them in for art projects and gets A's. Ryan worships Tubs.

When we were sent home from the war, I moved back to Hannibal and Tubs found me a year later after suffering a head injury. Both of us had disability money coming to us from the government for the rest of our lives. That and a whole lot of dead time. A lot—

a whole lot—of down time. More than anyone should ever have to bear.

Still no sign of Ryan.

"This sucks," Tubs says. "I think our wives are highly pissed-off creatures."

"If we bring Ryan back, they won't remember a thing," I say. I maneuver the banjo onto my lap and start fingerpicking "Happy Birthday" extremely fast.

"You know, that kid you got ain't leaving to get away from you. He's leaving to get *to* you."

The river narrows, we get low. I rest the banjo on my plastic knee. On the right the trees are all leaning in with groping arms. I can see roots and footprints and between blinks I think I can see an Air Jordan in the mud. By now Ryan might be in the Gulf of Mexico, hammerheads striking his young body. He might be drowned in a web of seaweed. There are points on our journey where the river is so wide we can barely see either shore. This is not one of them.

Tubs smokes incessantly. The copter swerves.

The ground's going by an inch at a time as we follow an elbow of brown water. I tell him I think I'm getting sick.

Tubs closes his eyes, his head rolls back.

"But keep going," I say.

"It ain't me, babe," Tubs sings. "We can go down at any time and nobody will ever know. All the people are gone now. Just me and you and my baby, a few birds, the sun and the moon, and Mr. Victor Charles."

His eyes are wide and scary.

"We're not in Vietnam, Tubs. We're not back and we'll probably never be back. We're just here to find my kid, remember?"

He blows smoke rings. "Roger."

I bring my hand to my face and squeeze the bridge of my nose, try to keep my face from crumpling. He looks at me and grabs my arm and squeezes it and I see that his eyes are blue surrounded by red. He tilts his head and pops his neck.

I look away, into the fidgeting shadows, and watch the leaves and light go by. There is a big field of electric transformers and a sign that says DO NOT ANCHOR GAS PIPELINES CROSSING.

The ground is going by so fast. We follow another elbow of brown water. There's no logic to our travels now. No logic. He could be anywhere, anywhere.

We've passed more than a couple locks and dams. They'll allow you to cross for free, Tubs has been telling me. I told him I've heard it'd probably tear a shitty raft right up. If it does, and my little kid gets sucked under, the undertow will pull him down so fast he won't know what to do.

Something in Tubs's eyes tells me he's elsewhere, and his hands may be working the reins and his feet the gas, but no, he's not with me anymore, not at all.

Water's rougher here, and rockier. We are deep into our reserve fuel, almost out. Tubs closes his eyes and his head rolls back. The chopper swerves.

"Tubs!" I say, scrunching my teeth together. And when he looks ahead drowsily, he smiles. Far ahead and way below, past a small sandbar, is a lot of white foam, a spillway, and a little before it I see the raft, which is caught up on a pile of sticks and rocks and jetsam that trails off to the bank.

Neither of us says anything.

Like a madman I swing open my door and drop the ladder down, sticking my fake leg out to prop the door from swinging back and slamming me in the face.

Tubs's knees rise and fall with both biceps working hard. I swallow, my heart stuck to my ribs. I see birds flying all around us. I can picture the Jesus bolt flying off, behind all the stress, and the blade just whirling down the Great Miss like a monstrous machete.

Tubs takes it slow. We continue to descend and move forward, until we can see the white foam, the raft, and now the dog. But no Ryan.

The helicopter is shaking so much the empty fuel containers are bouncing and clanking, nearly hitting the ceiling.

Now I can hear the dog barking. We lower another invisible

notch, so that we've nearly landed on the raft. I scoot near the wind. I can see the things piled on it: my full, soaking-wet duffel bag, a wicker basket filled with empty cracker boxes, a bunch of bananas, a carton of cigarettes, and then, when we drop down another fifteen feet, I can see a whiskey bottle full with nickels and pennies.

"Come on, come on," Tubs says. "Nice and easy, Beaver Cleaver."

I nervously lean over and can see Mr. Hooper wagging, barking at us like a trumpet. She's underweight, giant-pawed, black and brown, has short hair, a square jaw. She picks up a rotting fish with her mouth. Her hair hangs over her eyes and, standing at attention, she is definitely glad to see us. She has a purple bandanna around her neck. We're about fifty feet above the bunged-up raft as we let down the ladder.

"It's too high," I say. "Lower her more."

"Watch your step, nothing fancy," Tubs says. He has drunk himself sober. I can barely see straight, but can imagine Ryan underwater, his face in the gravel. I swing my plastic leg down and wiggle it onto the third-to-top rung, realizing I'm going to have to depend on my good leg and my arms.

"I can't do it, man," I say, now fully on the ladder, which has been pulled under the chopper by my weight.

On the distant bank I see a mysterious splotch of green smoke. Down two more rungs and I smell the poisonous smoke. The siren goes off, something makes a loud popping sound, I get startled so badly—my brain goes nuts—that I let go of the ladder. I try to reach for it as I fall, but my folded body falls through the air, my stomach surges, and I close my eyes as my head hits the raft. Down under I go. All I see is maroon everywhere.

Underneath, hurt and discombobulated, I try to get back up, get my bearings, my breath, but I'm off-balance because of my lucky leg, which is something of a flotation device. I follow my air bubbles to the surface.

A strong hand grabs me and I weakly hang on to a hip that reminds me of Lois's. I feel myself being dragged roughly over a thicket of sharp trash and rocks and wood and slimy river stuff. My heart sinks as the foot of my fake leg breaks off and hurries away. He has me around the neck in a stranglehold, and I'm being cut to hell.

Ryan drags me over to the short bank, coughing and panting, and when he can pull no farther, he sits beside me—between us are firecrackers—and stares at the river.

Ryan's skin is slick with oil, his wet hair shining with thick curls, his neck long and forward, eyes squinting and deep-set, his bottom lip still but his top one quivering. Ryan's freckled nose is sunburnt, his cheeks puffed like roses; and mosquito bites spangle him from head to toe. He is wearing faded torn jeans and no shirt. We're leaning back on our hands, which are descending into the black mud.

Tubs hovers above the bank, wobbling, about twenty feet up; when he sees he can't land there either, he flies above the sandbar, which is about three inches above the water and about three hundred yards from our side of the dock. The bird's engine coughs and sputters, its fuel tanks all but empty.

At last Tubs manages to set her down all in one piece, and then one final drama ensues. The chopper begins to slide into the river while the blades are still spinning. As it continues to slide in, getting lower and lower, until it is floating in the water, the door opens and Tubs jumps into the river. The helicopter slips more and then rolls over on its side like a whale as water swirls and bubbles around it. Tubs dog-paddles back to the sandbar with a lighted cigarette still in his mouth, he goes under, then rises like a dead man and climbs up part of the sandbar, and instantly sinks into the mud up to his thighs. With his wide, hairy, waterweed-covered back toward us, he fiddles with his front, his pants drop, and he takes a long low bow, shaking his naked booty at the world.

The only thing remaining above the water now is the tail end of the chopper, reminding me of the caudal fin of a giant radioactive fish. Then I see Mr. Hooper swimming toward us. Tubs dives in the river and swims over to the sunken helicopter, where giant gurgly brown bubbles are starting to bring up the Alpo, the remnants of the birthday cake, some unopened packs of Camels, some empty cans of Bud, and some very strange unclassified fish. Tubs meets the dog halfway, they both start barking, and at that moment I notice the raft is gone.

I rest my hand on Ryan's shoulder. The wind has picked up a great deal, and the clouds overhead lay an intense shadow over the river. I look at him again and he is still staring at the river, perhaps at the exact place where he saved my life.

Ryan shrugs my arm off altogether, and I lean back, exhausted, not knowing what to do or say. Ryan lights a cigarette, shakes out the match, and blows three perfect smoke rings.

Then Tubs makes it back—he's crawling up onto the bank—his face covered in brack, wheezing and laughing so hard he looks like he might have a heart attack right in front of our noses.

"We gotta get out of this place, wherever it is . . . Guatemala." My shivering arms are buried to the elbows in mud.

Ryan gives me a killing look, then he laughs. I'm feeling nauseous. "You're drunk." He laughs again, sniffles, coughs, and smiles. I can see that he needs braces. "Goddamn," he whispers, then he examines me and makes a disgusted face. He grabs the dog by the bandanna, clears his throat, begins to tie my shoe, and that's when I see my Bronze Star pinned to his belt loop.

Tubs says, "Hey kid, I hear noises. Over thataway." Tubs points west. "Freeway or something. She looks good, looks good, looks fine, looks fine . . ." As Tubs humps slowly away, still out of breath, Ryan, who seems more grown-up than ever, catches up to him, punches him in the kidney, puts an arm around him, and begins to tell his story. I had given the medal to Ryan for a good-luck charm years ago, and had always figured he'd chucked it in the Mississippi by now. I just look blankly back at the river, and give thanks that Ryan is alive while studying the prehistoric fish dead on the shore. Then I turn toward the highway behind me. As I sink slowly into the mud, Tubs and Ryan are already out of sight. I lift my lucky leg and plant my good foot, knee deep in Mississippi mud, and start after my boy again.

NAMING THE BABY

LUCY HOCHMAN

I lay on our kitchen table, in the dark, and continued the conversation while allowing my husband to complete the scene he was performing.

I said, "I was baby-sitting for a woman I didn't like. She was thoughtless. I mean, she went through life without thought. I was angry, or ashamed that a woman like that could have a baby.

"I was thirteen, but I had breasts. I was sitting with the baby on my lap and the baby was hungry, so he was pawing and whining. So I unbuttoned my shirt. I wasn't wearing a bra. I thought wearing a bra was a sign of weakness. I sat there and let the baby try to nurse. He tried sucking and gnawing and was very upset. I thought I could see my breasts turning gray."

My husband said it sounded pretty harmless.

I said, "Well, that's the most sinister thing I have ever done. And I don't think it was harmless."

He wanted to know if I fed the baby afterward.

"Sure I fed him," I said. "It was a baby."

I was letting him do what he liked to do. He liked to play out his impulses. He liked to turn his impulses into scenes. He'd think, "I wonder if I could—" or "I wonder what would happen if—" and where another person would know, "of course I cannot see into my wife's womb and identify the sex of my unborn child," and leave that thought for the next, my husband would play it out. He'd make the notion physical. As many notions as he had time for he made physical.

He finally turned on the light. He said he was not pleased I'd moved the flashlight apparently, as we were supposed to be able to find it in the dark; that's what it was for. I told him how uncomfortable I was, lying on the kitchen table, and how silly he was being about the whole project, couldn't I just tell him boy or girl? He turned the lights off again and bumped into something even though the flashlight was on. It was a big, expensive flashlight because my husband did a lot of research before he bought anything, saved up, bought cash. Also, he didn't want our name on the mailbox, wouldn't have a bank account, drove all the way to the electric company every month to wait on line, his down time. These were little things I noticed about him over the months. These little things I accepted about him every day and regarded as my greatest pleasures. What I found most interesting was his habit of constructing these scenes.

My husband finally made it over to me and pushed my knees apart. I'd already gotten rid of my underwear, but it was difficult to keep my knees apart because I was laughing so hard. My neck ached because I couldn't fit my head on the table, so I let it flop back while I laughed and he pushed my dress around, trying to see into my body with the flashlight. He said he couldn't see shit.

I said, "Come on honey, let me tell you, boy or girl, my neck is aching." He said that baby must be way up there because now he was seeing all sorts of shit, but no baby.

I said, "One time there was a sick horse when I was at the farm, and the vet came, this really pretty, prim little woman vet, and she was talking to us while she worked on the horse, telling us how her kid was just in a play, and she put her arm up the back of that horse all the way to her shoulder and was moving its internal organs around to try and fix it."

My husband said that sometimes if a person's heart stops in surgery the doctor has to break the chest open and massage it. They call it massaging the heart.

He finally got tired of looking in me, gave me a peck on each thigh, and I told him it was a girl. Then the next day at breakfast I told him I was just kidding, it was a boy.

Ever since we got married, he'd been saying "Honey, I'm home" all the time. Of course he said it when we were having sex, that was obvious, but he also said it when he was going through the mail, or watching TV, or anytime, as an icebreaker. It was the sort of thing that would keep our marriage alive unless I got sick of it.

He knew, of course, that he would not see the baby. I supposed he'd only wanted to have me on a table and look at my body with a flashlight, imitating a clinician. He thought that would be fun. Also, the moment itself was important, wondering about the secret inside me, the bulging cellular bundle that would affect the rest of his life, which he knew he would love but could not yet love.

On a more symbolic level, he wanted to give weight to a ridiculous moment across which his mind had wandered. What if the sun didn't set or turned purple or green? There is nothing to *do* with such a notion. Or what would it feel like to be dead? Again, nothing to do, though people keep trying.

What would it be like to have my wife lie on the table and look into her at the beginnings of another person? There is a possible step to be taken there. I wouldn't care enough to take that particular step. I *would* indulge him, my own favorite sport.

Sometimes my husband and I would get home from work at exactly the same time. We came at the driveway from different directions and when we saw each other, we'd race our cars to see who could get into the driveway first, which was ridiculous, because whoever won got blocked in. Then we'd sit in our separate cars and try to open the doors, step out, and close them simultaneously. We never got it to work, and we didn't even acknowledge that we were doing it, but sitting there in the driveway, we locked eyes in the rearview mirror, and it was intense.

I thought, when our marriage gets old and weary, he'll say something like we're going to wreck both our cars and we should quit racing at each other, life is not a game of chicken, and then I'll know he's not the man I married.

We were getting home at the same time one day, and he didn't even notice, he was thinking so hard about something. When he got out of his car he looked surprised to see me waiting for him. He didn't say anything until we were in the kitchen, and then he told me his friend Jim had punched him. I said, "Where?" and he said at work. I said, "Where?" and he said in the side of his neck, Jim apparently didn't hit very often, and his aim was off, good thing. My husband was slumping over his ginger ale, not so much shocked as confused. I said, "Well, why?" and he said he didn't know.

"When was the last time someone hit you?" I asked. He said he'd never gotten hit. I asked him what about at the park, because he'd hustled chess at the park when he was in school. He said chased off, sure, but no one ever got him. "Have you ever hit anyone?" I asked.

He said, "Sure."

Before I was pregnant, I used to chop wood. My husband never bothered to get the gas hooked up because the stove was electric anyhow, and there were two nice old fireplaces in the house, so we used them when it got cold. My pregnancy never bothered me as much as when it got so I couldn't chop well anymore. My swing was off, because my body was out of balance. An ax is out of balance, of course, because it's all head and a skinny, light body. It's the motion that puts the thing right, so it bothered me to think of how I wouldn't be using it and it would be lying around, top-heavy. It bothered me that my husband would go to the grocery store and pay cash for little bundles of shrink-wrapped wood that came with handles, lazy city boy. I thought that about him, but I didn't mean it.

We were lying around in bed, looking at the fire, and my husband had been amusing us with mother earth jokes. He'd collected the seeds from the orange he was eating and stuffed them into my navel. He got the spray bottle we used on the houseplants and sprayed me. I said, "What if I get sick of playing your straight man?"

He asked me if I'd ever watched myself behave in a way that I hated, and then continued to do so, even exaggerating what I knew I despised in myself. I said, "Of course I have." He asked if that was really the most sinister thing I'd done, frustrating that baby. I said, "Probably not. I probably don't even know it when I'm doing my most sinister things." He said my answer was a cop-out. It was the most sinister or it wasn't. He told me he always knew when he was being sinister. I said, "How do you know?" He said sinister includes knowing it. I said, "Maybe *telling* you was the most sinister." He said that answer was a cop-out, too.

I wondered if, when he asked me questions about myself, what he really wanted was for me to ask the questions back. It made me think I didn't care about the same things he did. What I liked, of course, were my own memories, and exposing secrets I only recognized as secrets the moment I told them. When I was thirteen and made that baby frustrated, when it beat its fists and growled, it hurt me, and I kept at it. I was so angry about not liking the mother that the baby's own confusion had nothing to do with it. I wasn't thinking of emotionally scarring the baby so that maybe it would grow to be fucked-up and cause its mother problems. I wasn't angry because that drip had a baby and I didn't. I was thirteen. I didn't want a baby.

In fact, in a pure kind of way, I stole the baby's individuality for a while, making its blank body exhibit my own feelings. It was almost a motherly thing, almost that connection you're supposed to have with your own baby, your little dig at immortality, the hope that it will be at least some of you. Mostly, there I was, staring my feelings in an actual face, and those feelings were desperate.

And after all, I'm sure, decidedly inconsequential.

I was letting him play out a scene. Occasionally, I wondered if I was playing along with his physical representations in an attempt to know him better. I wondered if he'd done these things when he was on his own, or if he was doing them as an attempt to let me get to know him. It's true, we weren't married before I was pregnant.

He wanted to cook a balanced meal that was all in blues and purples. He'd come across blue corn at the grocery, it had given him the notion, and he took it. What do other people do with their time, I wondered. What do other people do with the ridiculous things they think? I mean, how long can I go without urinating? I don't care if I ever know. My husband, if he wonders, and if he notices himself wondering, will try to know. And why act on one thought over another, I wondered.

He was slicing the beets he'd baked, staining his hands. He told me to guess what he was thinking about.

"Beets," I guessed. He said he was only thinking of beets indirectly. He said he was thinking if the baby was a boy, he wanted to name it James, after Jim. I had nothing to say to that at first. How could he want to name a baby after violence? Whatever Jim was before, his name, in our life, at that time, meant hitting without coherent reason. The name meant random, physical hurt. We sat down to dinner. We ate the beets, berries in yogurt, plums, and grapes. He'd found squid ink pasta and we ate that with the corn. We drank sangria. The kitchen was a mess. I said, "It looks like a battlefield in here."

He said, "By your silence, I take it, it is."

"What do you mean you don't know why he hit you? And when *you* hit people, why did you do it?" I asked, and I was angry. He said he didn't know why he hit people, it wasn't like hitting was a regular part of his life. He said there were lots of reasons, but he knew he'd never hit a person because of anything that happened right before he hit that person.

"Who did you hit?" I asked. "Why did you hit the people you hit? I don't believe you have no idea why he hit you."

He said it hurt him to hear me say I didn't believe him. He said when he says he doesn't know, he doesn't know. I said, "Are you going to ask him?" He said if Jim wanted to talk about it he'd talk about it.

I said, "Well, if it's a girl I will stand over it while it's sleeping, with my ax, when you're not looking, to think of scaring you." He said that was ridiculous, what was that supposed to mean. I said, "You want to talk sinister?" I said, "This is what's sinister. What's sinister is you, how you ask me questions and I answer them and then I ask you questions and you pretend you can't answer. And it's sinister, how you can spend time with blue this and purple that, and put orange pits on my belly, and all these things you do. Play chicken with my car when you know you leave first in the morning. Everything. All that. And how I lie on the table so you can look at me with your fucking industrial flashlight. And everything else. It's worse than sinister."

"Don't be ridiculous."

"That's right," I said. "Worse than sinister, it's ridiculous."

I wasn't angry for long. I began to think there was even more to having been hit by Jim than I'd considered. I'd been angry at the fact of the violence and its implication of further violence, and I hadn't considered it for what it was, essentially. A person moves his arm and it makes contact. After all, the pretty vet thought, I want to fix this horse, and so she plunged her arm into its body, and when the doctors wanted the patient to live, they plunged their hands into its body and rubbed its heart. I realized there must have been more to the incident than Jim's simple act of aggression. It had called up some serious questions for my husband, questions he couldn't easily signify, physically, and notions that were certainly far too complex for linguistic representation. While we were seeing if it was really possible to climb out a second-story window using a rope made of sheets, or attempting to have sex on a bicycle as we'd seen in a movie, some people were being mugged, battered, boxed, beat up, mugging, battering, boxing, and beating. The blows referred to incidents, but no particular incident. They referred to unanswerable questions like "What can I do?" Physical manifestations of the unknown and inexpressible, chords were being struck with every blow.

"What's it like to hit someone?" I asked him.

"It's like throwing a ball, but you never let go."

The baby was born, and I went out to chop wood as soon as I could. I'd been wondering if I actually loved my husband, or if I was simply trying to find out if I could. I was asking myself "What if I loved my husband, what would I do?" or "Could I love my husband? What would that be like?" When the baby was born, I'd said, "I'm not saying I approve of violence, but we can let his middle name be James." And James was his middle name, but that was what we called him, James. I lifted my ax and felt the weight of its head. I let it swing like a pendulum, and watched it find its fulcrum at my initiative. I let my arm act like a continuation of its handle, let the ax swing over my head and fall and bury itself in the wood. I wiggled it and pulled it out and swung again. I have never been hit.

We stood over the baby and watched him sleep. He was a strong, quiet baby. We didn't know much else about him yet. It had been a couple weeks since his birth and he was getting cute.

"Do you love me yet?" I asked my husband.

He asked did he act like he loved me, and I said he did.

"Do you love James?" I asked.

"I do love James," he said. He picked up the sleeping boy and went out on the porch and sat on the steps. I looked at them through the window. The sun was setting. I went out back and chopped wood until it got dark. Then I walked around to the front of the house, holding my ax. They were still sitting there on the porch, not doing anything. The more I watched, the more it seemed they were moving away from me, instead of simply joining the dark.

A few weeks later, Jim came over with his wife, to meet the baby. Right off, he and my husband shook hands. Jim said, "Sorry, man. I know it's been a while, but sorry." My husband said no problem, he understood. Jim's wife and I went inside.

"How's it going?" she asked. "Being married."

"He's a good husband," I said. "We've been trying to get to know each other. I was lucky."

"Jim told me what happened," she said. "It was terrible, how upset he was about it. Your husband can be frustrating to deal with."

"I know," I said. "But you shouldn't hit." I wondered if Jim ever hit his wife, but I didn't think it would help to ask. The men were on the porch, laughing about something and slapping each other on the back. I decided to let the conversation drop.

It was a good marriage, I decided. We knew all sorts of things about each other. We had the best baby stuff around, the mobile with the best motor, the crib with the best safety record. Sometimes when we sat in our separate cars in the driveway, and our son was beside me in his little seat, I'd see my husband searching for the baby's eyes in the rearview mirror, and it was intense for me to see this.

I did take a lot of time, thinking about why people hit each other, but in retrospect, it was only important because the issue happened to come up when it did, while my husband and I were still trying to make our marriage truly intimate, as if trying to fix something before it fully existed. When Jim's wife gave birth, she told me she thought of her baby as the physical manifestation of her love for her husband. Of course, I knew better.

While I was pregnant, remembering that unthinking woman's baby and watching my breasts swell even more than they had the first time I tried birth control—while I was noticing more and more about my husband, and feeling, mostly, impatient with what I took to be the projects of that period of time in my life, the new marriage, the pregnancy, all that potential—while I was immersed in all that, and swelled with it, I came to an almost soothing conclusion. Nothing, I concluded, is any good unless it leads to love. The rest, at best, is training, and at worst is wasted time.

But times change, if not people, if not what it feels like to be alive. It was when James started trying to talk, and was wobbling around the house and the yard, pointing at things with a furious look on his face, that I stopped believing in love in that way. I had trouble believing I'd ever asked a person, "Do you love me?" The words no longer represented anything for me, and I came to doubt that they ever really had. Some notions get life, I suppose. Or, no, it's not what I would call life. At least, and at best, they get recognition. I held my boy, and I played with him, and I continued trying to get to know him. Sometimes it was frustrating.

UNTITLED

ADAM PLANTINGA

Rejoice o child in your youth.

—*Ecclesiastes*

The cockatoos squawk and sweep overhead and under a low red sun, Sharman's tents roll into Dowmore Downs. The caravan stops in a clearing of heat and red dust. Soon hard men in suspenders and doughy hats inhale grit from the wind as they unload ring posts and mats, canvas and chairs, an iron bell and a chalkboard. The men set up an array of tents, all-enveloping and dull-colored, four smaller tents ringing a large one. A silver motorcar has been trailing the caravan and now it pulls up and Jimmy Sharman steps out to survey Dowmore Downs. A large boy with a gold ring in his nose and a smooth head opens the passenger side of the motorcar and greets the heat and the dust with a smile that cuts across his face. The boy puts his hand on Jimmy's shoulder and whispers something in his ear. Following Sharman and the boy are long carriages, impossibly long, pulled by muscled, panting horses. There seem to be men in the long carriages but when the carriages pull closer, the men are boys. Boys with the eyes of men. The boys are behind bars—the carriages are cages. The caged boys are Sharman's boxers.

On the outskirts of town, from an open window of the First and Last Hotel, a dark man with a hat pulled low watches them all come in. The dark man will leave the hotel and find another place close by, now that Sharman's boxers are in town. As he packs his bags, the dark man hears something on the wind that stirs up old memories. Old ghosts. Sharman, he knows, will be at Dowmore Downs for a month, perhaps, until the rains come. Then the caravan will move on.

Word spreads quickly. Sharman's boxers are back. Young boys run through the fields and tell the men, who nod and then return to their work. The blacksmiths and the grocers hear it from their customers. Men talk about it over cigars at dinner. The word reaches neighboring towns. The word is out. The word is everywhere. Sharman's boxers are back.

It is the first night of the fights and outside the tents the barker in his harsh monotone urges the crowd to step right up and get in on the greatest game of them all. The ticketman sells the tickets, and a man in a candy-striped suit takes the tickets at the entrance and hands out the fight cards.

The people stream into the massive, billowing tent. Those who are from the fields and the shops close to Dowmore Downs have walked in. Those who work at the big businesses have driven out from the city. They sit on long wooden benches in the dark and wipe their foreheads with handkerchiefs, for though the sun has sunk low, the air in the tents is unforgiving and thick. Some of the crowd seek out the two hatchet-faced betmen who take the wagers on the side: *"Twenty on Hans, twenty on Israel, twenty, twenty, thirty, forty on Rogers."* Money flies through the hands of the hatchet-faced men who handle the money like they are used to it, like it is an old friend. The dark man with the hat pulled low sits in the crowd and one of the hatchet-faced men approaches him and gives the odds but the dark man says nothing to him and the hatchet-faced man leaves.

Quiet settles in the stands. The bets have been made. Now all eyes strain to the center of the tent, to the ring. The ring is a spot of light in the darkness and Sharman's boxers stand in the darkness and wait for the bell. Those that are dark are swallowed in the darkness and those that are white look like faint phantoms. Near the ring are stairs which lead to an upper level where there is a box. Sharman watches everything from the box.

Rogers is first on the card and he moves with precision in the ring, an automaton. He does not hit hard but he hits often and soon his opponent's knees sway and buckle. He cannot stand and Rogers wins. The crowd cheers on his blows, a wave of energy surging through the stands whenever he makes contact. The cheers do nothing for Rogers and he does not think of the cheers as he steps out of the ring. The next fight is between a heavily muscled aborigine and a compact boy with long arms. The aborigine wins quickly, striking with powerful blows that smack dully into bone and muscle.

Those that are new to the tents and have not seen the fights quickly learn there are two rules. The first rule is no blows below the belt. The second rule is fight as many rounds as it takes until someone cannot stand. A bell signals the rounds but the boxers do not always stop at the bell because the bell is something made by men and what is going on between the ropes is a dance between two animals. The bell rings now for a new fight and a white-eyed boy explodes at the sound, bouncing around in the ring, hot fear shooting through his body that makes his arms and neck hum. He flies at his opponent, a wide, bronzed boy who takes one step back and hits the white-eyed boy in the throat. The white-eyed boy spins to the ground. The crowd jeers. He stands up and the bronzed boy hits him in the face two times. The white-eyed boy already hears the drums. He knows he is losing because he hears the drums, because the drums are in his ears, burning, beating out staccato bursts of pain. Sometimes the pain is white, and sometimes it is red, but always it beats. The round is over and the white-eyed boy kneels in his corner and hears the drums and the drums are white. While he kneels, the crowd stirs and hums and Toothman scampers into the ring with a bucket and cleans up the teeth and the spills. In the crowd, the dark man with the hat pulled low watches Toothman, who is small and hunched. Toothman used to fight but he was hit too many times in the eyes and now he cannot see well and cannot fight so he is Toothman and between rounds, he cleans up the teeth and the spills. The next round begins. The white-eyed boy is hit and goes down again, flailing down to the hardness of the canvas. The crowd surges and shouts.

It is the only game in town.

Late at night, after the fighting is done, the crowds have gone home, and the smell of straining bodies and sweat has filtered out in the air, Sharman's boxers are walked in a chain to the First and Last Hotel just outside of Dowmore Downs. The boxers have stayed in many hotels but they are all the First and Last Hotel for they are all the same: low ceilings, white walls, open windows in which the winds gust and hum, pulling the curtains out to play. Outside, the dingoes battle in the red dust and laundry lines bounce and sway, the clothing flapping in a grotesque dance. One of Sharman's men watches the front door of the hotel. He is the Doorman, who cannot be bribed even if there was money to bribe him with. At the Doorman's side is a long rifle that he is very good with. He can hit anything with his rifle. No one can run from the Doorman's rifle.

There are five floors and many rooms in the hotel. One hundred boxers fill up the floors, scattered mostly, sometimes together in twos or threes but mostly scattered. But in a large room on the third floor, six stay together. Rogers leads the six. It is not because he is the oldest—he is eighteen—but because he has a way of calming the others. And he has not fallen in the ring. He is blessed, they say. He has fought thirty-five times without falling.

There is not much in the large room. Some beds, some wooden dressers, a lamp that gives off light dimly. In the corner near the open window, Rogers does handstand push-ups against the wall. He breathes heavily with each repetition. Next to him is Jangler, shuffling, playing cards. Jangler is a year older than Rogers, and lean and red with long arms. Jangler always has problems with his ribs. His ribs jangle so the others call him Jangler, except Rogers, who calls him by his first name. Jangler has won eleven fights and lost twelve.

Rabbit Nix watches Jangler shuffle. Rabbit is small and scared and sixteen. Rabbit moves over to where Rogers has finished his push-ups and Rogers takes a worn book from underneath the bed and begins to read to him. Many of the boxers cannot read, but Rabbit is the worst off of them all, so Rogers gives him lessons. Rabbit sweats a lot even when he is not fighting. His eyes dart around and he doesn't say much. But that is not why they call him Rabbit. They call him Rabbit because he is always washing his hands, always cleaning himself like the desert hares. Rabbit is new and has only fought a few times. He has lost mostly.

Wilco sits on one of the beds. He takes up most of the bed because he weighs two hundred and fifty pounds. Wilco fights everyone else who weighs over two hundred and twenty pounds and he wins most of his fights. It is hard to hurt Wilco. Wilco is playing a counting game of sticks with Simon, who is aborigine and wears a cross around his neck and tells everyone about Jesus in a voice that still cracks. Simon hits hard and wins more than he loses.

Case stands quietly near the window, motionless. Case, fresh-faced and solid. Case who has been hit too many times though he is not yet seventeen and is slow now in the head. When he talks, only every fourth or fifth word makes sense. Case does not remember much, but he does have a distant memory of a New Year's party and sometimes he walks through the hotel room and imagines himself at that party and imagines the others in the room as the party's guests. The others are frightened when he does this because he speaks to them as if they were the guests at the party. But Rogers has said it is good for Case to do this and they should not think ill of him. Case wins a little more than half his fights.

When they are not fighting or training, they all have something to pass the time. Rogers has some poetry on loose leafs of paper and also a calendar on which he keeps careful track of the days and the seasons. Rabbit has board games and Simon has his Bible and Wilco has some faded books, adventure books mostly. Case has the New Year's party and Jangler has cards. Jangler plays Two Jack Up and Jump with the cards. Sometimes Jangler plays with Rabbit but usually he plays by himself because Jangler likes to make up his own rules for the games as he goes, rules no one else can understand. They also have something else. They will never fight each other. They will never fight each other because the boxers fight according to weight and none of them are close to each other's weight. In that they find comfort.

Rogers leads the six. Rogers, quiet, confident. Rogers who cannot fall in the ring. But there are other boxers in the hotel whom Rogers does not lead. Hans, Israel, Limmy, Rourke. Rogers does not lead them. They go their own way and avoid Rogers and his, grouping with those who are either bigger or smaller than they—

with those they will not have to fight. And Cutter. Rogers does not lead Cutter. For Rogers and Cutter both weigh the same, they both weigh two hundred pounds. Sometimes they brush past each other at the meal table or stand near each other in the darkness near the ring and there is an unspoken hate between them because sometime they will have to fight. Cutter is thick and bald with narrow eyes. Because he hits so hard, he has won forty fights and lost one. No one wants to go in the ring with Cutter because he smashes bone and breaks teeth and holds rocks in his hands when he is not fighting and tries to crush them. His real name is not Cutter but he is called Cutter because he smiles when he knows his opponent is weak. He smiles a big smile that cuts his face in two. He does not stay in the hotel with the others. Cutter stays with Jimmy Sharman at the lodge in the center of town, the lodge of dark wood and soft lights. The lodge is where the gentlemen stay when they are in town. It is where Jimmy Sharman stays when he is in town and Cutter stays in Jimmy's room with Jimmy because he is Jimmy's boy. Cutter has a gold ring in his nose that he does not take out for fights because Jimmy likes the gold ring to stay in.

Rogers is not a child, he has seen too much. Cutter is not a child because he is with Jimmy. But the rest are, children that put on thin gloves that weigh a few ounces and hit each other until someone cannot walk. Some of the boys were taken to settle land debts and some, aborigines mostly, were taken from the auction block. Some were just taken, off of the streets in Sydney and Melbourne, those it did not look like anyone would miss. They are taken and branded. A moment of blinding pain and unearthly smell, then the stomach gives up what it holds, a cold compress is placed on the brand, and a scar forms. It is Sharman's brand, a large X that sprawls over the left biceps. Now they are branded and they fight. They are orphans, runaways, and slaves. Because they do not matter, they must fight.

During the day they train. They have nothing else to do, for they cannot work and the fights are at night. But there is meaning in the training, meaning as the heavy bag thunks and the speed bag rattles and the jump rope whisks and whips until their arms and lungs burn, and there is meaning in the burn. After the training, the box-

ers assemble in a long tent where the Bakerman feeds them milk so
their bones are hard and will not break, and meat so their punches
are strong and snap, and rice so their knees are sturdy and will not
buckle.

After the meal, most go back to the hotel. Some do push-ups
there and some do sit-ups. At first. Then, when they stop fighting
for pride and start fighting because it is what they must do, then
they instead peer out onto the horizon, into the red dust. They listen to the wind and are silent and do not want to live forever. That
is when they say the days are darker than the nights.

Days blur together. Of the six, only Rogers bothers to keep them
straight. The fights continue. The fights always continue. The barker
works the crowd and the hatchet-faced men knife through the stands
taking bets and there are always fights. A blond boy, sweaty and
pale, bruised cheekbones the only color on his face, fights a boy who
is short and low to the ground and growls. After four rounds, both
of them gasp for air and cannot raise their hands anymore. The next
fight is a lean boy who fights against Case. The lean boy lands short
jabs that make a popping sound on Case and then skirts out of his
reach, then moves in again, beating a stiff rhythm on Case's head
and arms until Case is bloody and weak.

This is the place. Dowmore Downs. The people come from miles to
watch boys fight. There is no championship. There is no title.

Jangler is starting to get heavier. He has been eating a lot lately,
sausage and porridge mostly. Jangler has always liked to eat but
there was a time when his father told him when to stop and leave
food for his brothers and sisters. Now no one tells him when to
stop. Jangler is close to weighing as much as Simon. Simon has
been watching Jangler eat, and at the noon meal, he puts a hand on
Jangler's wrist when Jangler gets up for seconds. Jangler frowns and
sits back down. But he skips dinner that night and breakfast the next
morning and has only soup for the noon meal. At night he fights a
quick-punching boy with a low brow who hits him often and hurts

him. After the fight, the two of them whisper and nod that all is right. They will not have to fight each other.

The next day there are fights but soon an off night comes. Tonight no one fights. It is the time for leaning back and talking. The six of them talk a bit about how the war might be going against the Turks. They talk of the fights and Simon brings up the name of Jimmy Sharman. And from the corner, Rabbit, who has been washing his hands in a small basin, leaps to his feat and cries out an oath against the name. The others start at this, for it is not like Rabbit. They are quiet for a time as they all think about the name but it does not mean much to them. It is a distant name. They move to talk of Cutter and his gold ring that he does not take out for fights. And sometimes Rogers and Jangler, who are the only ones old enough to remember, talk about one of Sharman's boxers who may have gotten away. They did not know him well, for he was not one of them. The others circle Rogers and Jangler, entranced. It is hard to be sure of the fate of the one, Rogers explains. He overheard the Doorman insisting to Sharman that he got the one with his long rifle. But there was something in the Doorman's voice that spoke otherwise, something in the mood of Sharman afterward. Something in the wind. The others listen and nod and smile. He must have gotten away. One must have gotten away. Rogers breaks off from the story to give Rabbit his reading lessons and after a time, Jangler tells some jokes that are not very funny. No one laughs but they nod occasionally. Simon takes out his Bible and turns to the Gospels.

"Let me tell you about Jesus," Simon says and his voice cracks. He looks around, face hot. Rabbit giggles. Simon presses on, reading from the Book of John. The others listen and do not say much. After a time, Wilco takes out a harmonica to play but the others shake their heads and he puts it away. Simon keeps reading. Wilco reaches behind his pillow and brings out a small ball made of rubber and tosses it to Case. Case tosses it back and the ball plunks Wilco on his lower lip. Wilco frowns at Case and Case starts to giggle and then Wilco starts to laugh, his great body shaking. Soon the room echoes with the noise of laughter. Laughter unchecked. When the laughter has subsided, they look at each other with contented grins, as if full from a feast. There is silence in the room. Their grins disappear. There is a reverence for the laughter.

On the off nights, they drink. The bar downstairs is always open. Because Sharman has talked to the bartender, he is always happy to give them drinks. There are many boxers downstairs in the bar who drink, mostly in silence. Drinking makes the pain and the fear go away in the First and Last Hotel, for the doctor does not come so often to heal the bones and the bruises and the cuts. The whisky is the doctor, the boxers sometimes say.

But even with the whisky, the fear comes. Fear of losing too many fights. Losing too many fights means a meeting with Jimmy Sharman. And no one that ever meets with Jimmy comes back. They disappear. Only Sharman knows where they go. Somewhere in the heat and dust and red rock they go because they have lost too many fights and sometimes at night Jangler thinks he can hear their voices on the wind but he does not tell anyone what he hears. Jangler has lost many fights. But he does not know how many fights too many is. Sometimes Jangler cannot sleep because he does not know how many fights too many is.

Business has been good the past week and Sharman lets his boxers have an off night on the town. The shops and bars of Dowmore Downs are clustered tight and small and beaten down by wind and time. The dogs play in the streets. The boxers walk the streets and Sharman's men are all around them, big men with small eyes and with bellies that roll over their belts. Out on the street, a woman with a lipstick and a short dress beckons from the doorway and Rabbit looks at her and then looks at Rogers. Rogers frowns and pulls him away from the doorway. But as he does, he recalls nights he spent with another such woman, times that seem long ago. He remembers the quick stab of pleasure, the sickly sweet odor, the pale powdered skin, the dead eyes. Rogers moves Rabbit past the doorway toward a bar on the edge of town. They drink in the bar as Sharman's men watch. Cutter is in the bar, drinking with one of Sharman's men, and he sees Rogers and his face is dark and he says something to Rogers. But the drink slurs the words and Rogers does not understand him. Cutter says something else and Rogers gets up and leaves with Rabbit. Cutter watches them go. They return to the First and Last Hotel, where the rest of the six drink some more and talk whisky talk that makes no sense and soon drift off to sleep. But Rogers does not drink any more. He stays up late. He thinks of how he does not want to fight Cutter. And, as he often does, he thinks of the train. Rogers has been around long enough to know where to listen and he has heard a train might be coming in fourteen nights. He keeps track on his calendar. He looks at the sleeping forms strewn around him. They cannot come with him. They would be spotted, the lot of them traveling together. Besides, they could not make the journey. Too many miles of desert to travel between Dowmore Downs and the train. But they need him. Here. The train. They need him to survive. The train. They need him to show how to apply oil so punches slip off, how to breathe, how to fight down the fear. No. He has already shown. The train is coming in fourteen nights and Rogers will wait, slip, spring, move across the miles of desert and get on the train and head west. It is a long ways to the train but he knows the cockatoos will lead him to water and he knows how to tell directions by using his watch and watching his shadow on the sand. Rogers runs his fingers over his left bicep, feeling the raised skin where Sharman's hot iron left its mark. He falls asleep dreaming of trains, trains that cut their own course through the desert.

A week has passed and there have been many fights. Rabbit enters late one night after the others have already come in. He has just fought and lost. He is not hurt badly but he is crying because he does not wish to fight anymore. Wilco goes to comfort him but Rogers motions him away and all turn with somber faces until Rabbit's sobs have quieted. He must be taught not to cry. He must be stronger than that. Rabbit sniffles and is done. The tension breaks. Rogers comes over and urges Rabbit to wash up so he does not get the shakes. When Rabbit is done washing, Rogers gets a worn book with a rocking horse on the cover from under Wilco's bed and sits down with Rabbit for their lesson.

"River," Rogers says, pointing to a picture of silver water surrounded by trees.

"River," Rabbit whispers with red eyes and scratches the letters on the floor with a chunk of coal.

"Knight," Rogers says, turning the page and pointing to a picture of an armored man near a castle. Rabbit sees the picture and wishes he could be in that suit of armor. He would be safe there in the armor, in the castle. He could stay there and just watch people as they walked by. Rabbit begins to cry again because he has no armor.

Night falls and the crowd comes in carriages and some in motorcars and they kick up red dust when they come. The crowd watches the fights. They say "Ahhhh" sometimes and sometimes they are silent. But when the blows become thick and fighters are brought to their knees, the crowd chants and pulses, eyes bright, hats pushed back, alive, so alive, nerves charged, woven into the fight. The crowd jabbers and points and gestures and grins and pokes each other and nods. Some of the men have come straight from the fields and wear dirty clothes, but many are from the city and wear felt hats and smell of strong cologne. The few women there wear ostrich hats and clutch jeweled handbags. A thin man with a thin mustache who is the marshal of Dowmore Downs watches intently. He is slightly drunk, and punctuates the blows with a thrust fist. The marshal comes every night to watch the fights because he likes to see the boys fight but mostly because he has done well with his bets.

Tonight Cutter fights and wins easily. It is a quick fight and a messy fight that keeps the Toothman busy cleaning up the spills. The crowd roars its approval for they love Cutter because of his power in the ring. Wilco is the next fighter and he does well, punches sinking into his massive body that he shrugs off and returns with more force. At the end of the third round he spits up some blood, but the boy he fights spits up more and cannot rise and Wilco wins. After the fight, Toothman scurries into the ring with a sponge and his bucket and mops up the blood. Jangler fights as well. Early in the fight, he starts hearing the drums and soon he has lost and cracked another rib. The crowd does not understand what it means to fight with cracked ribs. They do not understand what it means to spit out blood or to be in a ring with a boy who wants to kill you with his hands. They do not need to know this to clap wildly. Case fights next and lays a stinger on a boy and locks up his arm. Case's next punch catches the boy on the jaw and breaks it. The boy flops over the ropes and into the sawdust and does not get up. Case's arms drop limply to his side as he is pronounced the winner. He peers over the ropes at the boy. Case's face wrinkles up when he sees the boy is not moving. Sharman watches from his box at the top of the stairs. Cutter is with him. Sharman takes Cutter's hand and squeezes it. The fights are beautiful to them.

Another off night comes, a welcome night, and they huddle when it gets cold. Rogers tells them he has seen a paper downstairs in the bar that says the Australians are beating the Turks in the war. The six smile and nod, all save for Rabbit.

"Who are the Turks," Rabbit asks.

"Our enemies," Rogers says. "We are at war with them."

Rabbit nods and takes a piece of coal and scratches some letters on the floor. Then Rogers tells what he has read of the foot races at Perth. There are more nods because some of them remember seeing the foot races once, the men in the brightly colored jerseys, the great flashes of speed, the ribbon at the end waiting to be broken. Case gets up while they talk and paces the room and they know he is thinking not of the races but of the New Year's party. Images are flashing through Case's head of china and a red tablecloth, of savory odors and the ringing laughter. He was a child then and he was in the corner. From the corner, he watched everyone. Case begins to talk and every other word sounds like "galosh" because he has been hit so many times in the head. But after some time, the others piece together what he is trying to say. He is saying that a woman sat by this table here, a beautiful woman in a red satin dress, and near the door was a man with a top hat who had a drink in his hands. They repeat this back to Case and he nods fervently and waves his arms, running from one corner of the room to the other. Rabbit backs away from Case and looks as if he will cry, and Rogers takes Case in midrun and holds him for a moment, and Case stops talking and everyone is quiet. Jangler is at the window and he has heard none of this for the winds are coming fierce and wild and he hears the dead voices that come with the winds. He covers his ears with his fists to drive them away. He counts again the number of fights he has lost. Thirteen. He counts again. Thirteen. He has lost thirteen fights. Is thirteen too many fights to lose? How many fights is too many?

It is noon and raining heavily. It is a storm. On the outskirts of town in a small room in a boardinghouse, the dark man with the hat stirs in his bed, awoken from black dreams. He cries out, remembering a day when the Doorman slept, when the long rifle slipped from his hands and was silent. He remembers the bounce and the clatter of a cargo train headed west in the rain. Across town, at the First and Last Hotel, Rabbit watches the dark clouds outside and peers out the window onto the streets below which have already turned to deep mud from the heavy rain. It is still some hours before the fights.

"Let's go out," Rabbit says hesitantly. The others look at him and he points to the muddy streets below. Simon murmurs something and Wilco grins and Rogers smiles in assent. They push their way out of the room, descend the stairs, and go to the door. Rogers looks at Doorman, who asks them where they believe they are going.

"To the street," Rogers says. "We'll be in sight."

The Doorman waits for a moment. There is nowhere for them to go. There are no trains. And at his side he has his long rifle. No one can run from his rifle. The Doorman nods. Rabbit grins, a big grin. He steps gingerly out into the street, then gathers more speed and slides headfirst through the mud. Case joins him, diving in, mud spattering through the air, and then comes Wilco, his 250 pounds propelling him past the others. Rabbit leaps to his feet and takes a handful of mud, hurling it at Jangler, who ducks and then dives in backward, laughing and waving his arms, forgetting the pain in his ribs for now. Rogers barrels in after all the rest feet first and comes up hobbling and holding his leg. He walks in a wide circle, testing his weight on his leg and wincing. They cluster around him and Rogers laughs it off but does not dive anymore. He instead watches soberly as the rest dive in again and again. The train comes in three nights. He cannot make it to the train like this. He must heal. The train comes in three nights. He watches the others and the laughter rings out and the rain comes down and the mud flies.

The next night the boxers are led to the tent and walk over cracked earth to learn there's been a mistake on the card. Rabbit is to fight Apple Hornsby but Rabbit weighs one hundred and thirty-five pounds and Apple weighs two hundred and two. Above, in his box, Jimmy frowns because it is bad business to have an unfair fight. But the fight cannot be stopped because the crowd is in their seats and bets have been made, bets on how long Rabbit will last. Most say two rounds. A hardy soul says three. In the box, a man with a crooked nose says something to Jimmy and Jimmy nods and says something low in return.

The dark man in the hat is in the crowd. He looks up at the stairs. He looks up at Sharman's box. The lights are blazing in the box. Rabbit is shivering in the darkness outside of the ring, waiting for someone to tell him he does not have to fight Apple Hornsby, who none of the six really knows but whose triceps are cut and defined and who outweighs Rabbit by seventy pounds. Jangler, Wilco, and Rogers stand in the darkness wondering if Rabbit will have to fight. Jangler bites his lip and Wilco clenches his fists and Rogers watches the crowd for Sharman's men to see if they will make Rabbit fight.

Silence. One of Sharman's men pushes through the crowd and approaches Rabbit in the ring.

"You're up, Rabbit," he says.

Rabbit slides underneath the ropes toward his corner. He is numb and tries to remember a prayer but stumbles badly over the words. The bell rings, could that be the bell already? and the crowd shouts, and Rabbit charges into the center of the ring, wired, nostrils flaring, eyes wide. He ducks Apple's fists and dances to and fro. He is quick. Perhaps he will last. The crowd's eyes are bright and their mouths are open. They like to see Rabbit dance. Apple connects on Rabbit's chin and Rabbit backpedals, hurt, swallowing sweat. Rabbit dances and Apple hits him and Rabbit dances and Apple hits him hard. There are seventy more pounds of force in Apple's fists than

Rabbit has felt before and he bleeds from the face, his eyes are rolling back, and he is twitching—his lips move but no sound comes
out. Apple hits him again and Rabbit goes down and flops around
for a while and the audience roars and thinks to themselves that
Rabbit looks like a fish. The dark man looks at Rabbit and there's
something in the dark man's face, sorrow? rage? It is gone now. And
Apple moves in to pick Rabbit up and destroy him, but now there
is Rogers at the side of the ring, Rogers who knows Sharman is
watching him and does not want interference in the fights but does
not care. Rogers stares at Apple, and Apple sees him and sees something deep and dangerous in his eyes. Apple moves away slowly. The
crowd comes to a hush. Rabbit is helped off the canvas, murmuring. Above, from his box, Sharman watches Rogers and does not
like what Rogers has done. Sharman turns to Cutter and whispers
something in his ear. Cutter smiles and nods.

The sun is red and the clouds surrounding it look like thin paper.
It is the last night of the fights before the rains come to stay, before the crowd goes back to the shops and the fields and the city. In
Sharman's box, the lights are on, they are burning fiercely, and the
dark man is in the crowd. There is a hum in the crowd, a buzz in
the crowd, and the buzz says, "Cutter is to fight Rogers, Cutter is
to fight Rogers." "Cutter has lost once," they say. "Rogers has never
lost," they say as they nod and gesture with their hands. The dark
man can hear laughter ringing out from the box. There are many
people up in the box because sometimes Sharman invites the gentlemen to sit with him and smoke and watch.

   The crowd is charged for the final night of the fights. They stamp
their feet and cry out. Jangler is first on the card. He has been losing
and he is scared because he remembers what he has heard on the
wind. But he fights a boy who is tired because he fought the night
before. Jangler ducks and pushes rights and lefts at the boy and fends
him off with his long arms until the boy is leg-weary and fighting
for air. Then Jangler moves in and the rest is easy. He wins and the
crowd is shouting for him but Jangler gets no pleasure from the
crowd, he tunes them out, and instead has the curious recollection

of carving the name Sally in a tree with a clasp knife. Jangler does not know why he remembers this now, it seems strange and distant to him. But as Sharman's men push him out of the ring to make way for the next fight, he has a faraway look on his face.

The crowd now scans their card and scream and chant. Cutter is to fight Rogers. The betting is fierce and will not stop. The hatchet-faced men run through the crowd, shouting and gesturing. Rogers comes out of the darkness into the light of the ring and rubs his leg, favoring it as he steps between the ropes and takes his corner. He feels his leg pull with every step and feels something cold in his stomach as Cutter comes from the darkness and slips between the ropes and smiles at him. Cutter's head is shaved smooth and he does not take the gold ring from his nose, not even for Rogers.

At the bell, Rogers and Cutter do not dance away from each other but pound like machines. Rogers moves easily for a moment but now he is leaning heavily on his leg and realizing he cannot do what he wants in the ring. Cutter has him against the ropes and is hitting him. The dark man is close to the crowd. The dark man remembers now the feel of the ring. He remembers Cutter who only has one loss looking into his eyes. He remembers how Cutter did not smile when he hit the canvas. The dark man looks up at Sharman's box. The lights are blazing. He looks at the stairs that lead to the box. One of the hatchet-faced men dances around the crowd trying to get more takers. He approaches the dark man and screams in his ear and the dark man pushes him away, flings him away, into the crowd. No one notices. All eyes are on the ring.

Cutter is sweating furiously and hitting Rogers and opening up cuts on his head. Rogers cannot get away because his leg has knotted up. He cannot get away from Cutter's fists because his leg is heavy and numb. He thinks of the train. He cannot catch the train if Cutter hits him like this. Rogers cannot remember when he last heard the drums but he hears them now as Cutter pounds his arms and chest, the drums in his ears, burning. Everything is slow and blurry now as it always is when the drums come. He cannot catch the train if the drums are in his ears. He tries to fight down the drums but they are strong and both red and white. He paws weakly in the air at Cutter and is staggered by fists and stumbles down for a moment. Cutter smiles. His smile splits his face and his teeth gleam. Above the fight, in his box, Sharman smiles as Cutter smiles.

"Take him," Sharman whispers.

The crowd surges to their feet. Sharman's boxers both cry out and whisper, Rogers has never gone down, but look there! He has gone down again! But now he is up, limping, leaning in, and Cutter hits him again and Rogers goes down and then gets up and stumbles —there's an odd look on Rogers's face, he looks like he's about to say something. The crowd moves forward in their seats, intensely interested in what he could be saying. But he says nothing and Cutter hits him twice in the head and Rogers makes a low gurgling sound instead and falls. His head bounces twice. The second bounce is bad.

The dark man has pushed through the crowd, he is close to the ring now. Circling the ring are Sharman's men. There are many of them and the dark man looks past them into the ring and understands why Rogers is gurgling—he has been hit so hard that he has bitten off his tongue. Most of his tongue lies in the middle of the ring. Toothman, clutching to the outside ring post, sees it too and stares, transfixed. In his time he's cleaned up teeth, lots of teeth of course, and blood and spit and even an ear once but never a tongue. To him it is beautiful. Cutter smiles his smile, teeth flashing in a grin of triumph. He picks Rogers up off the canvas and holds him there and hits him and hits him. Above, in his box, Sharman tenses.

"Yes, take him," he says, voice rising, leaping to his feet.

Some of Sharman's men around the ring watch the fight but now some are watching the dark man with narrow eyes. The dark man knows he cannot get past them to the ring. He cannot stop the fight. He pushes his way back through the crowd and as he goes, some of Sharman's men let out a shout, they know who he is, they remember him. They try to follow but there are too many of them to get through the crowd all at once and they get caught up in each other for they are not used to moving fast. The dark man cuts toward the stairs which lead to Jimmy Sharman's box, where the lights are blazing. At the bottom of the stairs is a man with a crooked nose and deep-set eyes who looks at the dark man with a glimmer of recognition, then shakes it off and rumbles that he cannot go up the stairs. The dark man clenches his fists. He smiles faintly, a horrible smile.

Cutter's fists are a blur, sinking into Rogers, killing Rogers. Rogers has fallen limply against the ropes. His left arm is entangled in the top rope. He cannot move and his face is numb. But he thinks clearly now. He cannot catch the train like this. He is losing. He is missing his tongue. How can he catch the train like this? Cutter's fists snap into his head and Rogers does not think anymore. In the seats, one man's face twitches as he thinks of his own son. "Stop," he croaks. "For God's sake, stop."

The dark man steps over a man with a crooked nose.

Rogers hangs limply from Cutter's thick arm. Sharman's boxers stand in the darkness and are silent. They have not seen this before. Jangler and Wilco and Case and Simon are among them in the darkness. Their shouts of rage fade out and their heads droop. The crowd stamps and whistles and shouts for more as Cutter holds Rogers and hits him and hits him and hits him. Cutter's left glove has come off now, the rotting laces have snapped, but he does not notice, he is locked into a rhythm. Cutter is not smiling anymore but has a flat look on his face, his mouth is slightly open, he looks almost sad, he looks almost like a child again. The ropes keep Rogers up. Boxers call it Rubberman, what Cutter is doing to him, holding up and hitting someone who cannot stand on his own. Rogers's eyes are rolled back and he is covered with blood from his mouth. Cutter is holding him up and hitting him, his bare left hand is crushing Rogers's face as he hits him again and hits him and hits him and hits him, he will not stop. The crowd throbs and pulses and chants, a thousand voices blended into one. The dark man has been taught not to cry but he has not learned, his face is wet, he is howling as he ascends the stairs to Sharman's box, where the lights are burning and the noise is burning and outside out of the darkness and the pain, the cockatoos veer off into the sun and the red dust of Dowmore Downs swirls and builds and flies.

INDIAN SUMMER SUNDAY

CRESTON LEA

In the darkness at the edge of the orchard I sit and drink and watch the Mexicans pit roosters against each other in a blue plastic swimming pool. It's the kind of cheap pool you see all over the place, on lawns and porches all summer long. There's maybe two dozen men standing around in a circle trying to keep quiet, just sort of chanting in Spanish or whatever. But they've been drinking too, and can't keep from crying out every now and again. Most of what I hear is the flapping of wings and the *skitch skitch* of talons on plastic. By the number of men in the circle I figure some of the pickers from the other orchards nearby have found their way over.

It is almost four in the morning on a Sunday and I have until nine o'clock to make a sermon. I am what they call a man of God. Or was. Maybe *was* is a better word. I harbor grave doubts these days. And I am, now, a month and a half drunk. So, for reasons that I cannot explain to myself, I've come to where I am not welcome in the middle of the night to hide in a hedgerow and watch these Mexicans fight roosters.

The sun isn't even up yet, but it's still hot as fire. The beer I've got is warm, so I'm holding off on that for the time being and concentrating on what's left of the gin.

They've got three cars around the other side of the pool with headlights on. I just see silhouettes.

It's hard to tell just how drunk I am. Hiding in a hedgerow on the edge of an apple orchard, by myself, watching a bunch of pickers play with roosters is a pretty dreamy kind of thing anyway, so who knows? Things always seem fairly lunatic when I'm drinking.

There's a lot of murmuring as a fight ends, dollars being passed around. A dark young Mexican with a flowery shirt steps out from the circle and walks toward me with a black rooster under his arm like a football, his other hand on the bird's head. He stops fifteen feet off from the hedgerow where I'm lying and gets down on one knee. The rooster is purring and sounds like it's got blood or snot in its throat. Even I can tell that it's close to death. The Mexican pulls a bottle of something from his shirt pocket and pours it here and there on the rooster's body, rubbing it in and talking to himself— or to the rooster, it's hard to tell. He's trying to save it. Then I hear him curse in a loud whisper. *Hijo di puta.* It sounds so close, my skin moves. I know I'm about to witness violence. Quick, he whips the big black rooster up by its neck and brings it back down again, like a bag of dirt, and spits at it, throwing his hands up and turning back to the circle of men. He takes about four steps before coming back and kicking the rooster across the grass to near where I'm hiding. Then he throws the bottle of salve after it, into the trees over my head. I hear it bump down through the branches.

After the Mexicans get into the cars and disappear it's quiet and dark and I feel very much alone lying there in the branches and dirt. I finish the gin off and go pick up the big black rooster. I can't see just leaving it there for the vultures and flies when moments ago it was alive and fighting for its life. Its neck is thick and soft except for the places where blood has thickened to paste. I can smell an antiseptic fruitiness from where they've spat brandy under its tail feathers to make it crazy for fighting. Its skinny tongue is drooped out of its mouth and I shake its head to keep it from licking my hand. And so I walk like that, a heavy dead rooster in one hand and four sixteen-ounce cans of warm beer in their plastic retainer in the other—back to my Buick at the edge of the orchard.

With the headlights off, I drive my car slowly by the light of the moon between rows and rows of twisty apple trees, looking for the way out of the orchard on a Sunday morning. I have five hours until I have to deliver the message to my congregation so I turn on the radio to see if I can pick up some notions from a radio-church crusader. But there is only an all-night call-in talk show, coming in loud and clear from someplace. And by the time I find my way to the orchard gate, there is a woman on from Bangor, Maine, who says with complete conviction that O. J. Simpson is innocent. As if she were there. As if she knows the truth of all things.

The road leads me over bumps and holes and eventually past the pickers' barracks. The three cars from the cockpit are parked up on the dirt yard between the long cinder-block buildings. Four Mexicans are out sitting on the cars. Their heads turn as they watch me pass and it unsettles me so I speed up to get out of there quicker. This day is the day they rest, Sunday. Yes, by and by, when the liquor wears them down, they *will* rest. Saturday night gives way to Sunday morning. Always has.

I have taken to driving up here to watch the cockfights on Saturday nights because they are of another world. It beats driving all night or, worse, sitting home in front of a pad of yellow paper with blue lines, trying to come up with something to say.

Farther down the road, two Mexicans are walking on the grass strip between the tire ruts. They are drunk, I can tell by the way they walk, heavy-like. I am practically on top of them when they hear me and turn around. They are just staring dumb, so I flash the lights and they squint, caught like jacked deer. One is fat and the other skinny, just like a joke. There is no way they will make it back to the other orchard on foot without waking up in a ditch first.

"You boys want a ride?" I say to the fat one, who stands on my side of the road. His eyes are half closed and he's wearing a T-shirt that says "Mess with the Best Die Like the Rest."

He doesn't say anything but comes back to the door behind me and gets in. He sits hard and falls over onto his side grumbling in Spanish. The skinny one seems a little less enthusiastic but gets in next to me, leans against the door. Neither of them says a word. They smell of liquor. I turn my lights on and drive a little faster.

The skinny one looks at me and then away again, out the window. "English?" I say. He looks at me again and I can tell he's seeing right through me. He doesn't even know where he is. The fat one snores in the backseat.

I reach for a beer where I have put them, on the raised strip where the gearshift is, and feel the greasy wing feathers of the dead rooster there. I find the beer and when I offer one to the skinny

Mexican next to me, he takes it and I try to hide the body of the
rooster under the seat while he fusses over the beer tab. He's having
trouble getting his thumb under the ring. I'm having trouble getting the rooster out of the way. So I quit trying. What does he care
anyway?

The dirt road turns to pavement with a bump and we pass by
a few dark trailers, pickup trucks in the driveways, empty *Union
Leader* boxes glowing bright orange under my headlights.

Out on the highway I drive the Buick south, toward Lebanon.
I figure they hitched their way north to the fights from the Eaton
orchards. It's as good a guess as any. The only lights on the highway are from semis driving north, from Boston or Hartford or New
York. Soon the skinny Mexican is asleep too, the can of beer between his legs. He has horrible buck teeth.

I take the Lebanon exit and pull into the huge overlit parking lot
of the Grand Union Superstore that went up last year or maybe the
year before that. I leave the car in the fire lane and go inside. There
are girls in red aprons sitting on the checkout counters and they
look over at me as the electronic door squeaks open to let me into
the light. I realize how I must look. Dirty. In the aisles, teenaged
boys are shelving boxes of cereal, relish, spaghetti from rolling carts.
I am the only customer in this bright enormous place. My knees are
tired. And I am dead drunk. Being in the light makes that fact very
clear to me. My feet automatically lead me to the beer and wine sec-
tion, where I stand and stare for a very long time before deciding on
the Genesee Cream. I carry the two six-packs back up to the register
and ask the girl what the time is and she presses a button on her cash
register which makes 5.12 flash on the little screen. My feet take me
to the Buick.

The fact is that I've been drinking for almost six weeks now.
I have lost my appetite for anything other than white bread, dry
noodles, sometimes a potato, which I figure to be the only things
that will soak up the excess alcoholic bile that is surely pouring from
my liver. The congregation has become a foreign thing to me. The
new people seem to come in droves. I can't speak a word to them
from my heart. There is nothing worse than having to speak with a

false heart. I don't know that drinking helps any, but it's the route I've chosen.

Outside, I see that the skinny Mexican is busy puking all over the parking lot. He's hunched over in a three-point stance like a football player, coughing and spitting. I get to my door and see that he has left a thin trail of vomit on the seat as well, which is really a painful thing to behold. I put the beer on the roof of the car and open the back door. A couple ungrateful Mexican apple pickers have made a damn mess of my car. The fat one is dead asleep. He's wearing green basketball shoes which are untied, and I yank on them and say, "Okay, my man, time to wake up." He sort of shakes his head and works his mouth, so I know he's on the verge of coming out of it. I reach over and yank on his ear and his eyes open up a little. The skinny one is sitting over on the curb, head in his hands, and the fat one gets out and plops himself down beside him. The buzz from the orange tungsten lights high above the parking lot is everywhere. I look up to see millions of insects flying circles around the lightbulbs. It's hot as hell.

"Vaya con Dios," I say, getting back into my car, like in the movies. I may be wrong, but I swear they both say it back to me, *"Vaya con Dios."*

Back on the highway, going north this time, I roll the window down to get some cool fresh air. I have to pry the bottle cap off with my teeth because I am lacking an opener. I slide the six-packs back under the seat and think that it's times like these when the size of an old Buick is a comfort in the world — a wall between you and what lies ahead. On the radio is Good Times and Great Oldies Guaranteed Ten in a Row, "Stagger Lee" by Lloyd Price. I turn the knob hoping to catch the gospel channel, but most of what I get is static. I chuck the empty into the median and brace the steering wheel against the dash with my pinkie to make sure I drive straight and true.

To the early sunlight coming at me through the windshield, I try one out. I say, *Our America is a place where the pursuit of selfish desire is defended all the time as a God-given right,* et cetera, et cetera.

I try the radio again. Nothing else besides static and low Quebecois voices coming down from Canada early in the morning.

It is dawn, and beautiful. With the windows down at 70 mph it is not half bad, cool at least, and it smells a lot less like vomit. The clock on the dashboard says 6:02. Three hours. And I have given my Book of Daniel pleasure-madness sermon twice already in the past six weeks. Last Sunday, not a single member of the congregation thanked me. Not one, and that has got to be a record. But then, I know I've been sleepwalking in front of them all. I know it.

I cannot claim that I possessed the deepest brand of faith. I cannot claim that I was ever 100 percent. But I've tried to say things that will help.

Yet in these days of early autumn the First Congregational Church of Pikestown is crowded. Crowded with Mexican apple pickers on top of everything else—doctors, teachers from the college, from cities. The church has become populated with new faces, brown faces. Rich faces. I am addressing a congregation of strangers, of newcomers.

I open another bottle of beer with my teeth and am convinced that my molars move a little as I do so. I am most positively drunk now. The Buick is low on gas. I take the next exit and taste the sourness of my throat and try to wash it down with beer. All of this is now. I can't think to remember before.

The sun is hard on my eyes. Up ahead is the new Cumberland Farms gas station, and I drive through a stop sign to get there. When I get out, I see that there are three little kids sleeping under one of those loose-weave patchwork blankets in the back of a wood-paneled station wagon. They look so nice in there, packed together with duffel bags and suitcases all around them. A little boy is sucking his thumb. I put my hands against the long rear window and lay my forehead there too. The windshield is hot already and I know it's going to be a day without mercy.

I hear the electronic chime of the store's door and look up to see two men come out, one after the other. One has a gallon jug of orange juice and a box of Donettes. The other one has a quart of oil. They look tired, big purple moons under their eyes. They notice me standing there and regard me in a way that you could call unfriendly.

"Help you with something?" one says in that way that means, really, I'd be happy to kick your ass right now.

I try to say some words, I'm not sure exactly which ones, but all that comes out is a dry sound from my throat. I am afraid he might come bump chests with me, he looks like the sort who likes to do that right before he catches you in the ear with a heavy roundhouse kind of punch. It seems that his brain is already set to throw it. But the other one is back in the driver's seat and the one looking at me seems to judge me not worth it and so he gets into the car, too. They back out and I try so hard not to look at them that I can't help but blink about a dozen times.

Inside the store, big Dwight Eider is in his white T-shirt and brown elastic suspenders, leaning against the counter and not talking to his big wife, Bonnie, who stands behind it. They stop talking when I come in and look at me. He nods. It is cool in the store, but I get two little packages of Fig Newtons from the display at the end of the aisle and pay for them and leave as fast as I can, the heat of their eyes on my back.

I could swear to God that the sun has gotten twice as bright. The heat from the asphalt feels like it's wafting up my pant legs and making my knees melt. The Fig Newtons feel like they're getting softer by the second in my damp hands. I am dying from the inside out right there. I don't even know why I have bought the cookies.

When I open the car door the first thing I see is the rooster stuffed halfway under the seat. Its tongue is hanging out onto the accordion-shaped shroud at the gearshift's base, gray and black. The smell of the skinny picker's puke hits me like a fist and I gag at the deathly sights and smells of my car. I don't throw up, but it's close in my throat for a minute. My saliva is all ropy and I have to spit it out onto the asphalt, where it darkens into little black spots. The car wants to be abandoned forever but there is no place to walk to.

I hold my breath and get off the lot and up to speed as quickly as I can, heading west, back toward Pikestown. I can't stand to look at the rooster right now—I have to get him out of my awful car and into the ground. It is all I can think about. He deserves a proper burial, a thing that I can preside over. And then the sky turns blue and I can feel my whole head well up with the fluids that come with tears. Something about the perfect beauty of the pine trees on the side of the road as I pull off the pavement and climb the rise to the Old Cemetery with the wasted body of a black rooster under my gearshift on a hot Indian summer Sunday makes me about sadder than anything I have ever known before.

I drive up through the cemetery toward the top of the hill. As usual, I am amazed that death has taken so many people in this tiny town. There are small American flags all over the place, left-overs from Memorial Day. The sun has bleached their little wooden flagstaffs pale. There is the recent grave with its pink marble headstone where I buried Vera Whitcomb, aged ninety-seven. How many weeks ago?

At the top of the hill, I stop in the gravel lot and pull the rooster from his place half under the seat. The blood has firmed up into little rocks under his feathers. I see the muscles of his legs and the meaty feet. There are cutters made from the folded red-and-white aluminum of a Budweiser can attached to his spurs by thin strips of duct tape. His comb has been ripped partway off his head and I see the dark patch of dried blood where it has been torn from the short red feathers of his scalp.

I go all the way over to the treeline where I mean to lay the rooster and scrape at the ground with my tire iron, but the heat has sucked out all the moisture of the topsoil and I just loosen crumbles of grass and dirt.

It is cooler within the shade of the trees and I break through the low branches until I find the clear spot where I lay the rooster out flat on a bed of red pine needles. With my hands, I scrape away the needles and twigs and dig a few inches into the black earth. Not deep, but enough to make a bed for him. I have to search for a while to find the five or six sizable stones I use to surround his body. Then I pile most of the pine needles from the clearing onto the grave so that it becomes a red lump in the center of a dark earthen circle. My own voice startles me when I hear it in the quiet of the woods as I say what I can remember of the Order for the Burial of the Dead over his grave. I shake some dirt over the mausoleum I have made and stand there in the woods seeing what I have just completed. Then I lie down and see my eyelids shut out the world.

The sound of the church bells banging out the hour of nine o'clock wakes me. I find my way back out of the woods and walk across the cemetery to the back door of the church with an emptiness in my stomach and the sun burning hot on my head. The members of the choir are there, in their white robes, their faces talking and smiling. The organ is loud from inside. I step back around the corner and brush the red needles and last night's dirt from my clothes. They all get quiet when they see me. No one shakes my hand as I pass through the crowd. From the top step, I can see my car at the other end of the cemetery, small, its door open, its gas tank empty.

Inside, I bump into a few more choir people as my eyes adjust to the darkness. The new deacon shakes my hand quickly on his way to the bell-tower door. In a few seconds I see him leap down the stairs with the heavy rope in his hands. The bell tolls. He's grinning, all teeth, and in a moment he is flying back up the stairwell, pulled by the weight of the bell. I get into my clothes and peek out across the transept to where the sound of commingled voices comes from packed pews. The young organist from the college conservatory is playing something too tricky. He's showing off.

There is an order of worship bulletin on the table by the door and I read it. It says, at the top, The Baptismal Christening of Margarita Dolores Dominguez.

At the change of the organ's melody, the choir files past me into the bright space of the church. I step out from the corner and follow them. The pulpit has been varnished since last week and is considerably darker. I finger it to see if it's as smooth as it looks. It is. I switch on the reading light and look out into the congregation. There are colors and I have to hold on to the sides of the pulpit to keep balanced. I am still drunk.

In the first row, a Mexican couple in dark clothes are smiling up at me with tears in their eyes. The father blinks and thrusts a baby girl in a long white dress up above his head, presenting her to me.

Matthew 15:11

BORGES RIDES THE CYCLONE

DAN O'BRIEN

Certain twilights, and certain places, try to tell us something, or
have said something we should not have missed, or are about to say
something; this imminence of a revelation which does not occur is,
perhaps, the aesthetic phenomena.

—*Walter Horatio Pater*

CAVETT: There is a story that your translator was trying to translate
the phrase "unanimous night."
BORGES: Yes, how priggish, perhaps.
CAVETT: And he said: "What on earth does this mean, 'unanimous
night'?"
BORGES: . . . I don't know, really.

—The Dick Cavett Show, *New York, May 1980*

Borges is lost.

He is a dying man these days, as he has been, he thinks, from
the day he was born. This day, a day almost night, a night falling
over Borges's blind eyes not like a dark hand passing through darkness, but rather a hazel, bluish mist, a luminous haze of descending
oblivion. In dreaming, blind Borges sees again. In fact, so vivid is
his dream vision that the waking world has become the less real of
the two, his present moments a liquid suspension of time, fantasy,
and philosophical speculation. His skin gauging the progress of the
setting sun; a passing child's balloon bouncing off his face; the mad
loop of carousel music; thinks Borges, All this is tomfoolery, all this
is a dream. Thinks Borges, Every crowd is an illusion, and I am just
the dream of another's sleeping mind.

Borges, coughing wet into his open hand; Borges, thinking,

Where am I? Thinking poetic things; thinking the words upon his lips, Where are you, Maria? As if composing an ode of sorts: My brittle lover, my sallow shadow, my night moving through mirrors, soft swallow, filling my bathtub, filling my cup, my hands. After all these years of loneliness, only you, Maria, only you could love me. I, being a melancholy man, wobbly dead eyes peering into darkness. I, being a brooding man, eternally standing upon the coattails of my own shadow, waiting for death, perpetually puzzled.

A shove—Borges is knocked down! falls against the curb; humid lipstick, a shoal of pistachio stench, shipwrecks Borges, slams Borges back into Reality, back into the present tense of things. He coughs again. Wheezes for breath. Where am I? he thinks.

"Excuse me," offers Borges (to no one who responds), says Borges tossing his head back, pulling himself up by his britches from the puddled pavement, steadying his body upright, slipping his cane quite accidentally through the wet ribs of a storm drain. These mazes! thinks Borges, chuckling, These houses of Asterion! Why do they never cease to surprise me? And wonders, tongue in his cheek, Is there a beast in the center of this labyrinth, to make this trip worthwhile? Where is the American minotaur that I must slay?

Borges sighs, Nowhere. There are no minotaurs, anymore. All the beasts Borges has ever known have dwelt exclusively in books, and Borges, always in the darkest corner of his library, always reading, always every day more blind than the day before . . . hardly a match for a minotaur.

Borges bats his lip with a handkerchief. Thinking, Old man, start walking.

"Ride the Cyclone," says a man from a wheelchair, scuffing Borges's wingtips, rolling brutal upon his shifting feet. Borges, wincing for the pain, smelling the sweat of chrome and beaten leather, pulls his foot back and turns, mouth agape, expecting an apology, receiving none.

"Excuse me," says Borges, again, this time not meaning it quite as much, wondering already (returning to walking, his walking stick tickling the buckled pavement before him like an insect), What is this Cyclone? A beast, after all, in the middle of all this mess? A

Grendel to the masses—immigrants and children of immigrants, the deficient in courage and the courageously deficient—every crowd is a sea of approaching ships! every human chest hauls in cargo at least the inspiration for a myth, at least the imagination with which one might dream oneself a monster, or a hero. Anyone can be a hero, thinks Borges, for the right price. In America, anything for the right price. Borges has only the change in his pocket.

So Borges, still walking, jangling his coins; Borges, as always, remembering.

"Let's go to Coney Island," says Maria; it is earlier that same day, early that same morning, breakfast at the Waldorf, honey tea and buttered toast, the musk of an old woman from the next table intruding, an old woman blowing her old breath through tight nostrils, and Maria, "Just this once," saying, "You need to cheer up," and, "Besides, who knows when we'll be in New York again?"

Borges coughs into his fist, swallows thick. Groping across the surface of the table, he fingers the butter knife. Lifts it, delicate.

"You've been there before, no?" says Borges, shaving grit from his toast, leaning his tired head into a warm palm of light; disinterested; supposing things.

"Yes, I've been there," she says. She drops her hand to the table, and lifts her cup, sips her tea. "You should really relax before the program tonight. You know how you get."

Borges scowls, knowing how he gets; imagining the program tonight, envisioning the American television host and a studio audience of five hundred, anticipating their feigned admiration, his own gut-churning modesty (motivated not so much by humility but by cowardice), his ardent desire to talk of anyone else's writing but his own: Cervantes, Dickens—even Sandburg if need be!—but not his own books. His own words, his own *life* even, is minuscule, is tiresome, and is best forgotten.

"What are you thinking?" asks Maria, her teacup lifting from the table again.

"Nothing," says Borges—but thinks Borges, closing his useless eyes, *I am remembering how to see.* Remembering last night's dream, in particular, remembering sight as an amputee remembers a limb;

Borges studies the implications this peculiar dream has to offer, a dream in which he is riding a train through the countryside, the hills and fields passing silently beyond and below the delicate translucent fiber of window; fields thick with dead snow and dead moonlight, the air above the fields being empty, a vacuum, the moon in the sky hanging like a drop in an overturned bucket.

It is a vision from which Borges, in his waking state, quickly deduces that all fields are separate, and all fields are divided; that all fields on this godforsaken planet—in this tired, spinning coin of a universe—are cut by fences, lines of black pine, or marked by boundary of crumbling fieldstone; and these fields (the fields he is conscious of, for Borges knows there exist larger fields whose boundaries and consequent area he cannot even begin to fathom) are only plots of earth cut from larger fields, factors of a divine number—*the number of God, perhaps!* Infinite plots of earth carved from the belly of the cosmos.

But this is too simple, thinks Borges. This dream is exactly what it is. Empty fields are nothing but a reminder of humankind's kinship of loneliness (a subject of which Borges has vast firsthand knowledge), and the subsequent observation that these fields reside within larger fields reflects, once again, the maddening equation of consciousness, the basic paradox of the limits of human understanding that is best demonstrated by trying to see one's own face without benefit of a mirror.

Regardless, Borges is now off the train (in dreams as well as in life, Borges finds the transition between place seldom recalled once completed), and he stands squarely before the door of a great church. As always, as is expected, Borges, disappointed at the blatant metaphysical implications posed by such an ungainly and obvious symbol, is nevertheless overcome with some primal urge, perhaps, to go through the door—but there is someone blocking his way! Someone he knows. A friend of Borges—an elderly doctor whose name escapes him now, but still, an old friend who has been dead from this world for twenty-odd years, and here he is alive! Immutable, august and statuesque, standing like a great Corinthian pillar between Borges and the heavy oaken door. He wears a white gown, and white gloves; an obscene stethoscope dangles from his neck; his mouth is covered with a surgical mask; he is veiled in a most clinical shroud of mystery.

No matter, thinks Borges in his dream. This is my dream, after all, and he, my old friend, is not dead within the universe of my dream, and so I will speak with him politely, catch up on old times, laugh perhaps as we used to, if the fit seizes, and then I will ask him, when the time is right, and politely, of course, if he might be so kind as to let me pass.

Borges opens his mouth to speak, but his voice has died. He finds it difficult to breathe. The air is cold, and biting; he concentrates, remembering honesty is the best foundation to any conversation. "I forget your name, friend," he says at last.

The doctor lifts his eyebrows, piqued. His bristly goat's chin juts out before him, cuts the night air between them.

"Borges," he says, words muffled beneath the surgical mask, the doctor's breath ballooning the fabric, "how could you forget my name?"

Borges shrugs. "I got old," he says, "and forgot many things."

"We used to play chess," says the doctor, still hopeful.

"Did I ever play chess?" asks Borges.

"Yes. But you always lost."

Borges smiles sheepishly, hoping to charm the doctor. He is about to remember the doctor's name; but no sooner has he thought to remember the name than he has forgotten. Isn't it always that way? thinks Borges.

"But friend," says Borges aloud, "I did not forget what you look like."

The doctor frowns, folds his arms across his chest. "What do you want?"

"To get in," says Borges.

This makes the doctor laugh, for quite some time uninterrupted, and Borges begins to feel childish, a bit humiliated. He is about to turn and go when the doctor grabs his arm.

"I will let you through this door," he says, his icy grip spreading a chill like an arthritis into Borges's very marrow, "If you can answer me this one riddle."

Borges cannot believe his good fortune. He loves riddles! He's read all manner of riddle, in all manner of book, and even if the doctor should happen to present him with a riddle he's never heard before—say an *original* riddle (if there is such a thing), or a riddle snatched from some ancient mythology of a culture in which he is not yet well versed—why, at least Borges is familiar with the archetypal structure of riddles. And furthermore, thinks Borges, *everyone knows there is only one riddle that cannot be answered.*

"My riddle is this," says the doctor, bending at the waist (he is quite a tall doctor, taller than Borges remembers). "Are you ready?"

"Yes," says Borges, nervous yet confident enough to tease, like this: "I'm all agog."

"You may pass through the door," says the doctor, "only when you have found—" he is all mystery and drama, this doctor, a gloved finger crooked moonward, "only when you have found . . . *happiness!*"

Bah! thinks Borges, back at breakfast, back at the Waldorf, This is a pathetic riddle! Not what you would call Schopenhauerian in any sense, not a riddle of the universe—not a riddle of the solar system, for that matter!—it is a riddle not even worthy of a second-rate Sphinx. Thinks Borges, What is wrong with my muse, my Holy Ghost, my subconscious—whatever you call it—that it cannot come up with a better riddle than that? Repeating the riddle, When I have found happiness? Borges answers, Never. The only happiness in life is knowing that in time I will be dead. Thinks Borges, It is little consolation, but comfort enough, to know that one day I shall be dead and all but entirely forgotten.

"Stop dwelling," says Maria, reaching across the table, knocking a sugar spoon from the sugar bowl, lifting his hand in hers. She can be unkind in her kindness. "You are such a depressing man."

Borges, shrugging, "I was just thinking, When will I be happy?"

Maria laughs. "When we go to Coney Island," she says. She pats his hand, quite serious now. "All your life, Jorge, you never have any fun. It will do you some good to have some fun."

Borges pulls his hand back to cough.

"You see," says Maria, scolding. "You're getting sick again."

Borges waves his hand before his face and spits into the napkin.

"Okay," he says, after he has thought it through. "Let's go."

Now, Borges stops walking. Now, in the present, standing on another corner, his blindness reeling with the dizzy heat. Borges, being tired, being hungry, stops remembering for a moment and, groping clumsily, slumps against a streetlamp.

"Ride the Cyclone," says a man—another man? (Borges is sure it is not the same man, it is not the same corner.) But who can know for certain? There are so many corners to stand upon. Borges wonders, Have I moved at all? or only dreamed I have moved? No, thinks Borges, such circular reasoning leads only to ruin, will drive one straight out of one's mind, and besides—this he is sure of, there can be no doubt—I am here. Time has indeed passed, as evidence the sun's conspicuous absence, the twilit warmth sliding off his face like a glove from a hand. He is not dreaming; the proof being these people here—people Borges would never intentionally dream of in a thousand years; these people are loud and ill-mannered; these people are crowding Borges, pushing and sliding over Borges like water over a stick in a stream; or, being hopelessly morbid, thinks Borges: *like water over a corpse*. He coughs again, his throat raw like mulch. He has lost his train of thought; he begins to worry.

Maria? he thinks. "Where are you?" he says, this time aloud, by accident—no one answers. He concludes he's not been heard, even speculates he never spoke.

He taps his walking stick against his toe. He taps a little harder, until it smarts.

"Yes," he says. "This is where I am." The crowds begin to thin.

Maria, being sighted, being sharp and all bone, being always somehow glad to be living: Maria is not one to get lost. She is one for finding things, she is one for looking and for taking, as she looked for Borges many years ago, as she found him and took him and cared for him. But being more than twenty years younger, being guilelessly beautiful, Maria has never been quite real to Borges. Even naked, offering her body to his blind sight, to his keen, trembling hands, she has been like something only imagined, something always felt in darkness, her true self felt only partially, and even that, with great inadequacy.

Perhaps she is not altogether real to Borges because he has never truly seen her. He has seen all the things he loves, saw them in the years before the blindness took him. Having stored these images in his head, these memories stacked and catalogued like cherished manuscripts in some ancient Babylonian library, Borges has enjoyed the luxury of having every memory at his beck and call, and would conjure them at will, when musing, or against his will (nightly, in dreams; sometimes in his nightmares). But he has never forgotten the easy sights that have brought him joy: the almost alliterative power of a fuming sea; a small boy, head stricken with unruly cowlicks, laughing like a son, somebody else's son; the wheel of a gardener's capsized wagon spinning gently in the morning, great clops of mud dropping from the filthy circuit; the minutia—that is what he has loved. The individual, living letters of God's wholly incomprehensible name.

Borges remembers when he was newly blind, that wet autumn afternoon in the conference room of a hotel in Buenos Aires, when he first met Maria; she was interviewing him for some paper, asking questions of art and literature, of solipsism and Descartes, quoting words he'd once written and at once forgotten, crossing and uncrossing her legs with unnerving frequency, with alluring auditory grace. He, Borges, dropping insipid response after insipid response like pebbles from his lips, his attention drawn exclusively to an erection swelling deep inside his trousers, simultaneously surprised and invigorated by this unexpected resurrection of libido. The remainder of the interview, all he could think about was the cool smoothness of her stockinged thighs, one leg lifting against the other, crossing above the knee, sliding down again, one leg caressing the other like a wave rising and slipping from the smoothest shore.

No, thinks Borges, Maria has always been somehow lost to me. No matter how many hours spent memorizing her flesh, his hand splashing the length of her body from throat to ankle, his heavy hand resting upon her belly, or her thin voice tickling his gray chest;

Borges has spent almost all of his blind years with Maria, and he has no idea what she really looks like.

"Stay here," she says to Borges, maybe an hour ago, helping him onto the curb like an invalid. Having left the train and walked an interminable distance, Maria is determined. "I'm going to get you a hot dog."

Borges groans. He does not want a hot dog. Moreover, he does not like being treated like a child, which is happening more and more these days. Which is happening right now.

"I don't want a hot dog," he says, suddenly hearing the seagulls shriek, imagining they circle like vultures overhead.

"You can't come all the way to Coney Island and not get a hot dog," she says. And, touching his hand, "You stay here," his cold, white-knuckled hand and the knob of his black cane, "I'll be right back," she says, and waving, "Don't move," she has walked away.

Then Borges, alone, grimaces. Sulking in his black suit, profoundly suffering, the librarian as martyr. Borges thinks, This is not at all what I imagined. Something pleasant, something peaceful, perhaps, but not this. An amusement park is a most deceitful name! for Borges finds little amusement in screaming children and impostor argonauts. And so it occurs to Borges that in a moment he must start walking (walking being his body's chosen expression of impatience), and in another moment, separate from this moment as two grains of sand in the same desert are separate, he will be standing on another street corner, a corner very much like this one, a carousel's anemic trickle of melody licking his ear like a dog, perhaps remembering this very moment. In a moment, Borges may sense all that is to come, and he will be inexplicably drawn to solving last night's riddle.

In his dream, Borges says to the doctor friend, attempting to talk reason, to be somehow sly, "Friend, tell me. What is behind that door?"

"Why should I tell you?" asks the doctor.

"Why should I answer your riddle, if I don't know what is to be my reward?"

The doctor thinks it over. "Very well. Beyond this door, Borges," he says, "is a train."

"A train?"

"Borges," says the doctor, "you of all people should know that the world is full of such trains."

Borges, who has often thought this himself but lacked the sufficient nerve to say it aloud, replies, "Yes. How true."

"But," says the doctor, "I am not guarding just *any* train. I am guarding a train within a church!"

Borges, confused. "A train within a *church?*"

"A train running through a thousand churches, each church housed within the other, no church any smaller, yet churches all within the same church, each identical but for the religion practiced upon its altar, each religion the same but for its different god."

The doctor friend pauses, knowing he has Borges's full attention.

"Riding on this train," he continues, "one may travel through all churches known to man, churches of both intellect and spirit, churches of most secular thought and churches of animistic magnificence, and thereby the passengers of this train will attain all manner of knowledge, and gain objective understanding of all things absolutely." The doctor smiles, wryly. "Of course, if you have not found happiness before you board this train, the trip could kill you. I know this. I am a doctor."

After a pause, Borges replies, "I do not believe in an absolute truth."

"It matters not what you believe. Absolute truth exists, independent of you."

Borges shivers with a sudden chill—to be told that the world exists independent of one's beliefs! that is a most cruel heresy—and begins coughing, hacking, his chest seized as if squeezed in some massive hand. This is rare, thinks Borges as his coughing fit subsides, I do not usually dream myself sick.

The doctor has Borges by the wrist and is taking his pulse. "You're running out of time, old man. You are most definitely dying, and quickly at that!"

"Then let me through," says Borges, struggling to step round the doctor, to reach for the doorknob, but the doctor is impassable.

"But you have not answered my riddle, Borges."

Borges replies, "I refuse to answer such a stupid riddle."

The doctor frowns. "You will not be allowed to ride the train until you have answered my riddle."

And this is precisely where Borges wakes up; back in the present, Borges stands in a gravel ditch. The smell of axle grease, of greasy popcorn, the sweet rot of cotton candy moldered in a garbage can; the park, dripping with a sticky residue of sound, is all but empty. Here and there a voice calls a name—not Maria's voice and not his name. This is now, thinks Borges, this is real. You have been walking, Borges, and thinking too much.

"Ride the Cyclone?" says a boy. His voice is broken and raw, but gentle, and Borges can hear a ball of keys jangling; he is a worker.

Says Borges, without thinking, "Yes, I would like to."

"Got a ticket?"

Borges, checking his pockets, pulls out a quarter, a dime, a nickel. "No, I don't have a ticket."

"You ever been on a roller coaster before?" asks the boy.

"No. What is it like?"

"Fun," says the boy. "Scary as hell."

Borges turns his head up; a drop of rain explodes on his forehead. "Are you blind?"

Borges replies, "Not always." He can hear the distant traffic, the water hissing like a desert; the sky opening with rain.

The boy's hand touches Borges's elbow. "Come on," says the boy, "before it starts raining for real."

Borges stumbles in the gravel, confused.

"Don't worry about the ticket," says the boy. "This is the last ride." Borges, through a turnstile, shuffles across pavement—never-ending pavement—his cane skipping through granite and puddles, the boy's thin hand fluttering on the old man's arm like a bird. Then, "It's free," says the boy, and suddenly Borges's foot is flat on a step, he steps up, he feels the boy's other hand touch his old man's calf.

"You're going to have to sit down, sir," says the boy.

"Thank you."

Borges sinks into a seat. A metal bar descends, pins him in place. The boy backs off, stepping heavy. "Hold on," he says. "I could get fired for this."

And then the great beast awakes. The groggy Cyclone coughs, sputters, rises from the ground.

Borges lifts into the sky. Thinks Borges, rising, What am I doing? If I could see, what would I be seeing? Climbing the sky like a Pegasus, the clack and thunder of this mechanical monster (could the Cyclone really be a monster? would a monster bring me so much joy?) lifting against gravity, against what is undeniable, against what is real. Thinks Borges, This is really quite fun. Thinks Borges, I wish Maria could see me now, on my own, taming the mythic Cyclone, and at my age! Thinks Borges, How stupid I have been, how wasteful to stand on street corners, to lose myself in labyrinths of memory; wonders Borges, as the Cyclone curves upon its peak and slides into that motionless gap preceding the inevitable drop, Tonight, the night unanimously presents itself free of symbol, free of intellect, but what on earth can it all mean?

GEESE

ZZ PACKER

We were trapped in a room with a grapefruit and a banana.

The five of us all sat down noiselessly on the floor in front of the just-rinsed plate. Ari was about to speak to us about the grapefruit and the banana. Washed in from the shores of the Philippines, Ari was the official renter of the small flat in which we all lived. Ari spoke English the way a faucet drips water.

"Those," Ari sighed, "is our last."

We all knew what Ari meant when he said "Those is our last." It meant that besides paprika and salt, the grapefruit and the banana were all we had to eat.

My six-month visa had expired and the Japanese were too timid and uninventive to hire anyone on the sly. There are usually only two lines of work for American *gaizin*—teaching or modeling. Modeling was out—I was not the right race, much less the right blondness or legginess, and with an expired visa I got turned down for teaching jobs. The men who ran the interviews knew my visa had expired. That put a spin on things, the spin, specifically, being that they expected me to sleep with them.

The *sararimen* that passed me in the subway stations would proposition me with English phrases they had tutors teach them on the side—"Verrry sexy," they'd say to me, looking around to make sure women and children didn't see them. And even on the *tokkyuu* itself, where every passenger, it seemed, took a seat and immediately fell asleep, the emboldened men would loudly whisper, "Verrry chah-ming, daaark skin," raising their eyebrows in brushstrokes of innuendo.

I finally took a job working at an amusement park. Summerland, it was called. In Tokyo, anything vaguely amusing has an English name.

My specific job was operator of the Dizzy Teacups ride. That's how I met Ari. He was my coworker, which meant he and I would alternate mop duty whenever a kid vomited.

Ari and I found ourselves unamused and jobless at the end of the summer. I could not see myself back in Baltimore with my mother and her cats: my mother frantically clipping coupons while the cats lazily positioned themselves in the warmest parts of the tiny apartment. On the morning that I left for Japan, my mother and I sat for ten minutes discussing whether or not she should get another cat. She finally came to the conclusion that we—she—couldn't afford it. That morning, I could feel a silent insurrection coming on, and finally she blurted, "I don't know why you have to go to Japan to earn money and have fun. We've got cats right here." She tipped the last bit of Courvoisier from the bottle and into her mouth. For about twenty minutes she ran around doing things to remedy her hypochondria; she rummaged about the refrigerator for lemons, washed her hands and gargled, then she spat in the kitchen sink and made a face like a woman unhinged. Noticing that the Courvoisier was gone, she worked her way over to the bar and brought out a Glenfiddich bottle with a lipstick stain around the top. She took a quick but satisfying swig. "Take some pie," she said. She brought out a boxed-up cherry pie from the freezer.

"It's frozen," I answered. "I don't like frozen pie."

"Well," she said, finishing off the scotch, "I can't help you."

Ari finally found a job, I didn't. He invited me to live with him awhile, so I did.

And so did Petra and Zoltan. Petra had once been a model but had fallen down an escalator. It ripped her face into unequal quadrants of permanent pained surprise.

"Can't you just put makeup on it?" I'd asked. She looked at me and blinked her Pine Sol–colored eyes. She began to cry. Zoltan had to hold her as if holding two repelling hemispheres of a girl together as she wept. She had to pay for the surgery and had no money to speak of.

"No," Zoltan explained to me without really explaining. "No, she cannot just put makeup on it."

Petra and Zoltan, as I understood it, were an item. They loved each other in that dangerous Eastern European way of soft glances, hard, sobbing sex, and fistfights. Zoltan had hit her with his large open hand and she took it with the stiff hard body of a boy in basic training. Within the hour she had pressed a good portion of his hand onto the electric range. The hand formed several huge, strawberry-like blisters. But still they loved, and that same night they shook the bamboo shades with their passion, came out of the bedroom which the men shared, and sat down to eat crackers dusted with paprika.

After the hand-on-the-range incident, Zoltan and Petra ate their crackers and Zoltan went to ice his hand. Petra continued to sit in her corner with cracker-crumb whiskers around her mouth. She began to cry. Her crying baffled me, but I paid no attention to it. I had given up trying to understand her. Or any of them, for that matter. Things made them cry and sigh. Things dredged from the bottoms of their souls brought them pain at the strangest moments.

The only time I'd seen Petra laugh was when Zoltan had brought in a marionette for her—a foolish waste of thieving energy—and bobbed it upon her powdered navel. All at once, Petra's scars managed to dream out a smile. She sat in a corner and sneezed paprika and tears while I continued the farce of looking for a job in the *gaizin* paper.

Zoltan maundered about with the look of a beast trying to understand human speech. Watching him move about the room was like watching a cruising yawl sail into port—it could take sunsets, moon-risings, and daybreaks before anything substantial happened. The pictures he tacked on the walls were from his bodybuilding days, long before his Tokyo diet of crackers and fruit. The pictures showed him oiled and bulging, as though he were constructed of hundreds of five-pound bags of hard pressed sugar. For some reason he had given up bodybuilding—although he maintained that he was winning prizes right up to the time he came to Tokyo. If he were pressed further than that about his past, Petra, invariably orbiting Zoltan like a satellite, would begin to cry.

Then Sait came to live with us. He had a smile like a sealed envelope, had a way of eating as though he were horny. Whenever we talked for a length of time he would bob his head like a pecking bird and hiss "Yesyesyesyes—I see. . . ." We got along.

But little by little, he began to despise me. Why? I had no earthly idea. At least, not at the time. Whenever I asked Ari and Zoltan what Sait thought of me, why he continued to slip into a scowl when I came around, they insisted that Sait was just strange that way. So each night I had to listen to him hiss affectionately at everyone else but me.

Sait had married a white woman instead of the woman he was supposed to marry, and his family, her family, the whole country of Morocco, it seems, disowned him. He had moved to Tokyo in hopes of opening a business but the money that was supposed to be sent to him was not sent.

"They know! They know!" he repeated in reference to his crime, in reference to the people who did not send his money. Whenever he thought of this injustice, the sealed envelope of his mouth turned into an open half-drooling box of shame and wonder. When he thought on how life had gone wrong, how his wife had left him, how his family had done him wrong, he usually turned to me, as though I were somehow responsible.

One night, I felt something at my throat. I awoke to find Sait glaring over me in the Cookie Monster pajamas Ari and I had gotten him from Summerland. The present was more for us than for him; before the pajamas he had slept and gone around the flat naked. It was only seconds after I saw that it was Sait standing over me that I realized that what was at my throat was a knife. I screamed and woke up Petra, who turned on the light, went to her corner and promptly began to cry. Ari and Zoltan turtled out of the men's, saw Sait posing the knife at my throat, saw that I was still alive, and looked at me hopelessly, as though I were an actress, failing to play my part and die on cue. Sait threw the knife down on the fiber-fill of my sleeping bag. When Zoltan saw that it had nothing to do with him, he went back to sleep. Sait rattled off accusingly at me in his Arab tongue with his Arab eyes and finally had to be led into the hallway by Ari. They spoke for a while. I sat straight up in my bra of decaying green lace and men's hockey-stick boxers. I brought my blankets around me.

I had urinated on them.

Sait tried to slam the door violently, but the door was broken, refusing to make the proper dramatic coda; Ari told me not to worry, Sait wouldn't try to kill me again. Nevertheless, I was resigned to certain death. I took a bath with dishwashing detergent and put on the same bra and the one pair of jeans that I hadn't sold. I wrapped myself in someone's musty sheet. I lay there.

I guess that was when I had one of those hazy ten-second dreams one normally sees only on soap operas. Right behind my eyelids, I was back in Baltimore and my mother's cats were dropping sardines in my mouth.

"I can't take it!" I screamed. I was suddenly alert and awake and must have screamed the words several times before Zoltan sleepily yelled for me to shut up. Petra sat in her corner with a stray tear running in a rivulet along one of her scars. It was whorishly beautiful and I wanted to kiss her in my madness. Zoltan would probably smack me if I did and Petra would probably begin to cry again. That is what I was thinking while Ari was suddenly beside me, talking to me in broken English that I hadn't the energy to try to understand. More thoughts which I didn't recognize as my own began to run through my head, but Ari lay beside me and put his arm around my neck. Petra went into the bedroom and soon she and Zoltan were going at it, panting and pounding at each other till it seemed as though one of them might dislocate the springs of the weak mattress.

Ari lay beside me, a fresh-baked loaf of vividly musky human fragrance. His arm was the smoothest I'd ever felt, the hairs felt as as though they were extensions of liquid skin. I wanted either a saltine-cracker kiss or a lurid stomach-rumbling rendezvous with the two of us in his thin sheets, and nothing in between. I nudged him. He politely rolled away from me.

"You should wear more clothes," he mumbled. He was half asleep.

"I can't take it," I repeated, more softly this time. I tugged the sheet closer to my chest. Ari suddenly turned toward me. He knew that I was not even talking about Sait anymore. Not even talking about Petra and Zoltan. He knew I was talking about hunger.

"Can't take?" he asked, as if I had announced some unutterable evil. "But you must!" he managed to yell without actually yelling, turning out the light with his velveteen arm.

When we sat around that grapefruit and banana, we looked at them as though we expected them to perform. Ari sliced up six pieces of banana and six pieces of grapefruit. I watched his arm make each slice. I wanted to ask why he sliced up six pieces of each instead of five. To make it seem like we had more? To have an old maid's portion left over? I didn't bother to ask. I had given up asking questions.

We all sat there, Sait looking from side to side, Zoltan staring straight at the fruit, Petra holding on to Zoltan's arm like a child hugging a tree trunk.

"Enjoy," Ari said with all the solemnity of a mortician displaying caskets.

Ari would not steal. When we had asked him for money to buy food he had said he didn't have any. Which was true. Japanese banks automatically deduct rent and utility bills from your checking account, and you are left with whatever is left, whether it be nothing or less than that. Ari, whenever he could, sent money to his family in the Philippines and the rest went to crackers and cheese for us.

The rest of us used to steal food. Zoltan had swiped packaged steaks, Sait had swiped fruit and bread and one time even couscous, opening the package and pouring every single grain into two pants pockets. Even though I would never have stolen anything in America, stealing in Japan gave me the same giddy, weightless feeling that cursing in another language did. You did it because it was unimportant and foreign. And so I stole. Spaghetti, rice, fruit, and

Oreos. But Petra outdid us all. She went in with a sack taped across her stomach, put a sweater in it—to look as though she were pregnant—and began shopping. When the sack got full she'd go to the bathroom and put her sweater on and pay for a loaf of bread. She did this for a while. I couldn't have gotten away with it. I stuck to spaghetti and Oreos.

But Petra's trick didn't last for long. She went to get Zoltan a watermelon for his birthday and the sack gave way. She gave birth to a watermelon, which split open wide and red, right in front of her. The store manager, a nervously smiling Japanese man in his forties, brought her to Zoltan, telling him, in smiling, broken English, to keep her at home. The manager seemed frightened by her. She cried.

Since then, the stores in our area have been suspicious of foreigners, pregnant or otherwise. They know our faces. We'd all been caught. We'd all made mad dashes down the street, losing ourselves in crowds and alleys.

Most times we didn't even have the money to get on the *tokkyuu* to go steal food elsewhere. It was impossible to jump the turnstiles. They were all electronic. We didn't even go outside the one-bedroom flat, knowing that we would see people selling food, stores selling food, people eating food, or people whose faces reminded us of food, and that was too much for us to bear. I would try to practice writing *kanzi*, Zoltan and Petra would try to get up the energy to have sex. Sait would sit next to the window and stare outside, mumbling in Arabic.

And then we simply gave up. We gave up thieving food, whispering food away from frightened children, soaking our fingers in the compact dumpsters, feeling for the rotten fruit desserts of happy families who'd moved on to other meals. We were still hungry, but some alloy of disgust and indifference checked our most human instinct, the search for food, and propelled us into our stagnant one-bedroom dementia.

Most people don't understand that there are two types of hunger; one in which you'll do anything for food, the other in which you cannot bring yourself to complete the smallest task for it. I had done almost anything for food short of sleeping with men for money, and even the thought of those offers—"very charming" and "hey sexy" did not clang so sharply in my ears as they once had. I was too lazy to take the echoes seriously. Lazy hunger, lazy hunger, traps us all, somehow. The proverbial deer caught in headlights has that look on her brown face, and so it is with hunger; it is not the fact of being trapped and stunned, but the sense that for one second before she dies, she is relieved.

Sometimes I would take a crate and sit outside our stoopless apartment building and try to recreate the neighborhood feeling I'd had at home. The sun would shine hotly on the pavement and the movement of people everywhere, busy and self-absorbed, would have to stand in for the human music of Baltimore. The corner grocery stores back home were as dingy as they were lively, and the men who loitered inside them seemed more focused, needy, and hardwired playing lottery numbers than their Japanese counterparts who visited Pachinko parlors. I was not the homesick type, but I missed the black and Latino kids, always either extremely plump or extremely emaciated, who, at the end of a day of screaming and biking on sidewalks and defying any type of sleep, sat down on cement stoops to swab their scrapes with alcohol. For a few minutes, the daydream would work, even in Japan.

Once, in Taito-ku, Tokyo, a cellophane popsicle wrapper had nestled up against an ornamental ginkgo. It was gaudily beautiful with stripes of orange ooze from where a kid had licked it and buds of homesickness crept into my chest. Then, seemingly from nowhere, a Japanese streetworker, humbly brown from daily hours in the sun, conscientiously swept the little wrapper into his flip-top streetsweeper's box, and it was gone.

One day after work, Ari said that we must go to the park. We all looked at him uncomprehendingly. Sait went into the bedroom. Zoltan stood there, blockish, his flesh dripping from his bulk like leftovers clumsily wrapped in plastic. He looked as though he had somewhere to go, but had forgotten where. Petra bit her fingernails, her sunset-blond hair in unwashed clumps, framing her scars. I asked Ari why, why we had to go to the park.

He didn't answer.

"Let's go," he said. Packing up the cheese hardened on the ends, the paprika, the box of crackers, a plum. Zoltan got Sait out of the bedroom and once we all stood erect in the living room, as if we had nothing further to say to each other, we all left. Ari locked the door.

Dazed with the sunlight, we sat down, surrounded by an autumn of traffic-light yellow ginkgo trees. For the most part, the sky was gray, punctuated with fibrous clouds, each flaunting a gold diapered bottom like light reflecting off quilted foil. The Japanese families sat like cookies arranged on a plate. The family closest to us had a kid as bronzed as I was, a holdover from the summer, biting into the squared-off sandwiches I had seen mothers unwrap at Summerland. The girl was almost entirely pink and singing "Coke is it!" while the mother was talking to another mother who bounced a swaddled *akatyan* on her nonexistent hip. The father dozed off on a blanket of red and white squares.

The boy nibbled at his sandwich as we watched. When he saw us staring at him, at his sandwich, he ran to his sister and pointed. Five *gaizin*, all together, sitting Buddhalike, was too much for them. You could tell the boy wanted to go right up to us and ask us questions in the monosyllabic English he had learned from older boys who had spoken to *gaizin* before. Did we have tails? If so, would we kindly show them to him and his sister? Do we come out at night and suck blood? He would look at me and ask if the color rubbed off. He wanted to ask us these questions and more, if his limited English permitted, but the girl had enough shyness for the both of them, and held him back, a frightened smile on her face.

Ari took out the crackers, the cheese with the hard ends, the paprika, the salt, and the plum.

"I lost my job," he said.

Sait, disgusted with nature, both human and scenic, turned to look at the food which Ari had spread about on Petra's Slavicsmelling picnic blanket with the care one lavished on a feast. We mustered out our sorries to Ari.

We ate the cracker sandwiches with sliced plum and cheese on top. Then Petra spoke.

"I do not like cheese," she said. Everyone looked at her, as she held her lip out, her eyes declining to blink, her hair the only motioned part of her. Zoltan grabbed her arm. Petra had taken her slices of cheese off her sandwiches and Zoltan grabbed the slices with one fist and thrust them at her. They fell humbly into the folds of her shirt.

"You don't have to eat them," said Ari. But Petra knew she had to eat the cheese, that the cheese mattered. She ate them and looked as if she might cry, but didn't. We sat for a while. The food melted in my stomach just as the sunset melted, their synchronized fading seemed to make the whole world go dimmer and volumeless. Then I felt a sharp pain, as though the corners of the crackers went unchewed. None of us spoke to each other, and that seemed to make the pain in my stomach worse. The rest of them watched the people and the lake and the sun, now only a sketchy thread of light.

"Look," Sait said. We looked.

Geese. Stretching their necks, sunning themselves in the absence of sun, paying no mind to humans. Zoltan stretched his absurdly thick neck, and seemed, for a second, like he might be a goose as well. Zoltan bolted up and ran after the geese in the way children do, but his large blocky legs attempting to run made me too sad to watch. But he was running all over, and there was no way I could not see him unless I closed my eyes. He kept at it for a while, a family or two turning to watch the monstrous *gaizin* until he stopped. When he came back to our blanket he tried to sit down as though nothing had happened. His large hands dusted off the blanket before he sat down. But he was never successful pretending anything, and he fell into Petra's ugly gray corduroy shirt and began to cry.

"Why was he running after them?" I whispered to Ari. But as soon as I saw Sait's face, as dim as a brown fist, as soon as I saw the way Petra's sunset hair leaned over Zoltan's body like a veil, I knew. The geese flew hysterically for a bit, then landed again, waddling away from us. Picking up bits of crackers the Japanese had thrown just for them.

It was a week after we saw the geese that Ari sliced up our grapefruit and banana into six pieces each. I watched them eat. Sait, with a face that no longer said "Yesyesyes—I see" to anyone anymore, took his banana slice and put it underneath his tongue. He would transfer the warm disk of banana from side to side in his mouth until it had grown so soft that it slid, like liquid, down his throat. He nibbled away at half of the grapefruit, tearing the fibers, which clung from fruit to skin, with his bitten-down lips. The latter half he irreverently popped in his mouth. Petra let her slices sit for a while and finally chewed the banana, looking off from the side of her eye as if someone had a gun pointed to her head. She wrapped up her grapefruit slice in a bit of leftover Saran Wrap and went to the bedroom to lie down. Zoltan rubbed his eyes, put the banana slice on the flat side of the grapefruit, and swallowed them both whole, grapefruit peel and all. Ari ate his slices with delicate motions, and smiled afterward, as though it was not the best meal he'd had in his life, but definitely a tasty one. It was the kind of nonchalance that made me sick.

I ate my fruit like any American would. I bit into it.

Two other pieces sat on the plate, their perfect lonely shapes testaments to geometry.

"Anybody want those?" I asked. No one said anything. I looked around to make sure. No one had changed. I ate the last two pieces of fruit. Everyone's face looked the same. Anemic, terror-stricken, watching, watching. Everyone's face had that same starved look.

I ate the last pieces, wiped the grapefruit juice from around the corners of my mouth, looked at the semicircle of foreign faces around me.

I had done the wrong thing.

I borrowed enough money from Ari to catch the *tokkyuu* to Akasaka. That fare was money for crackers. I promised to return it by the day's end, I tried to hug him for lending me the money, but his body adopted a rigor mortis which pushed me away.

Akasaka was a banquet of neon and flesh, the *sararimen* humping whatever appeared most electric at the moment. When I got there it was going on noon and the *sararimen* hurled by, smiling with their colleagues, bowing for their bosses to enter the subway doors first. Mothers shopped, factory workers sighed, shopworkers chattered with their only friends—other shopworkers. The secretaries—the Office Ladies—all freshened their lipstick and straightened their hairbows.

I stood in the station and read an old magazine I'd brought with me. Finally, a *sarariman* came up to me.

"Verrrry sexy," he said to me.

He paid for the motel with a wad of yen. CAN RENT ROOM BY HOUR! screamed a red-lettered sign on the counter. We ascended the dark winding staircase; he followed me. The room had only a bed and a nightstand. He watched me undress and felt my skin only after I had taken everything off. He rubbed it as if he were trying to find something underneath. The insides of my closed eyelids were orange from a slit of sunlight which had strayed into the clinically neat room. The *sarariman* shook me. I opened my eyes. He raised his eyebrows, looking from me to the nightstand. The nightstand had a coin-operated machine attached.

"Sex toy?" he asked, in English.

"No," I said, in Japanese.

The motel-room sheets were perfect and crisp. They reminded me of sheets from home. I touched the *sarariman*'s freshly cut Asian hair, each shaft sheathed in a sheer liquid of subway sweat. The ends of the shortest hairs felt like the tips of lit, hissing firecrackers.

He was apologetic for the short length of time. "No problem," I told him in Japanese. He wanted to meet again. "Maybe," I said in English.

I left with a wad of yen. The price for selfishly eaten fruit. I took a seat in the station and leafed through the old American magazine I'd brought with me. I stretched my neck to observe the city on ground level. I watched flocks of alert employees return to work.

But I didn't want to go home just yet. I'd wander around Tokyo on the *tokkyuu* a bit. I decided to go to Shinjuku, that garish part of Tokyo where Pachinko parlors pushed against ugly gray earthquake-resistant buildings; where friendly, toothless vendors sold roasted *unagi*, even in rainy weather; where the twelve-floor department stores scintillated with slivers of primary colors, all the products resembling toys. The subcity of Shinjuku always swooned, brighter than Vegas, lurid with neon and Japanese pictograms. In the heart of Shinjuku one would find skinny prostitutes swishing by wearing miniskirts and pouty red lips, darting into doorways without signs and, seemingly, without actual doors. It was nothing like home, and when I walked its streets more than a year ago, I felt as though I had escaped something.

The traffic-light yellow ginkgo trees bowed rapidly to our locomotive as it blazed through flocks of geese in an otherwise empty park. No one seemed to notice the geese, or anything else for that matter. I did not let the motel room bother me as I rode the *tokkyuu*. It was so easy to forget that man. I didn't even know his name. I did not know the names of the commuters, and I did not know the very people I'd lived with. Even in the hectic lunch-hour life of Tokyo, the passengers wore the faces of early-morning commuters, a face that I had begun to understand. The geese started up apprehensively, as they had that day of the picnic, and picked up speed with confidence. Westward, westward, their wings spoke, and I imagined them flying back home without me. Westward, they flew, as I thought of how, just hours earlier, in the high morality of the waking morning, how everyone, absolutely everyone, struggles to a seat and falls promptly, deeply, asleep.

FLAMINGO

BENJAMIN PESKOE

I

Cathy paused, fingering the day pass in her pocket, as the hospital doors slid open before her. She blinked several times against the bright fall sunshine, and when her eyes had adjusted she searched the curb and the parking lot beyond for her mother's car. She didn't find it but she wasn't expecting to; she was down from the floor fifteen minutes before her mother had announced she would be there to pick her up. She gathered her coat more tightly around her: it was one the hospital had loaned her for the day, and the rest of what she wore—green sweatpants, a T-shirt, fuzzy slippers, and wool socks— she had borrowed from a pool of hospital extras as well. She had arrived at the hospital with nothing but her purse and the nightgown she wore; now the purse was all of her own that she had with her. The nightgown still carried a smell which made her stomach clench.

The hospital lawn covered a huge, steep hill, and down past the trees she could see a neighborhood of small brick houses. They seemed like little miniatures, as distant from her as if she had been viewing them from the window of an airplane, and it comforted her that she could not even hear the sound of the cars as they passed on the busy road below. Her mother would be coming from one of the houses in that neighborhood—the house where her mother lived, and where she herself had grown up, was less than a mile away. The lawn that spread out before her was one where she and her friends had once gone hunting for buckeyes that dropped from the trees. She remembered the nervous laughter and shouts with which they had greeted the blank pale faces that sometimes appeared in the hospital windows. She turned to look back at the windows and saw that now they were mirrored. She moved to a bench to one side of the doors and sat down.

Cathy hadn't wanted her mother to come at all, but of course she had insisted. Her mother always insisted. She would want to come up to the floor to thank the nurses for all the wonderful care they'd given her daughter—for saving her life, practically. "Well," Cathy could hear her saying to them, "let's hope this third time's the charm! God, thirty-eight years old and having to start again like you were twenty-two, you know?" Then she would laugh and look into the face of each nurse in turn as she kept laughing, handing over whatever present she had brought for them—probably something sweet, and probably seasonal: Thanksgiving pies or a box of holiday chocolates.

Her mother was right on time. Cathy traced the car's path as it wound along the road up the steep hill. Her mother pulled around the circular drive and stopped in front of the hospital doors. She leaned across the passenger seat, hunched her shoulders to her cheeks as she grinned, and waved. Cathy smiled back without moving. She fingered the day pass in her pocket and reminded herself that the whole trip would not take more than a few hours. She would go home and gather some clothes for herself, and then she would return for five more weeks of treatment.

Cathy waited for her mother to get out of her car and come around and then walked over to meet her. "Hi, honey," her mother said. "How's my girl?" She was a small woman, several inches shorter than Cathy, with a body so slender that it could have belonged to a girl of twelve. She had a bright, open face, and behind the boxy lenses of her glasses her wide eyes seemed perpetually amazed. She wore a plaid sweater of lime greens and hot pinks against a black background, the long kind that extended down below her hips so that she could wear tight leggings without exposing too much of herself. Once out of the car she moved both hands to her lower back and took a moment to arch and stretch it. *"God,"* she said. "Dr. Vargas says I'm really not supposed to be doing any driving for at *least* another week." She paused again to massage the area around the base of her spine. "I could re-strain it," she said, and looked at Cathy.

On the phone the day before she had told Cathy of the morning a week ago when she came to pull Cathy from her bed and take her to the hospital. (Cathy had needed to have her mother tell her this, because she herself remembered nothing.) Not only had her mother sprained her back, but she'd gagged at the smell of the house—on the phone she'd kept using the word "rancid": "Honey, there's *got* to be something rancid in there, I just know it," and "Let's be sure when you get home to check for what's rancid," and, as an afterthought, "I heard on the radio this morning that there's a rock-and-roll band called Rancid now! Can you be-*lieve* it?" So—and this Cathy had used to keep herself hurting and furious through half the previous night—when her mother arrived, her first step, before even speaking to Cathy, had been to close all the windows in the house. "Well," her mother had said, "I knew where we were going—it's not like I hadn't been through it twice before!—and if somebody didn't close the windows the neighbors would've called the Health Department! Besides," she'd added with a laugh, "it was getting cold in there!"

"Consider yourself lucky, mother," Cathy said now. "At least I didn't weigh very much. I was less of a burden than I could have been. You could've pulled a muscle." She pictured herself as she had been in the mirror of her hospital room that morning: she hadn't been so thin since high school.

"Well, kids can be burdensome!" her mother said, and laughed. "We just do the best we can! See, then you don't have to worry about what's lucky or unlucky or this or that. Just keep on breathing!" She looked down as she lifted a finger to her mouth to bite at a pink nail. Her laughter faded and her face grew concerned. "And then you've got to hope your kids'll understand someday, honey," she said sincerely, without looking up.

Cathy repeated the words like a nine-year-old mimicking, muttering them under her breath: " 'And then you've got to hope your kids'll understand someday.' " Inside the pockets of her coat she dug her nails into her palms. "Why should they understand?" she said aloud. "Why would I even want them to? There's not anything *to* understand."

"Oh," her mother said. "Well, do you think you'll be all right when we get you home? I was thinking about that refrigerator of yours. You probably ought to check it and put a stop to whatever's growing in there before you come back. Better now than later! Of course, with that *smell* it's not likely you'll notice the refrigerator. God, that smell would've puked a buzzard!" she added brightly.

"I don't think there's anything *in* the refrigerator, Mother," Cathy said. "I wasn't getting out to do much shopping."

"Oh, well, one never knows!" her mother said. Then she began to dig in her small purse, which hung from the crook of her elbow. "Here, dear, I brought you this," she said and held out a small plastic package. "I asked Dr. Vargas what might help last time I saw him—of course I didn't tell him why *exactly*—and he gave me this. It's a little elastic band that fits around your head so that these plugs hold into your nose. Dr. Vargas said they give them to the orderlies down at the hospital for cleaning the most awful things. They're fresh-scented."

"Mother!" Cathy hissed and snatched the little package from her mother's hand. She wanted to shriek but she stopped herself with the thought that someone might hear her (although there was no one around). She took a deep breath to gather herself. She put the little package in her pocket and then said calmly, "I'd like to go home now." She reached for the handle on the passenger door.

"Well, listen, honey," her mother said, "I've got something in the backseat there that I want to take up."

"Mother, please. Please just take me home."

"No, now, I want to. It's such a thankless job they have."

"Send them a card!" Cathy shouted in a whisper. "Knit them something! Anything! But later! Just take me home!"

"Oh no, dear," her mother said, unfazed and still smiling. "I won't forget my manners. It's just a small thing, and they've done so much for you. Lord knows it's a miracle. My first thought was to bring them Daddy's best bottle of bourbon—the one he's been saving?— but then I thought he might miss it," she said and laughed again. "Lord, he'd have killed us both!"

"Probably," Cathy said as her mother's laughter faded. She turned to look up at the massive red-brick building; its mirrored windows were full of blue sky. "So what is it this time?" she asked.

"Oh, I just brought a bottle from the liquor cabinet instead, one of the cheaper ones," her mother said and laughed again, but tentatively, and when Cathy did not turn to look at her she ceased altogether. "It's just some nice Halloween candy, dear," she said then. "It was on special."

"I'll wait here," Cathy said and put her hand again on the door handle.

"Okay," her mother said. She went around to the other side and reached into the back for a brown paper grocery bag. "I won't be gone a second. I'll be right back." She smiled and took a few steps toward the entrance, but suddenly she turned around laughing and said, " 'Rancid' as a rock-and-roll band! I just couldn't be-*lieve* it!" She must have noticed Cathy's body go absolutely rigid—so taught that it did not even breathe—because at once she went back to Cathy and with her free hand touched her daughter's neck. "If I've tried to teach you anything, dear," she said, "it's that there's *nothing* in this world so bad you can't laugh at it and keep going." Then she squeezed one of Cathy's hands and let it go, turned around, and stepped off purposefully toward the hospital entrance.

Cathy watched as her mother walked away, her black leggings glinting in the sunlight. She walked around to the driver's side of the car and peered down through the window. The keys were still in the ignition and a tiny toy horse dangled from the key chain. She opened the door and got in. She looked out the window in the direction of her mother's house; she pictured her father sitting at the little table in the kitchen, his huge body hunched into a small chair. He might not be doing anything, she imagined, just sitting there, sipping a drink, passing the time until her mother came home. Then he might just sit there all night and go on drinking—or he might find some reason to erupt—there was no way to tell—and her mother would just laugh and joke until he was calm again. In her anger Cathy pictured her mother's wide, innocent eyes and hated them—she hated that they never seemed to be touched or altered no matter what the viciousness. Cathy lifted one hand to the keys in the ignition with an urge to start the car and go. She thought that some of the nurses up on her floor would actually *like* her mother and pity her for having the daughter that she did. The thought made her want to scream, but instead of screaming she put the side of one palm in her mouth and bit down hard. She bit until she gagged at the pain and then she felt better. She sat up straight. In the rearview mirror she spotted a cab at a taxi stand around the side of the circular drive. She checked in her purse to be sure she had money and then left before her mother returned.

II

The flamingo still stood in the front yard. That was the first thing she noticed. It was nearly three feet tall and made of cheap plastic, and it stood to one side of the porch steps, facing away from them. She used it to point out her house to the cab driver as they approached. Without it she would've had to count the house numbers to tell which was hers, which was part of the reason why she put it up originally—to act as a landmark. The houses on her street were all old and brick and as deep as they were wide across the front, mostly similar and spaced almost evenly, with a little variation, like cars in a crowded parking lot. She paid the cab driver and walked across the front yard so that she stood in front of the bird; she stared at it against the background of dark green shrubs which bordered the porch. There was a yellow splotch of dead grass around the spot where the metal rod poked into the ground—dogs in the neighborhood that got loose from their yards liked to come pee against it. She scratched at the splotch with her slipper and looked around her. Up the street stretched the row of houses, and a row of yards, and the gray concrete line of the sidewalk; there was a row of old oak trees in a strip of grass between the sidewalk and the curb. Her younger son had kept getting lost in this neighborhood; he would walk past the house and if her car was put away in the small garage he kept on walking. Nothing less conspicuous than the flamingo had been able to tell him where home was.

The flamingo had come with them when they left Hawaii. It was almost ten years old; she dated it from the birth of her younger son, her second, the one who kept getting lost. It was a gift to him from her mother. Her mother had sent it to him with a cloth diaper hanging from its beak; the attached note said it was a tropical stork that they should stand in the front yard to announce the birth.

("But Mother, there *aren't* any flamingos in Hawaii!" "Well, there are now!")

Cathy and her husband and their older son had already lived in Hawaii for a year and a half when the baby was born. They had a little house on a hill which looked out on the bay. They couldn't see the water of the bay themselves, but from their back porch they could see it reflected in the side windows of a house behind theirs. The weekend after she brought the baby home from the hospital she and her husband had slept outside. She remembered it was dark and that they had fallen asleep drunk and happy, but that during the night he fell out of the hammock. She woke up to see him sitting there naked on the wood of the back porch with a smile on his face. "Whoops," he said, and laughed, and then lay out flat so that he could look up at the sky. "Do you realize where we live?" he asked after a while. The baby was near them asleep in the stroller; their older son was inside in bed. "It's paradise! It's almost November," he said, "and I know I've been drinking a little, but look at this—I'm naked and it's almost October and go ahead, look at me, no goose bumps. It just feels perfect." He could sometimes get so giddy when he drank, she remembered. After a few minutes he spoke again. "Look," he said, and stood up smiling. The sky was cloudless and in the light from the moon she could see him clearly. "It's paradise. We live in paradise." The flamingo was leaning against the porch railing. He walked over to the railing and picked it up, pulled off the diaper, and then held it so that it covered his groin. He half-turned and stared for a long time at the shadows of the mountains in the distance.

"It's just so peaceful here," he finally said.

"Yes it is," she said. She drew a slow breath and studied him for a moment, as if putting a finger to the pulse of his sobriety, and then said, "Buzz and Mary brought over two books of children's stories about Hawaiian legends today for Davey. I'd like for the kids to learn Hawaiian. You know, in time. When they're old enough."

He didn't answer and she saw that his face was still turned toward the mountains. She bit her lip. "Let's always stay here," she said. "I don't ever want to go back."

"I know what you mean," he said. "It's so peaceful."

"No, I mean it," she said. "Or, at least, wouldn't it be nice if you just stopped going to the library for a while?" she asked. "I mean, can't all those articles and journals just wait for a while? Let's just enjoy being here. You can catch up again later, can't you? I mean, it's just such a beautiful place, sometimes it seems awful to me to spend any time in a library."

"I know, I know," he said, still holding the flamingo in front of him. "We're going to have to leave soon, anyway. I really should enjoy it while it's here."

"But we don't have to leave," she said, so eagerly that the hammock began to sway beneath her. "You could renew your fellowship"—the fellowship with the Public Health Service had been Richard's means of avoiding Vietnam, two years and then back to begin his career as a doctor. "We could stay two more years, and after that, who knows? I mean, really, why should we leave this place?"

"Oh, c'mon, Cathy—" he said.

"No, Richard," she said. "I mean, think about it. I know you've never really given any thought to staying here, but I have—I've thought about it a lot. I've been meaning to talk to you. I've just been waiting. I mean, what more could we want? Our parents are so far away, and we have our children, and—I just feel like an *adult* all of a sudden, and I can't believe it, but it's not a bad thing. I actually like it."

"No, I know what you mean," he said. He set the flamingo against the railing and then sat down on the porch steps. She dropped her head to the pillow and stared up at the moon.

"I mean, I get up every morning at dawn," she said, "and I open my eyes and I know it's going to be a beautiful day. Don't you ever feel that?" she said. "How amazing it is to open your eyes in the morning and just *know* it's going to be a beautiful day? Here I actually *want* to get out of bed. I actually *want* to do the things I have to do."

"No, I know what you're saying," he said, staring out across the backyard.

"I mean, I feel like I knew I wanted to stay here for a long time even before I got here, even before the plane landed," she said. He laughed under his breath without looking at her and immediately she felt embarrassed for having said it—she hadn't intended to tell him that, but she really *had* felt that way. "From the window of the airplane," she said, "I just stared down at the ocean and it was so blue and it stretched away forever, and at first I was thinking of Mother and Dad, hearing her talking and seeing him staring, but after a while I forgot them, or just couldn't hear them—like I lost the signal—and I laughed—do you remember me laughing?—and I looked down at the blue ocean and said, 'Thank you' for that. I mean, you could do your fellowship here, couldn't you?" she went on. "At the university?"

"Maybe," he said. "It's not the best program."

"But Richard—"

"I said maybe, okay?" he said. "That's enough for tonight." She was silent. After a moment he came back to the hammock, and they did not speak again that night.

The next morning he did not mention the talk they had had on the porch the night before, and he did not mention it the next day, either. She waited for a week before she asked him if he had looked into fellowship programs at the university yet. No, he hadn't, he said. After another month she went to the university herself for information and an application; she left them on the kitchen counter for him. He took them, but she never saw what he did with them.

That night when she cried he held her in his arms and said, "Please don't cry. I know we've been happy here, but it just seems like happiness means we're not facing up to things."

She pulled away from him. "What's that supposed to mean?" she said. "What things?"

"Well, if we're really happy," he said, "shouldn't we be able to be happy anywhere? I mean, if the happiness is attached to this place, then maybe there's something wrong with it."

She rolled over so that her back was to him, feeling offended and trying to think. She heard him sit up against the headboard and she pressed herself closer to her edge of the bed. She could tell that he was gathering steam, that his eyebrows would be raised and the vein on his forehead pumping, and she did not want to look at him. "It's not like I wouldn't love to stay here, because I would—you know I would. But, well, I mean I always feel like I'm on vacation here," he said. "It's impossible to live in a place so peaceful and not always feel like you're on vacation. This isn't the real world. Sure, we're happy here, but who wouldn't be? It's not a happiness we've earned. It's nothing we've achieved. It's no challenge we've met."

He waited for her to answer but she didn't know how to begin. She had tried every subtle means at her disposal and she had failed. He was set on leaving. She had told herself that if it came to this (and she had known it would), she could, after all, keep the kids and stay behind without him. She did have a choice. But now that the choice was there to make she couldn't bring herself to voice it.

"And it's not like we weren't happy before we got here, right?" he asked. He went on expounding and she just let him go. She watched the curtain flutter against the open window, only half listening, as he compared their life there to a life in Disney World and wondered what skewed perspective on reality their children would be plagued with. In her mind she was thinking that she loved him and she hated him, that she wanted to leave to make him happy but that she also wanted to stay. But she couldn't tell him any of that. She just let him go on talking until finally she heard the pause and long breath that told her he was about to finish—"All I'm asking is for you to be reasonable and try to see this like a rational person," he said.

"I don't want to be rational," she whispered to the open window.

"What's that?"

"I want to stay!" she shouted.

He touched her gently and said, "Honey, we're leaving."

"I know," she said and began to weep. After a moment she began to weep more intensely, turning so that he could see her face.

It was less than six months later, when his job with the Public Health Service ended, that they left Hawaii, and she wept nearly every day of that time. Her crying got her two more weeks. He himself would leave on the scheduled day, but the plane tickets for her and the kids were dated two weeks later.

Her closetful of bright clothes—floral prints and silks, vivid floral patterns that she loved because they were loud and unlike anything she'd worn before—she packed away and shipped back to the mainland on a boat in a huge trunk. With the kids she took him to the airport to see him off, and afterward what she remembered of his departure was how upset he'd been that they were caught in traffic. He'd been irate; the airline had said he needed to be there an hour early. His reservation might be canceled. When he was gone she went to the beach every day and built sand castles and watched every sunset from her back porch, sipping cocktails and smoking. She didn't let herself wonder what it would have been like if she had stayed without him, or even merely threatened to stay. She found herself smiling brightly for her kids and speaking in perky exclamations, when often her body shook with anger.

She flew with her children to Los Angeles and from there to Denver, where he had found an opening. The plane had lifted off from Hawaii in the morning, and out over the edgeless blue ocean she remembered how she had felt at first seeing it on their trip out, how her mother's voice had seemed to recede, and she wondered if that voice would come back to her again, bright and exclamatory.

Over the next six years she unpacked the floral prints from her huge trunk three times, each time in a closet larger and more lavish. She always unpacked the clothes, although she never wore them or even spoke of them. By the time they finally settled in Indianapolis she kept them on wooden hangers in plastic cleaner's bags in a closet lined with cedar.

Richard began to make more money than she could spend, and not for lack of trying. She could spend all she wanted and he didn't care. She could show him everything that she bought and he still didn't care. Anytime she thought of Hawaii, she was inspired to purchase, and she thought of Hawaii often. When she found that she couldn't or wouldn't spend beyond her means, she began to drink more—if not in place of spending then at least in addition to it—especially during the day once her kids began school.

She remembered going out to the front yard to wait for her kids as they came home each day from school; that must have stopped, she realized, as her drinking picked up, but she had no idea of how it had stopped—she could only remember a later time when she no longer waited for them. Did it end gradually, she wondered, or all at once? The worse things got, the more time her husband spent at the hospital. Finally, in desperate boredom, she had begun to attempt some hobbies: a painting workshop and a gardening club and a ballet class. In the ballet class, at the first lesson, she had pulled a muscle in her back and been bedridden. That was what she had been waiting for, she now realized—an excuse. She never really got up again.

In bed she had time to ponder. She rearranged their room so that her side of the bed sat next to a window ("Pretty good for a pulled muscle," Richard said, but that was all). She liked to sit and look out on her neighbors and watch them move from car to house and house to car. It's a life that bores you to death, she thought, but a lot of people live it. She couldn't tell whether or not she still felt like an adult—sometimes yes and sometimes no. She was no longer sure what she had meant by that word "adult" that night on the porch in Hawaii. She felt she'd known when she spoke it, but now she wasn't sure.

Her husband took the children while she was in treatment the first time. When she got out she signed the divorce papers. She went home and packed her things and her children's things, and with her children she moved to Louisville, the city where she had grown up. The house to which they'd moved was the same house in front of which she now stood, and as she looked at the flamingo she wondered if her husband hadn't been right about happiness. Happiness just meant they weren't facing up to things, he had said. Shouldn't they have been able to be happy anywhere? But those were questions he had never asked her after they left Hawaii. She thought of her drinking—the first and most lengthy bout, before the divorce, and the second one, here in Louisville in this house with her children, as a result of which they were taken from her to live with their father, and this last time, the third, when she had taken a drink her second week home from treatment—and she only knew that each time it happened more easily. Her questions now were of surviving, of staying sober, of being able to endure a life without her children but which was still full of the guilt of knowing what she had put them through. She did not expect that she would ever be happy again, but she didn't feel she deserved to be.

III

Now, in front of the house and her flamingo, she felt in her pocket for the nosepiece that her mother had given her and took it out. It was a small, white, square package. The glossy white plastic was blank except for the word "Nosegay" printed in small black letters and the outline of a little flower. She stuffed it in her pocket again and looked in her purse for her keys. She expected that her mother would come after her when she found her gone, and she wanted to avoid that. She looked up the street at the row of houses and realized that without the flamingo her mother would not be able to pick out which one was hers. Her car was all that her mother could possibly recognize, and that was put away in the small garage at the end of the driveway. She pulled the flamingo free from the yellow splotch of dead grass. She took it and climbed the steps to the front porch, her mother's voice again filling her head. "Lord," she heard her mother saying with a laugh, "it was either here or the liquor store, but I thought I'd try here first!" She went inside.

The smell made her nauseous. She wanted to leave the door open, but remembering her mother she set the flamingo aside and then shut the door and locked it. She held her nose with one hand, and with the other she reached for the nosepiece. She held her breath as she opened the little package and put it on.

She moved through the dark living room and into the kitchen. It was not as bad as she had expected. One sink was full of dishes in gray putrid water; the other sink was empty, and in the drying rack on the counter several plates and glasses had been neatly arranged. Apparently at some point she had thought to do dishes. She pushed up her sleeve and sank her hand into the scummy water to pull loose the drain plug. As the water drained out she pulled the overflowing bag out from the garbage can. It was the garbage, she thought, that must have made the bulk of the smell, although with the nose plugs in she couldn't tell for sure. On top were two empty cans of macadamia nuts and the debris from an emptied ashtray. Beneath that she saw some old broccoli and a large piece of fish which looked as though it had never been cooked. She tied the bag off and set it outside the back door, and then began to clean mechanically, first scraping the crusty food from the plates strewn about the counters and then stacking them in the sink.

She went down to the basement in search of clean clothing. The basement was where she always did her laundry. Stretched across the whole length of the basement was a clothesline, and on it hung all the clothing from Hawaii that she no longer wore but that she had never wanted to give away. The clothes were so light that the clothesline hardly bowed at all under their weight. She ran her hands through the dresses and blouses and pantsuits, pushing the hangers back and pulling up the plastic so that she could look at each one in turn. She remembered how she had looked in the mirror of her hospital room that morning—she had not been so thin since high school —and she felt herself grow excited at the thought of being able to fit into many of the clothes again for the first time in years. She had an urge to take off her hospital clothes and put on a silk pantsuit, to stuff a suitcase full of the things which hung there, but she hesitated.

She suddenly remembered a morning when she was eight or nine years old, standing in her mother's walk-in closet and looking at all the bright beautiful clothing there (back before her mother's tastes had turned to hot pinks and lime greens). That morning she had stood in the closet and tried on the clothes, imagining what it was like to be her mother, a grown-up. She spent a whole morning there until her mother walked in on her; Cathy was frightened at first, but then her mother laughed and joined her. "Where did you get all these?" Cathy remembered asking. "How come you never wear them?" Her mother put a finger to her lips. "Oh, I can't, dear," she said. "Daddy'd have my hide if he knew I had these. See," she said, "that's what you have to do when you have a husband." She laughed and smiled. "If you see something you like, *buy* it—but you've got to hide it! Now, there are some people who would just not want to buy a thing if they weren't able to wear it. And there are others who if they bought it would wear it no matter what for all to see. But I like the middle path—if you ever hear anyone talk on the radio about the Buddhist religion you'll learn about this—which is to buy the clothes and hide them, and that way everyone's happy and no one gets upset!"

There in the basement Cathy took off her hospital clothes and dressed herself in a green silk pantsuit printed with small violet flowers. She stood still then, lit up under the dim yellow glow of the bulb on the ceiling, the nosepiece still in place, caught up in the prospect of being able to fit into all those clothes again. Not that she would ever wear them out in public—they were too loud for anywhere but Hawaii—but she was pleased to feel connected again to the person who had once worn them. For several minutes she looked through them again, one at a time, until finally she remembered where she was and what she needed to be doing. She *wasn't* the person she had been in Hawaii, and she felt sick at the thought of how selfish she was being, how forgetful of her kids. She switched then into a sweater and a pair of dark corduroys which she pulled from on top of the dryer. She pulled some other clothes from the dryer, too, and gathered them all in her arms together with the clothing from the hospital. She went to the couch in the living room, where she took her time folding the clothing.

Finally, she went upstairs to her bedroom. With the curtains drawn the room was pitch black; the light that flowed in through the open door cast a straight bright shaft of light across the dark outline of her bed in the far corner. She turned the light on and straightened her nosepiece. The covers and comforter were tangled in a heap in the center of her bed. The white sheets were streaked gray and black with ash from her cigarettes and spotted yellow in two places with overlapping ovals. The floor was a mess of dirty clothes and dishes and overturned, empty bottles; the drawers to the dresser along the wall next to her all stood open and its surface was totally hidden beneath piles of loose clothing. A fine layer of black soot covered everything where the smoke from her cigarettes had settled out of the still air.

Her TV remote control and cordless telephone were on the little bedside table among a grove of green wine bottles. Two of the bottles were still full, she noticed, and clustered around the bases of the bottles were some paper cups, a crumpled package of cigarettes in which a few still remained, and several shiny little screw-off metal caps. Toward the time when her drinking became heaviest she had taken to buying the cheapest wine she could find, the kind that didn't require a corkscrew.

Her little color TV stood facing the bed on the dresser. She sat on the edge of her bed and tried to remember what had gone on while she lay there. One of her few memories was of herself lying with the remote control in hand, flipping through the cable channels in the dark room and suddenly stopping at the Home Shopping Network. A woman's hand was demonstrating a dazzling diamond bracelet against a blue curtain in the background. She had been transfixed by that blue curtain; it was the same pure deep shade of blue as the ocean she had seen on her way to Hawaii. She had no idea how long she had stared at the curtain before fumbling for the phone on the bedside table and attempting to dial the number on the screen. She remembered a sudden panic when the color on the set had faded out for a moment before coming in again. Finally she got the right number, and after the woman at the other end finished greeting her (she remembered her mother's voice in her head telling her to be polite and wait for the woman to finish) she had tried to order four of those curtains. She wanted to do her whole room with them.

Now, with one hand absently fingering the remote control, she looked out through her open door and across the hall to the door of her younger son's old room. She remembered having gone through both her sons' rooms after she came home from the hospital the last time. That, more than anything else, in fact, was what had landed her right back in the hospital again. She had sat Indian-style on the floor of her older son's room and looked through all the books and crumpled papers from school which had been scattered on the floor with food wrappers and crumbs and dirty streaked underwear. She hadn't been able to put out of her mind thoughts of what she had done to them.

When she spoke with them afterward on the phone they told her much that had happened of which she had no memory: missed visits and birthdays, even a permission slip which her younger son had needed her to sign when she had not been able even to grip a pen. They had told her of a time when the three of them took a shortcut on the way back from a fast-food restaurant one afternoon and ended up in a gravel quarry. The sounds of their voices closed in on her again and she reached for the package of cigarettes and some matches on the nightstand. She took them and walked to the door; she closed it, turned out the light, and made her way back to the bed. She sat down and lit a cigarette in the darkness. She used the little light of the cigarette to search the nightstand for an ashtray, but, not finding one, she tipped her ashes onto the floor. The glow of the cigarette reflected off the wine bottles on the nightstand. Two of them were full, she remembered. She sat for a long time, hunched over on the edge of the bed, smoking and rocking herself gently. She lit a second cigarette off the end of the first, and then a third, her last, off the end of the second. Two of the bottles were full. The doorbell rang.

She sat up straight. It had to be her mother. She moved from the bed and walked quietly down the stairs to peer through the peephole on the front door. Her mother's face stared back at her, full of worry. Her mother bit at a fingernail, knocked again, and then turned to lean against the door so that Cathy's sight through the peephole was filled with the back of her head. Cathy pulled her face away from the door and leaned her shoulder against it. She needed to breathe deeply through her nose but the nosepiece stopped her. She wondered how her mother could possibly have found the house. The doorbell rang two more times. When she heard the door to the mail slot being lifted outside, she barely had time to move out of the way before her mother's fingers poked through the inside. "Cathy?" she heard her mother's voice say. "Cathy? I see that flamingo. I know this is the right house." Cathy saw that the flamingo had tipped over from where she had leaned it against the wall; it rested now at an angle against the windowsill, poking out in front of the curtains. She huddled herself against the wall in the dark shadows of the living room. "Cathy?" her mother said again. After a moment she said, "Oh, Lord," dejectedly and the door to the mail slot fell closed.

Cathy waited a moment and then looked again through the

peephole. She saw her mother standing still in the middle of the front walk, facing out to the street, her arms held out rigid a few inches from her sides. Her little purse stood next to her on the concrete. Cathy turned away and said softly, "Laugh and keep going, Mother." She began to laugh, but the laughter turned to tears and she slid down to the floor. A minute later she heard the door to her mother's car slam shut, and she felt sickened that she had not answered her. Again she felt like screaming and again she put the side of her palm into her mouth and bit down hard until she gagged at the pain. When she pulled her hand from her mouth she saw two distinct but overlapping sets of teeth marks, one fresh and one still faintly visible from where she had bitten herself while sitting in her mother's car. She looked at them and thought, "I want to scream at my mother and I bite myself. I want to scream at myself and I bite myself. What's *wrong* with me?" She closed her eyes, opened them, and turned to stare up at the ceiling. "Jesus," she said aloud, feeling desperate and afraid, "I need a better question."

She hurried back upstairs and pulled a little suitcase from her bedroom closet. She took the suitcase to the living room, her stomach full with fear, and filled it with her clothing. Then there was a search for the phone book; she found a number and called a cab. She drew back the curtains and took the flamingo away from the window to sit with it on the couch as she waited. Her children's fingerprints were lit up by the sunlight on the window glass. Stroking the flamingo absently with one hand, she stared at the fingerprints.

In the fingerprints on the glass she saw a whole history of failures. She held the flamingo and thought of her kids and what might have happened if she had decided to stay in Hawaii. She felt that they had had a real chance for happiness there, but that since then she had failed them completely. She felt that it was killing her to remember all she had put them through, but she also felt it would kill her to let it go. She thought of her car stored away in the little garage. She saw that she could get in the car, and drive to the liquor store, and fill up the trunk, and then find a hotel room. She could kill herself that way—it would be over—or she could return to the hospital. The choice seemed to unfold itself plainly before her: if she drank she would die, if she went back to the hospital she would try one more time to stay sober. She felt as if her future had been stripped of its possibilities, as if it had been handed to her small and bare, but it was completely her own now. The thought comforted her: she no longer had to worry about losing anything. The cab arrived but she did not see it. The driver honked twice but the sound did not register. She sat rocking herself as she still held the flamingo. The fingerprints on the glass transfixed her; she gazed and gazed at them as she felt the power of the choice she was offered.

MANNA WALKING

DAWN KARIMA PETTIGREW

The cashier in the A&P is the kind of blonde poured out of a bottle. She sneers as Manna pays her with many-colored food stamps. Manna has a college degree and pays her taxes. Since she sees these cartoonish food coupons as her fair share of Uncle Sam's apology for making soup out of Turtle Island, she ignores the girl's curled lip.

The smirking girl rolls her eyes as she tosses Pampers and canned goods into a plastic bag. Manna considers commenting on the less-than-stellar customer service, but the red "A&P" embroidered over the girl's polyester-smocked heart is the same shade as the ink on Manna's food stamps. Manna saves her breath. The cashier chews circles around unnaturally rosy bubblegum as she tosses Manna's food stamp change onto the black conveyor belt. Manna says nothing.

The chewing girl cashier sighs melodramatically as Manna organizes the rainbow of food stamps and change by denomination. She folds each coupon neatly into her seed-beaded wallet before leaving the checkout line. Wheeling the baby and the groceries out of the icebox of the A&P into the broiler of the blacktop parking lot, Manna decides that it would be tragic to work so hard to be President and then end up engraved on a food stamp instead of a dollar bill.

Making their way across the parking lot, Manna and the baby pass the Cactus Flower Trading Post. The place sells mostly cacti. In Gallup, that's a little like selling sand or hundred-degree temperatures. Tourists, dreaming of turquoise beads and woven blankets, come to buy the handmade souvenirs. The store convinces customers that the ceramic coyotes and palm-sized hogans are made by the industrious Navajo women on the brochures instead of Mexican children with swollen stomachs and flies on their faces. Manna forgives the store for its pots and even the mock kachinas, since it has a display of garden hoses and sprinklers out front and the sprinklers are turned on. Figuring that the plastic bag is like a shower cap for the groceries, Manna pushes the shopping cart full of baby and groceries into the synthetic shower. The droplets bless them like good-night kisses.

Standing under the sprinkler, Manna contemplates larceny. It would be easier to manage the miles between the A&P shopping center and her HUD house with the baby in a cart. The baby is singing and beating the bar of the cart with a plastic bottle of violet juice. She has excellent rhythm, and for Manna, that settles it.

Aside from the baby's powwow songs and the fact that they are both downpour-damp, they look just like any other shoppers walking across the lot. Except they keep on walking. Walking away from the burned-out ampersand on the neon supermarket sign and the sale on sprinklers and almost-genuine Navajo ashtrays, Manna pushes her cart through weeds, rocks, and amber-glass shards until they reach the highway.

Manna matches her steps to the beat of the baby's banging. Half a mile into the way home, shouts interrupt the baby's concert. Manna forces herself to intend, in her heart, to return this shopping cart someday, so that she will seem more innocent if the A&P has sent its forces in search of fugitive customers.

As the shouts come closer, they have nothing to do with the stolen shopping cart or the supermarket. "Hey darlin'," they say, crude calls in the threatening tones cowboys use for Indians. Manna attempts to hear the rattling of the metal cart over the broken bottles, smoked-down cigarettes, and road's-edge gravel instead of the men's suggestions for her hips, lips, and thighs. She has seen ranch hands and rodeo riders head into the Navajo nation for years. They act out cable-TV Westerns through double-up rapes, hit-and-run pinball, and target practice. True to the movies, when the cavalry finally rides in, they rescue the cowboys, not the Indians.

"Hey, hey, hey," the carload of men shout insistently. One wheel of the ill-gotten cart turns back toward the A&P. Manna promises God that if He preserves her life now, she will accept the rest of it without complaining. She silently begs God to make the men vanish, to make the cart pick up speed. The baby has stopped singing.

The white men in the blue car pass Manna. The car pauses, creeps backward, slowing to a stop. A single boot emerges from the backseat. Manna leans into the shopping cart and pushes, running into the heat of the sand.

Her shoes betray her. Slipping from the side of the road into sand, Manna falls. She feels her flesh tear as she slides into the cart, encounters the ground. The baby shrieks as the cart lurches forward. Manna opens her hand and grasps for the wheel. Sand scrapes the side of her hand. The cart stops.

Manna closes her eyes and concentrates on sitting up. Her lower lip is warm and sticky. She has bitten a sizable half-moon out of it. She blinks twice, staring into the scaryhouse mirror of an upside-down white face.

"Hey darlin'," he says. "You all right?"

He straightens and Manna sees the baby, who has folded her mouth into a disturbingly round O. Manna waves her wounded hand and the baby smiles slightly in reply.

The man tips his hat at Manna. He smells of Marlboros and Doublemint, and the twang in his apology reminds Manna of songs on the jukebox.

"My name is Randy," says this man in a cowboy hat. Manna hurts too much to answer him.

"I'm sorry if I scared you, darlin'," he continues. He drops to one blue-jeaned knee. Manna flinches as he begins to brush sand and stone from her left leg. "We seen you and thought you might want to ride a ways with us. Didn't know you had that little bit up there with you though."

Manna's body agrees to sit up. She wonders if the men decided not to be up to no good before or after they stopped their car. That the man in the cowboy hat thinks that the baby belongs to her is fine. Babies are safety. If you manage to keep them clean and fed and alive, they just might ward off everything from skinwalkers to Saturday-night cowboys. This baby is getting to be a handy person to know.

Cowboy Hat Man holds out a bandanna printed with neon banjoes.

"Can you spit into this for me? I wanna get some of that mess off your leg."

Manna's calf is torn and peppered with dirt. When she opens her mouth, nothing falls into the bandanna but blood.

Cowboy Hat offers Manna a ride, says he's sorry he scared her. He says all this again and once again for good measure. Manna wonders if he is only sorry that she hurts too badly to be a good time or ashamed in front of the baby, who is staring at Manna's bleeding lip and rag-wrapped leg like they are not to be trusted.

"Here." Cowboy Hat offers Manna a sun-scarred hand. "Let me help set you on your feet."

Manna shakes her head at him.

"You want a ride then? We can take you as far as the Gas-n-Go." Cowboy Hat motions toward nothing in particular.

"No," Manna says. She concentrates on standing steadily, without swaying. "We'd rather walk."

"Suit yourself," Cowboy Hat says to Manna's back. She has turned around to comfort the baby, who is stained with tears and splattered with grape juice. Manna listens to the drag of cowboy boots over sand. When she turns around, the men in the car are gone.

Manna repents of taking the shopping cart. She leaves it exactly where it is and earnestly expects that God will return it for her when He gets the opportunity. She lifts her groceries out of the cart. A three-for-a-dollar can of peas falls into the silence of the sand, and Manna leaves it. The sun will strike its golden lid someday, and a hitchhiker will, for a moment, imagine that buried peas are treasure.

Sliding her wrist into the handles of a bag that thanks her very much and asks her to please come again, Manna prays that God has seen fit to make the batch of plastic that birthed this bag strong. She lifts the baby onto her bruised hip and prepares to walk the rest of the way home.

The desert yawns at Manna. She promises herself that, in spite of her aching leg and swelling lip, she and this baby will make out just fine. Manna resolves to pray as often as she breathes.

LIKE A CROSSING GUARD

HOWIE AXELROD

It all started with that damn Mustang. See, if that night had never happened, with the empties rolling around the backseat and the mad run to upstate New York, I never would have been in reform school in the first place. I'm not saying I'm an angel or anything, but I'm no goddamn criminal. The weird thing is though, it wasn't the flashing blue lights or Tim hitting me in the head with a bottle that surprised me most, but what happened once I got here. I mean, you'd think all of us "delinquents"—whatever the hell that means—would kind of be on the same side. Not that we'd have to go ganging up on the guards and causing some riot with choppers and megaphones like in the movies, but at least that we'd act in that spirit. Like we'd be allies or something. But the way guys look at you here, it's like you're the reason they got sent away. I mean, it's like just your existence is the direct cause of them being here.

My trip started with an old piece-of-shit military bus driving me and four other reform rookies the six hours from the DSS in Boston (that's Department of Social Services, for all you angels out there) to Treasure Island in Maine. The officers made us sit staggered so we wouldn't get any ideas about having fun or stirring up trouble—heaven forbid the little delinquents might want to talk to each other. It was just as well though; from the looks of these four, they'd probably never seen trees and they definitely hadn't seen a white person who wasn't a cop, judge, or DA. I mean, I'm not trying to be racist or anything, but these dudes were black, city-black, the kind of guys that make my dad roll up the windows and lock the doors. While they sat looking back and forth between whitey-juvenile-delinquent me (yes, we do exist) and the trees rushing past outside, I started daydreaming about my days up at Camp Hiawatha. I was thinking maybe reform school would look something similar. Hell, I knew it wouldn't be cushy or anything, but it was still going to be a lot of kids living and doing all the same stuff together. Difference was, these guys weren't going to be rich and spoiled, and they damn well weren't going to lie sniffling in their beds every night thinking about home. I sat there on the one-seater in the back of the bus, picturing what it would be like if the whole bunch of us delinquents were at camp. Wouldn't that be something—all of us "screwups" running around those manicured fields and hollering down on the docks. Those campers never did. The way they got all whiny about doing activities, you'd have thought it was Camp I Don't Wanna. They just sat on their beds and wrote letters to Mommy and Daddy and their trust-fund accountants. Goddamn pansies. I had to make fun for myself at that place, and I did an all right job of it. One hobby that kept me busy was making blowtorches with my Cutter's and the lighter my counselor hid behind his socks. I lit the whole back wall on fire one time and got to use the little red extinguisher they kept in the bunk. Nobody had ever touched it—I bet they just put it there to make the parents feel safer when they dropped off their little darlings.

But driving past all the guards and barbed wire on the way into Treasure Island cut short those fond childhood memories. Instead Alcatraz and chain gangs and scenes of me singing "Nobody Knows the Trouble I've Seen" started running through my mind. I saw my dad looking at me over his *Boston Globe* at the breakfast table, saying in his firmest lawyer voice, "This should be good for you, Richie." Right, like the milk and the orange juice, my trip to reform school would start me off on the right foot—reform school part of this nutritional adolescence. Dad hadn't said much else, he just straightened his paper and disappeared again; I guess he figured his duty had been done. My mom on the other hand had wanted to "talk it all through." How did I feel about going, how many times a week would I write? How this, how that . . . how the hell did I know? I told her I'd never been there before, and seeing as how I wasn't a goddamn fortune-teller, I couldn't very well know. That made her pipe down a little, and the intro voice-over to another episode of *Geraldo* was enough to steal her attention. A regular genius, my mother. Her beady eyes narrowed and I could see little worry lines mustaching her upper lip. During the commercial before the show she looked at me standing in the doorway and patted the cushion next to her for me to sit down. As if I had been waiting there because I was interested in goddamn transvestites.

Why this place was called Treasure Island I couldn't figure—the military's idea of a joke, I guess. A real laugh riot, those green-boys. I'm not a pyro or anything, but the whole base just looked like it *needed* lighting up. Gray buildings, gray roads, gray grass burned by the summer sun. Just too much fucking gray. The bus did pass some guys playing basketball. The court was about a half a mile from the main part of the base and it was right next to the road. The fence was almost on top of the sidelines, and the metal nets were the kind that give a cold clink instead of a swish when you sink a shot. I could see a few tufts of grass struggling up through the pavement. Some guys were playing what looked like a pretty good game, so I figured the place couldn't be all bad. But I knew we weren't going to be roasting marshmallows around any campfire either.

The bus let me and the other four guys off in front of the Star barracks and they told us to report to the officers at the desk. I hoisted my duffel onto my shoulder and walked in. A muscular black guy with a shiny head directed me to my room, and told me to take the half hour before dinner to get settled. Before I could ask any questions, he closed the door and was gone. Nothing so welcoming as a door shut in your face. My room didn't look much like a cabin. The floor had carpeting that wasn't really any color, dingy brown I guess you'd call it, and the windows had grates on them so the light that came in had a jagged look to it. On either side was a bed, a metal locker, and a bureau. The lockers looked like they had been ripped from some high school hallway by a former resident, or inmate or whatever the hell you call us, and the bureaus had all kinds of shit carved on them: naked women, dragons, birds. Not exactly Picassos, but I guess if you give a guy enough time he's bound to start thinking he's an artist.

My roommate's side was all made up—his bed had a black comforter and a bright red pillowcase. It kind of took me by surprise, that cheery red. Made me feel strange too—like it belonged in some kid's room with teddy bears next to it, or outside on some convertible that was driving in the sun. Here it almost looked captured, like some exotic animal in a city zoo. It's hard to explain I guess. The rest of the room fit, though. On his dresser he had a Family Size Vaseline Intensive Care, a bandanna, and Old Spice deodorant. My side just had a piss-stained mattress. A regular shot out of *Better Homes and Gardens.*

First thing I did was put my sheets on the bed. Whenever I move into a new place, and I've been in a couple, I make my bed to make it feel a little more homey. I'm not faggy or anything, it's just that if you move around as much as I do, you have to find a way to make anywhere home. I don't mean to make it sound like I've had the roughest life, God knows I don't need any damn pity, but I did bounce around a few foster homes before getting adopted by Mr. and Mrs. Right.

I looked at the other bed to see how they did it. I had heard how some places could be real strict about bed-making. His sheets were pulled tight and he had perfect hospital corners—not the kinds you fake by pulling a little extra blanket out, but the real thing. It was really something, those neat little corners and that bright red pillowcase sitting on top. Like my roommate was just the model happy-go-lucky delinquent or something. But hell, at least he wasn't a slob. I wasn't looking for him to be my best bud or anything, but I didn't need any trouble either.

I finished making my bed, put my clothes away, and was getting into a fresh T-shirt when two guys busted in. I stalled a little before pulling my shirt down—I didn't think it would hurt for them to know I wasn't somebody to mess with. Hell, I know I'm not cut like the guys on the covers of those bodybuilding magazines, but I'm not the skinny kid I used to be either. Back in sixth grade we used to play sports every day after school in front of my house. Football, kickball, baseball, whatever it was, I usually got picked last. I wasn't a spaz or anything, I just wasn't too well coordinated. The shrink my parents tried to make me see jotted down lots of notes and started making noises to himself when I told him about that. I don't know what he was getting all huffy about, he probably never played a sport in his life. Shit, I wonder what his childhood was like. I started lifting a lot during high school though, I had a weight set in my basement.

For all my reps, these guys weren't impressed. One dude had a visor and all he said was, "Aw shit, Sean got a white roomie."

"Ain't no thing," Sean said. He was more concerned with putting Vaseline on his hands than with sizing me up.

"So when do you eat around here?" I said. They looked at each other like I was speaking some foreign language. I don't know which word was so goddamn confusing.

"We goin' now," Sean said.

I knew I wasn't going to get any engraved invitation, so I fell into step and Sean locked the door on the way out. They talked as if I weren't there, and I figured I'd wait until they asked me something before opening my mouth again. Sean was lanky and kind of sharp-looking. He had pointy ears and his eyes were narrow like a cat's. His friend Kemo was broader, but had a softer face. He laughed whenever Sean made a joke.

I remembered how much I hated when freshmen would try to get all chatty with me every fall. My junior year there was this one kid J.P.—you'd have thought we were best pals the way he talked to me. He was one of those real bouncy kids, like a small puppy or something, always yipping at your ankles. He was a nice enough guy, I guess, just real irritating. I never did punch him though. Sean and his boy didn't look like the kind of guys to use a lot of restraint.

At the commissary they piled heaps of steaming mush onto our trays. No plates, just the thick cardboard trays with the bumps to tell you where to put the different foods—if you could call them that. Commissary mush tends to run, so those dividing lines didn't do a whole lot of good. I sat down with Sean and Kemo at a table with another guy named Lucius. Lucius and Sean were really dark, and Kemo's skin was lighter, like the way my mom likes her coffee— lots of milk. Lucius asked who I was, and Sean said I was his new roomie. Lucius said he coulda figured that, but he wanted to know who I *was*. So I told them my name was Richie, and that I came from

Brookline. They sniggered a little, and Sean asked what a boy from Brookline was doin' in a place like this. That got another laugh—their heads cocked back, white teeth flashing. I told them that it was a long story, but Lucius said that if I was gonna be hangin' with 'em they'd have to know what I was in for. I smiled, and began in with my long story that really wasn't so long.

I told them that my friend Shitty—"Shitty?" Kemo's eyebrow jumped up to his visor.

"Well, his name is Tim, but we all called him Shitty because he was drunk half the time. Anyhow, Shitty had this girlfriend up at Ithaca, that's a college in upstate New York."

"Oh," Sean said. "Ithaca's a *college*, we thought it was a fuckin' prison." A real receptive audience this guy.

Horny Kemo on the other hand was too excited to realize his intelligence had been insulted. "Your boy was seein' a *college girl?*" he said.

"Yeah," I said. "He stayed back three or four years so he was twenty and his girlfriend was a freshman. Anyway, after a typical Saturday night out with the guys, drinking beers and smoking weed back behind the pond by the Davis Apartments—"

"Right by Route 1," Lucius said. His voice was low and solemn-like, like the way people talk in libraries. I didn't know what he was so serious about, but it made me feel like I had been talking too loud. The Davis was right next to the border between Brookline and Roxbury. On one side of the pond you had run-down tenements with winos on the stoops, and on the other high-rise condos.

I lowered my voice. "Yeah. Well, after the night there, Shitty and me were walking up the steps to his place and he said he wanted to go see his girl. So I said, yeah, that's cool. I thought he was just saying it the way you wake up in the middle of the night and say something like 'I'd love a steak right now,' even though you know there's no way in hell you're getting a steak at three in the morning. But he said, no man, I really want to go see her. Seeing as how our ride had just pulled off, I told him that the only way up to Ithaca was hitchhiking or in something stolen. He didn't care, and he said he was going with or without me. Shitty was like that, real bullheaded.

He always had a thing for this Mustang his neighbor had, and he said he could make it up to New York in no time. I told him he was crazy, but next thing I knew I was shining a flashlight on the lock so he could jimmy it open. He knew I could hotwire because like a dumbass I had bragged about it when my brother taught me, and he slid into the passenger seat so I could do my work. Once I had that baby purring, I wasn't about to go to bed either. We stopped over at my house to grab some beers and we were off."

"You stopped in front of your own house with a hot ride?" Sean asked with a grin.

"Yeah, I guess we did."

Kemo and Sean nodded their approval—some sort of warped bond of delinquency I guess. Lucius didn't say anything, he just kept on looking all serious, like a minister or something.

"Shitty was real intent on getting to his girl quick, and he started driving about an hour into it. We were just drinking our beers and going about a hundred miles an hour when I saw the blue lights."

"Five-oh," Kemo said, shaking his head and grinning. As cool as he tried to make it sound, just thinking about it made my mouth get all biley. You'd think that being in the damn reform school himself Kemo would know that five-oh, or the fuzz, or whatever the hell else you wanted to call them, wasn't some joke.

I ignored him and started again.

"I knew we were busted, and Shitty panicked. He started throwing the bottles out of the car and he caught me in the side of my head. I don't know why he was so worried about empties with us already sitting there in a hot ride, but I guess he was just acting on instinct or something. The dumbass. Not to mention he threw them out my window, like throwing them into the woods instead of into the road would make it all okay. Anyhow, I had been caught pushing dope at school and doing some other shit, so I knew I wasn't getting out of this one with just a couple of fines."

I took a big gulp from my bug juice.

They didn't say much for a while, they just pushed their food around on their trays. I didn't know what they were thinking about, maybe why they got sent here. Kemo finally muttered, "That was bad about how y'all stopped for beer." He turned to Sean. "Your roomie is all right for a white boy."

On our way back to the rooms Lucius asked me if I wanted to play spades with them. Sean was quick to ask if I knew how, and I told him I was a little rusty but that I'd be all right. I didn't tell them I had learned during "card hobby" at overnight camp, and I figured there was no reason why they really needed to know. Card hobby was actually the only activity I liked at that camp. We'd play poker, hearts, and spades, and just sit around like a bunch of gamblers. All the other kids in it were older, and they were cooler than the losers from my bunk. We sat out on this screened-in porch, looking out on the lake. Anne—this lady who had been at camp forever—lived in the house year-round. She was all crotchety when she was running the waterfront, but on those card nights she just warmed right up. It was like the old records she put on took her back in time and made her a young woman again or something. She'd walk around the tables and give us juice and M&Ms, which probably doesn't sound like much, but with the slop they served in the mess hall, it was. We didn't have any beer or cigarettes, but we savored those M&Ms like they were imported cigars and we were real gamblers.

Anne's husband had died a few years back in a boating accident. Sometimes she talked about how they used to play bridge every week, but she'd usually stop herself short. We listened politely (she did give us M&Ms), but I think the other kids never really understood what she was getting at. I'm not saying I did either, I mean, I'm no goddamn mind reader, but I liked listening to her all the same. I always tried to give her an extra thank you at the end of the night, to kind of show her I understood or something, but she just nodded and shuttled me out the door with everyone else. It's always like that—you try to be nice to someone and they don't even get it.

I didn't expect Lucius to be handing out M&Ms, but I was excited for some cards. Sean and I pulled folding chairs in from our room to Kemo and Lucius's down the hall. They were already sitting across from each other and Sean muttered something about I guess we got to be partners, too. Lucius had a pad in hand and was setting up a scorecard; Kemo was busy shuffling. If he had turned his visor straight instead of keeping it cockeyed, he would have looked just like one of those dealers in Vegas. I didn't mention it—I knew better than to try to tell a black kid how to wear his hat. Shitty got his ass kicked once for telling a kid his hat wasn't on straight. The kid told him my lid's on straight motherfucker, and Shitty said yeah, that's right, it's just your face was put on wrong. Shitty's not the smartest kid I know.

Sean gave a quick recap of the rules because, he said, he didn't want me screwing up. We figured out how many tricks we wanted to bid, and with Sean talking shit about how he was gonna win *even with me* as his partner, and Kemo saying we didn't have a hope in hell, and Lucius not saying much, but just grinning like he saw something in his cards which none of us knew about, we began. The first few tricks were pretty routine, and I took my first one with the ace of diamonds, then led a low diamond to play it safe. Kemo slapped down the queen of spades and declared, "The Bitch is back, niggers, and she gonna whup your ass." Sean fired back with the ace, saying, "That ole bitch ain't worth the shit on your ass, nigger." They all started laughing, and I laughed too, but it made my cheeks feel like when I've smiled too long for pictures. I guess that word's just always made me feel kind of weird. The way it snaps at you, "nig-ger," it kind of makes my head jerk. But hell, I figured if they were saying it and laughing at it then it had to be okay. I mean, I wasn't about to go complaining about it.

The next time it was my lead I fumbled deciding what to throw. With a mock Puerto Rican accent Kemo said, "C'mon man, it's on *jou.*"

I figured I could make a little fun of myself too, so I looked at him all serious-like and said, "Who you callin' Jew?"

They got real quiet. I could hear the hum of the lights, and faintly, somewhere down the hall, rap was playing. I shifted in my chair.

"What," I said, "jokes aren't allowed in this place?"

They looked at each other for a second. Only their eyes moved, not their heads. Then slowly, Lucius broke into a grin, and it was like someone had let the air out of a balloon—I mean all that silence just rushed right out, and in an instant they had all busted out laughing. I mean really laughing. Sean and Lucius laughed deep and loud—like they were releasing something from their gut. Kemo's was higher and more nervous.

"Shit, man, that nigger said who you callin' Jew," Sean said, holding his side.

It took me a second to realize who he was talking about. I've been called a lot of things before, but never that. I kind of liked it though, I don't know why. We played for about an hour, and I felt more and more like I was hanging out with my buds back home. I'm not saying my friends are black, or that they talk like that, because they don't, but they talk shit just the same. I still had the feeling though that one false move, like me slipping and saying nigger the way they did, would bring it all crashing down. I've been in my share of fights, but I never felt anything like that pause before I told them I was kidding about the whole Jew thing. It was like they were bracing themselves for war, not just some school fight that gets broken up before little Billy gets a bloody nose.

Me and Sean ended up losing, but he didn't seem too bummed. He told Kemo and Lucius that we'd get them back tomorrow, and I figured I had myself a partner. I said, "Later, guys," as we walked out the door but part of me wanted to say more. I don't know what exactly, I mean I'm not any sentimental type like my mom. She cries at AT&T commercials and shit like that. I guess they reached out and touched her sappy ass. She even cried at that stupid show *Family Ties* when Malerie's boyfriend got into a motorcycle accident. But the thing with me walking out the door was just that Lucius had asked me to play. I knew I'd say something that would come out sounding stupid anyway, so I just followed Sean back into our room.

We brushed our teeth together in the community bathroom with the cold tiles and the cold fluorescent light. Sean wore flip-flops and I figured I should get a pair too. The only other time I had brushed my teeth in front of people was at camp, but I usually just waited and brushed my teeth after those pansies. They giggled and had white foam dribbling down their chins and generally looked like a bunch of morons. But me and Sean, we were just brushing our teeth, not saying anything, and doing it all kind of in sync. It's not like we planned it or anything, but he liked to do his bottom teeth, wet his toothbrush, and then do the tops for another few seconds just like me. I doubt he noticed. He was too busy checking himself out in the mirror. You never know who's going to be vain, but Sean certainly had a weakness for himself.

After he put some goop on his legs and arms, he flicked off the light and slipped between his sheets. From the way he dolled himself up, you'd have thought he had a midnight date. I knew saying good night would sound too much like John-boy, but I wanted to say something, so I told him that Kemo and Lucius seemed like good guys.

"I don't know Kemo too good, but Lucius's been my boy since we was little."

"Did you go to school together?"

"We didn't *go* to school together, we cut school together—we was in the same gang."

"Is that what you all are in for?"

"Speak up man, what'd you say?"

"I just asked if that was what you guys were in here for."

"See it's like this. We wasn't the kind of gang to steal cars and go 'round shootin' people. I don't know what kind of shit you seen on TV, but that ain't it. Sure we sold some drugs to make cash, but mainly we was a gang for protection. So we was all real tight, you see, like a family, and we watched each other's backs."

"So you got caught selling?"

"Naw, we was real careful about all that." I heard his covers rustling, and he turned toward me. "See we was at a party, not far from the Davis Apartments, and everyone was just dancin' and havin' a good time. But Lucius's brother, this cool little G, he was workin' on some girl, and this girl's dude wasn't havin' it." He stopped for a second and let out a breath. "He shot Lucius's brother in the head. That's when all hell broke loose."

He paused. I could hear the ticking of his alarm clock—each tick not making the kid's death seem any farther away or older, but closer and more suffocating. Guys were always bringing knives to parties, like some sort of metal prick they could pull out of their pants and show around. I never saw any guns in Brookline, but I guess it's pretty much the same shit—everyone's got something to prove.

"How old was his brother?"

"Fifteen. He shoulda known better than to be messing with that dude's girl, but he was just always dancin' and smilin'—he didn't care with who."

"Did Lucius ever get the guy?"

"Naw. Our boys are keepin' track of where's he at. Lucius says he don't want to kill him, just that he don't never want to see his face again."

I shook my head. I couldn't imagine Lucius actually killing anyone, but he seemed too proud to let it slide.

"We'll see what happens when we get out of here," Sean said. I heard him roll over and kind of sigh. "This shit ain't over," he said.

A little while later he was snoring. In camp I used to plug the little bastards' noses so they'd pop up snorting and coughing. Sean's snore was loud and even peaceful in a weird kind of way. I didn't mind it so much, and I wasn't about to go waking him up, so I just let it carry me off to sleep.

The next day didn't start off with any surprises. We woke up at seven, ate more mush on the thick cardboard trays, and I headed off to take all kinds of tests so they could place me in the right level classes. I'm pretty good with English, but numbers give me trouble. I'm honest about it—hell, I know I'm no Einstein. My parents wanted me to take some tests in elementary school so they could see if I had "learning disabilities"—which to a ten-year-old kid sounds a whole lot like retarded. I wasn't going to take any retard test, and it pissed my parents off big-time. It was like they wanted to know what kind of problem I had so they could tell their friends, "Yes, Richie has a slight learning disability," then they'd lean in real close and whisper, "He's *dyslexic*." And they could shake their heads, and feel sorry for themselves for picking me instead of some smart kid. I wasn't going to make it that easy for them, and shit, I didn't want someone tell-

ing me I was retarded. I never got any extra help, which I guess I
needed, and now those tests drive me crazy. I walked out of there
feeling a little spacey and I stopped by the commissary to pick up
some food. They wouldn't be serving any more mush until dinner,
but I could snack on some Rice Krispies. I know Krispies without
milk sounds a little nasty, but you take what you can get.

I was on my way back to the room, trying to work up enough
saliva to keep my mouth from feeling all tacky and mealy, when I
saw Sean talking with Lucius, Kemo, and a few other guys by the
door to the barracks. He called me over. They were laughing and
joking, just like they were on a street corner back in the city. For
some reason I felt happy to see them—it's funny the way every-
day stuff like talking with your friends seems more meaningful after
being by yourself. I guess you feel the connections more or something. I mean, who cared if I messed up those stupid tests?

"I wanna show you something," Sean said. He was grinning.

"What?"

"I'm gonna show you something. Put your hand out." He pointed
to the hand holding the Krispies.

Everyone was smiling, just waiting for Sean to do something
funny. I thought something funny was coming too, but I felt a little
nervous. He had a queer grin.

"What's up? What do you want with my hand?"

"Just put it up," he said. "I wanna show you something."

Everyone was watching now, and I didn't want to look like a
chicken or anything. I held out my hand.

Sean looked back at his boys, then still grinning he brought his
hand crashing down on mine, spraying the Rice Krispies all over the
walkway and steps. I could hear their laughter buzzing in my ears,
and I couldn't separate that from the stinging of my hand and the
heat rising in my face. I stared at all those little white pellets on the
ground, then at all the black faces waiting to see what I would do.

"Aw shit," one of his boys said. "Sean done done it now."

"That ain't right, Sean," Lucius said as the laughter was dying
down. "He didn't . . ."

Sean silenced Lucius with a glare.

I swallowed hard and looked Sean in the eye. "Go get me another box," I said.

"What?" he said.

"Get me another box of Rice Krispies."

His thin eyes slid to his boys on his right, then back to his boys on his left, but no one was saying anything.

After a moment he said, "Whatever, man." He held up his hand like a crossing guard and turned his head.

"Not whatever. I want you to get me some more Rice Krispies."

His head snapped back toward me. "You want me to walk all the way back to the commissary to get you some fuckin' cereal?"

"Yeah, I do," I said.

"Shit man, what I wanna go walkin' all the way back there for?"

"What'd you wanna go knockin' my hand for?"

I could feel his friends bristle at my mimicking him. I didn't mean it like that and I was feeling real uneasy.

"Aw, I was *playin'*," he said. "I guess *some* people can't take a joke."

I heard a few sniggers. My face was hot. I kept my eyes on his, like if I could keep them riveted there hard enough it would make all those other faces go away.

"Well, I'm hungry," I said, "and I wanted to eat those. I know you were joking, and it was funny and all," even though it wasn't, "but I want some Rice Krispies."

Again he turned back to his boys.

"Just get the man some cereal, Sean," Lucius said. "He's straight."

A few of the others pitched in similar things. I could feel some of the flush leaving my face.

"Aw, man," Sean groaned.

Nobody said anything for a while.

"I'll walk over with you," I said.

"You wanna hold my fuckin' hand?"

"No."

"Then why don't you just get them yourself?"

"Walk over with the brother," Lucius said.

"Forget that."

I tried again. "Sean, let's not do this right now."

Lucius told the other guys to come on, and he started walking inside. Kemo hesitated, but Lucius shot him a look and he followed. As the group filed off, Lucius poked his head back out the door. "I'll see you guys later for some cards."

Me and Sean stood there looking at each other. Just two guys standing on a field of burnt grass with flecks of cereal scattered around. The ants were picking their way through, like Cocoa Krispies with feet. Sean stared off toward the basketball court.

"At least the ants will eat well tonight," I said.

"Yeah."

He stood there with his arms crossed, following the ants with his eyes. Without looking up he muttered, "I'm getting pretty fuckin' hungry myself," and he kicked the Rice Krispies box out of his way. He moved his head a couple of times and his hands kept jerking around like he was talking to himself, or at least thinking real loud. I could hear my stomach rumbling.

After a while he said, "I'm goin' to the fuckin' commissary, but I'm goin' to get me an orange."

I didn't say anything.

On the walk over he kept his eyes on the ground and he kicked at the acorns, sending up little clouds of dust. I could tell he didn't feel like talking.

"Sean . . ." I said, but I realized I had nothing to say. With some people all you have to do is start in, and even if you're not going to say anything they'll finish your sentence. Shit, some people will explain your whole thought. But not Sean—he didn't even look at me.

"What?" he said.

"Nothing." I paused. "I guess, well, I don't know."

He could tell I didn't know what the hell I was saying.

The sun was merging with the trees behind the fields, and for the first time the camp looked something other than gray. I felt kind of light-headed, like I didn't know exactly where I was or what was going on. Maybe it was just those tests and my empty stomach, or maybe just being in a new place.

Sean was walking all straight and dignified beside me, and I couldn't resist trying to talk to him. "I'm sorry," I said. "It's just I couldn't be looking like a fool before people know me here."

He grinned.

"What's so funny about that?" I said.

"Naw, it ain't like that." He paused for a second and he could tell I was still looking at him. He stared back at me, and somewhere in that look something must have clicked, because he started in. "Well, I got here before Lucius, and I never told nobody this, but my first day here some big dude stopped me on my way back to the barracks."

"You were eating Rice Krispies?"

"Naw, stupid, that shit's dry. I had me an orange, and he smacked it right out of my hand."

"What'd you do?"

"Nothin'. He had this big group of guys around him, and I knew they'd kick my ass, so I just pretended like it was cool. But that night I got so riled up thinkin' about it I couldn't sleep. I went and found his room."

We turned up the long concrete walkway to the commissary.

"What happened?" I said.

He smiled kind of crookedly. "I beat the shit out of him."

He kicked at the ground, but we were on the cement now and his toe just kind of caught.

I thought about it for a while: him breaking into some guy's room in the dark, his fists slamming into a sleeping face. I don't know why, but I pictured his red pillowcase, some kid's face asleep on it. It didn't seem like something Sean'd want to do, beating up a kid like that. I mean, I could see a part of him getting in there in the dark, seeing the guy sleeping, and then wanting to turn back.

We were at the doors to the commissary and I turned to look at him. His eyes were narrow and dark, and I bet he was thinking about that night too. For the first time I noticed that his eyebrows had these crazy arches in the middle of them, like boomerangs, and one of them had a little scar in it. It's weird, but they made him look thoughtful and fierce at the same time, like some war general or something. I don't know if it made me scared of him, but it did make me think for a second about what those eyes had seen. I mean, shit, seeing your friend's little brother get shot—that's gotta do something to you.

Inside the commissary, he reached behind the counter to a fruit bowl, and I walked to the cereal bar and got myself another box. To tell you the truth though, I wasn't really hungry anymore.

We started back. The air felt real heavy, and I could hear our footsteps on the path.

"Well," I said, trying to lighten the mood, "it's a good thing we cleared this up now. Tonight you would have been pretty easy to find."

I started laughing, but his look cut me short. He wasn't glaring at me or anything, I think he was just trying to figure out where we stood. I guess with most people you know where you're at, you know who's tougher and it's all pretty clear how you're supposed to act. But with me and him, we just didn't know. Then again, maybe he wasn't looking at me to figure out who had the upper hand. It was more like he was looking at me the way you look at something you've never seen before. Like I was some strange exhibit at the Science Museum or something. I don't know. We didn't talk on the way back though. He just ate his orange.

I didn't sleep that night. There was no way to tell what was going on in his head. Shit, I didn't know what was going on in mine. I just waited up wondering if he was going to kick my ass, wondering if I would ever really know him, or myself for that matter, or any other guy in this godforsaken place.

I talked to my mom on the phone the next night. Dad had a meeting. She asked me what my roommate was like and I told her he was black. She wanted to know what he was in for and I said gangs. She told me to be careful and I just said, "Yeah, whatever." She told me not to "whatever" her, and started going off on some shit about how he's probably done drugs and has a lot of rage, and how she saw on *Geraldo* how some gang member had done something or other.

"Mom," I said, "you don't even know Sean."

But she kept on going, "And you think you do? These people

will be nice when they have to, Richie, but I'm sure he has a lot of issues to deal with, and if I were you . . ."

I stopped listening. I just held up my hand like a crossing guard.

"Richie . . . Richie, are you there?"

"I gotta go, Mom. Some guys are waiting to play cards."

WAITING GAME

MARIE ARGERIS

They all hoped that TV might change their lives, all but her father, who cursed as he gripped the wheel tightly, gassing and braking the car in the thick Los Angeles traffic. Polly had stared at the back of his head on and off for seven hours, and when he leaned forward as he did often to stretch his back, she could see drips of sweat on his neck slowly making their way down to his perspiration-soaked collar.

"Move, goddamn it, move," her father yelled, slapping the beige steering wheel with the palms of his hands.

She looked over at her mother, whose eyes were closed. Polly wondered if she was asleep or just pretending, and watched her intently for several seconds, finally detecting movement in the eyelids that indicated feigned sleep. This came as a relief to Polly, reinforcing her belief that anyone who could sleep through her father's driving must surely be an alien. It also proved that while her younger brother, Darren, did come from another planet, her mother did not.

They had driven all the way from Santa Rosa for her mother, who would audition the next day for *Card Sharks,* the only game show on television where contestants could win cash instead of prizes. Polly and Darren would get to see Hollywood, Disneyland, and the wild animal park just outside of L.A. Polly didn't much care about the sights, she just kept thinking how if her mom won the audition she might be asked back on the show and win a lot of money, then finally all the fights about money would stop and possibly they could get a new car with air conditioning.

Polly picked up her book of Mad Libs and fanned herself, which offered no relief except to circulate the mid-August valley heat throughout the vehicle.

"Damn it," her father said.

Since they reached L.A. the curses had come consistently, like hiccups. Polly knew the swearing would stop when her dad pulled the keys out of the ignition, not sooner.

"Bastard!"

"What's a bastard?" her brother asked.

"It's a kid who doesn't have a father," Polly replied.

"Well, what's a kid who doesn't have a mother?"

"Stop asking dumb questions," Polly said, turning to her brother, unsure of the answer herself. Darren sat directly behind her mother. Polly didn't remember ever choosing to sit behind her father, but she figured she must have, since she was the oldest, and never sat on her mother's side. She thought hers was the best side except for those times her father decided to spit out the window and particles of spittle would make it back in again, sprinkling her face with a fine mist.

Polly stared out her window. She hadn't seen so many nice cars so close together since she accompanied her parents to the car dealership to test-drive several brand-new Plymouths. She wished they could afford a new car instead of having to rely on the Pacer, which kept breaking down.

"Son of a bitch," her father said, hitting the dashboard with his palm.

Polly knew her mother would win the audition, even though Polly always won when they played at home. Her mom was prettier than most women who had made it, and more enthusiastic. In Polly's opinion, that was more important than how well her mother played, especially since it was a card game and heavy on luck.

Polly and Darren had been auditioning their mother throughout the summer break. Each morning at ten they would watch the show, hoping to glean some new insight on the cards, examining guests for how they reacted when they turned a card correctly, and studying how the host, Jim Perry, related to contestants.

"You jerk," her father said, braking suddenly. A permanent frown had creased his face since they passed through San Francisco. Polly tried to recall the last time her dad had been happy while driving. Road trips and anything having to do with the car made him uptight. The car was his domain; he packed it, he drove it, and when any obstacles arose, he swore and lost control, knowing that no one but himself could fix the problem.

The last time she remembered him truly happy was two summers ago, when they were driving back from a trip to Crater Lake. They had been listening to the Giants pregame show on the radio when "The Star-Spangled Banner" came on. Polly and her brother began to sing and her father joined in, loudly and boisterously, as the car sailed down the empty stretch of freeway. Their voices got louder and more cacophonous, until they reached the song's pinnacle moment: "the laaaand of the freeeeEEEEE." Her father's deep voice resonated throughout the car and seemed to lift it up off the road. She could feel her face get red as she strained for the note from within the depths of her chest. She felt light-headed and giddy until she realized her father had stopped singing. The car slowed and their voices trailed off when they heard the siren behind them. They remained silent while the radio crowd cheered and the highway patrolman wrote out a hundred-dollar speeding ticket.

"These assholes can't drive."

"Hawaii," her brother said, hitting Polly hard on the arm. They had been keeping track of license plates since the trip began, and any new one was worth a slug.

"I don't see Hawaii," Polly said, hitting her brother back.

"It's up there," he said, hitting her again.

She grabbed a tuft of his thin blond hair and pulled it toward her sharply.

"Don't lie, okay?" she said loudly into his ear, releasing his head with a shove.

"Asshole," her brother sputtered as he lunged at her, beginning to cry.

"Polly, do you want to get us in an accident?" her father yelled, reaching his arm over the seat in a failed attempt to separate them. "Eileen, do something with them."

"He said 'asshole,' Mom," Polly said, pushing her brother away.

Her mother opened her eyes and turned around to face them. "I know, and if I hear it again I'm going to make your dad pull over. Now listen. If I do good at the audition, we may be able to come back and I may win a lot of money. And who knows, Darren, maybe we can take a trip to Hawaii and see lots of those license plates. But if I have to yell at you, then I'm not gonna have a voice to cheer with tomorrow, and I won't win."

Polly considered her mother's words, thinking how great it would be to tell her friends that her mom was going to be on TV.

"What if you don't win, Eileen? Don't get your hopes up, or theirs," her father said. "We're not going to Hawaii."

"I could win, Gary. Odder things have happened," her mother said, leaning back on the seat and closing her eyes.

Polly scooted closer to the window, hoping her parents wouldn't start fighting again. She considered keeping a tally of their fights and her fights with her brother, thinking the score would be close to tied. Polly fiddled with the plastic latch that opened her window outward an inch, wishing it rolled down like a normal window. She longed to be up front, where she could rest her hand on the roof the way her father did, and feel the wind taking her hair all directions.

Polly sat on one of the double beds in the motel room and alternated watching the morning news and her mother blow-drying her hair next to the TV set. The anchorman was talking about the hostages in Iran again. 298 DAYS flashed over the picture, and Polly wondered what it was like to have to wait that long in a strange place, never knowing if you'll be released. She smelled a funny burning odor and looked at her mother, noticing that every few seconds she brought the dryer too close to her head, allowing hairs to catch in the fan before breaking off.

"Just once, Gary, I'd like a motel room with a coffeemaker inside. Just once."

"When you win that million, honey," her father said.

Her mother was silent as she continued drying her hair, brushing it back with short jerky strokes.

"We'll go to Denny's, you'll get your coffee, and it won't be instant, okay?" he said.

"Can we do magic fingers?" her brother asked.

"Yeah," Polly said, hoping their father would allow them the three minutes of bed vibrations that could be bought for a dime.

"We're going," he replied.

"It doesn't take long, Dad," Polly challenged, knowing her father wouldn't budge. He always made them leave when they wanted to do something fun.

"No, Polly," he said, turning to her mother, who was applying makeup. "Your mom wants to drive through Beverly Hills."

"Yes I do," her mother said, glaring at him through the mirror. "And if it wasn't for me we'd never go anywhere."

"We'll wait outside," her father said as he opened the motel door, exposing the dim brown room to shards of daylight which made it look old and plain, not clean and new as it had appeared the night before. Polly would rather have stayed with her mother, but she couldn't ignore the sunlight and her father's command. Polly and Darren leaned against the hood and watched their father repack some of the contents of the trunk. He hadn't said much since they left the room, and Polly worried he was angry. When her mother emerged, they were inside the car waiting as it warmed up.

"Mom, do you know what you're going to say when they ask you what you do?" Polly asked as they pulled out of the parking lot.

Her mother turned around to face them. "I'm a second-grade teacher from Santa Rosa, California, and I love reading, cooking, and most of all surfing, which I do every weekend." Her mother brushed her hair behind her ear with an exaggerated flourish, and smiled at the small audience.

"Don't forget us," Darren said.

"And I'd like to say hello to Polly and Darren, if I can, Jim?"

"Woohoo," Darren cheered, clapping.

"Really play up the surfing part, Mom," Polly said. "That's gonna get you on."

Polly had come up with the surfing part after she noticed that every contestant had some kind of unique hobby or quirky habit: the man who collected Barbie dolls, the woman who traveled to Alaska to dogsled. Her mother was a swimmer, so it didn't seem so farfetched for her to be a surfer as well, even if her hair wasn't blond.

"What do you think, am I ready?" her mother asked.

"Yeah," she and Darren shouted. Polly could see her mother's mood had improved, which was a good sign, since the audition was at one o'clock. Polly hoped the drive through Beverly Hills would keep her mom happy, otherwise she might forget to be energetic at the audition.

"Can we get a map of the stars' homes?" Polly asked.

"No," her father said abruptly. "We don't have the time."

"Let's get the map, Gary, and you guys can go back while I'm at the audition."

"Na, it's a tourist trap. Why do I need to spend a day showing my kids millionaires' houses?"

"I want to see Lee Major's house," Polly said.

"Yeah, the Six Million Dollar Man," Darren said.

"That's what you need to afford a house here," her father said.

"You know," her mother said, turning around to look at Polly and Darren, "before I met your father I had a boyfriend from Beverly Hills."

"You did?" Polly asked. "Was he a star?"

"No, no."

"Oh hell," her father said. "Why don't we just drop in and say hello? Maybe he'll let us spend the night."

"I am kind of curious," her mom said, smiling.

"Why'd you break up, Mom?" Polly asked.

"Well, for one, I met your dad."

Polly had seen pictures of her mother when she was young. In her favorite photo her mom sat inside a tiny convertible wearing dark sunglasses and a scarf over her head. Her skin was smooth and pale, her smile perfect, like a movie star's. She imagined the two driving through Beverly Hills, her mother trying to keep the scarf from blowing off and her boyfriend reaching over to help her, both of them laughing.

Polly looked out the window as they drove up into the hills, passing enormous houses with bright green lawns and bushes trimmed perfectly into all kinds of shapes. Her mom might have been living in one of those houses if she hadn't met her dad, she thought. As they continued upward the mansions became less visible from the street and mostly surrounded by walls.

"Dad, stop," Polly shouted as they approached an estate with a busload of tourists milling outside. "This must be someone's house."

"Stop, Gary, for a second," her mother said. "Let us have time to look."

"Nah, what's the big deal," her father said, passing the bus that was parked outside the gate. "You can't go in."

"It's a beautiful house," her mother said. Polly looked at the white mansion, which had columns along the front, and a lawn as big as a golf course. She wondered who could be inside.

"Mom, maybe when you win we can buy a house like that," Darren said.

"A new car, stupid," Polly said. "She's not going to win a million dollars, only ten thousand or something."

"See what you've done," her father said, watching the road. "Now they think they're going to be rich."

Her mother didn't answer, and continued to look out the window at the houses, which got smaller and smaller as they made their descent from the hills.

After stopping at the drive-thru McDonald's, her father dropped her mother off at the studio, deciding not to park in the lot because it was too expensive. Instead he found a space near a fountain across from the studio where they could wait and feed the meter. Polly had a hard time waiting. She threw a penny in the fountain and made a wish that her mom would be asked back.

"Dad, you make a wish," Polly called to her father, who sat on the other side of the fountain.

"Yeah," Darren said.

"Okay, there," her father replied.

"You have to throw money in," Polly said.

"I play my way."

"Come on, Dad," Darren yelled. "And tell us your wish."

"It won't come true if he tells it."

"All right, all right." He paused and searched for change in his pocket. "I wish your mother would come out of that studio so we can get the hell out of here," he said, throwing the coin in a grand gesture.

"So do I," Darren said.

"Oh, that was a wasted wish," Polly said, disappointed. For the next forty-five minutes she and Darren fished out other people's pennies and threw them back in, wishing over and over again that their mom would make it on TV. In an hour she emerged from the building.

"Mom, over here," Polly yelled to her, waving. Her mother waved limply and crossed the street.

"How did it go?" Polly asked.

"Did you make it?" her brother asked.

"Well, I don't know." She shrugged, looking downcast. "The producer said he only kept me to the final round because he wanted to give me the benefit of the doubt, but he said I could still get chosen. I'll know in a few weeks," she said, sighing. "A woman who drove trucks made it, and a big man called Tiny."

"Oh," Polly said, discouraged by her tone of voice. "I'm sorry, Mom. Maybe you'll still make it, though."

"Now you've disappointed them," Polly's father said. "What did I tell you?"

"It's okay, Dad, I don't care," Polly said.

"What do you mean, what did I tell you?" her mother replied. "What are you doing for them?"

"You're feeding them nonsense, Eileen. Letting them think this trip is going to make them millionaires."

"I never told them that and you know it."

Her father took a few steps toward the car, raising his voice with each movement. Polly moved out of his way. "Yeah, and when I told them the truth you made me into the bad guy, when I was just being realistic."

"God, Gary, you can't even let these kids have some hope." She shook her head. "Okay, fine, you're the good guy, and I fill their minds with fantasies and lies. Shit, that's fine with me. I'm trying to have a vacation here, but I'm not enjoying it much."

Polly felt her face get red, as if a crowd had surrounded them to watch her parents fight. Her father turned and unlocked the back door, swinging it wide open. "Okay, get in the car," he said, straining to keep his voice even. "Kids, get in. We're going to enjoy our vacation. Let's go."

Polly and her brother filed into the backseat of the car. Her father walked around to the driver's side.

"I'm not going anywhere," her mother said.

"What?"

"I'm taking a vacation, and if this is your idea of a vacation, I'm not going."

Polly listened from inside the stifling car, wishing she had the power to threaten them and make it stop.

"We came on this goddamn trip for you, remember?" Her father raised his voice.

"I don't think so Gary, it's always about what you want."

"Get in."

"No, I told you I'm not going."

"Where're you gonna go?" he asked accusingly.

"My cousin Helen's, in Santa Monica."

"Get in the car, Eileen."

"I'll find my own way there, Gary."

"Right."

"I will."

"Fine."

Her father got in the car and slammed the door. He forced the key in the ignition and turned it. The car almost started, then died. He gassed it roughly and tried several more times.

"Dad, let's just wait for Mom," Polly pleaded.

"Shit."

The ignition caught and he did not wait for it to warm up. He pulled the car out of the space and it died in the middle of the street.

"Piece of shit," he yelled, pounding his foot so hard on the gas pedal Polly thought it would come out the front end. It re-started with a shudder. Polly looked back at her mother, who had begun walking down the sidewalk, and waved her over. Her brother did the same. She wasn't sure if her mom saw them or not, but she did not join them in the car, or wave back. Polly hoped her mom would find her way to Helen's. Her father didn't stop at the next stop sign, or the next. He waited until her mother was out of sight before stopping, where the car again died.

Darren looked like he had died and gone to heaven, Polly thought as she looked over to see her brother smiling, eyes closed, as the magic fingers took effect. Her father had been pumping dimes into the box next to the bed every time her brother asked him. On the other bed, Polly had been attempting to read her book about a girl who dressed up as a boy and traveled alone in a covered wagon to California, but her father kept distracting her by getting up and changing the channel. He had picked up the phone twice and slammed it down, and each time he did it Polly shot him a glare. She hadn't talked to him since they had left her mother, except to order dinner at Kentucky Fried Chicken.

She tried to concentrate on her story again but she kept having to read the same paragraph over and over. She tried to remember why her friend Carmen's parents got divorced, and recalled Carmen saying it happened after they had a fight about who would take out the garbage. At the time she hadn't believed Carmen, but now it seemed possible.

Polly wished she had refused to get in the car when her dad asked, or had tried to get out when it died. She didn't know why she just sat there. Reluctantly, she broke her silence.

"Why don't you call and see if Mom's safe," she asked.

Her father hesitated. "Why doesn't your mom call us, you mean. She's the one who walked away, Polly. Get it?"

"Get it," she mouthed his words to his back. She wanted to call him every swear word in the world. Instead she held it in. "She wants us to be worried," her father said. "It's all a little game of hers, Polly. She wants me to call and she wants to be missed."

"I miss her, Dad," Darren said.

"Dad, just call, please," Polly pleaded.

Her father mumbled something to himself and pulled the phone book out from under the nightstand. He flipped through it and slammed it shut, then picked up the phone and dialed.

"Santa Monica. Helen Samuels," he said abruptly.

He wrote a number on the cover of the phone book and dialed again.

"Helen," he said. "It's Gary checking to see if Eileen's made it there." He paused. "Thanks," he said, slamming the receiver down. "She's there, okay?"

"I wanna talk to Mom," Darren said.

"It's too late kiddo, you've gotta learn to speak up," he said, walking over to Darren and giving him a playful poke in the stomach.

"Can I talk to her tomorrow?" he asked.

"Maybe. It's time for bed. Tomorrow's a big day," he replied.

"Can I go swimming?" Darren asked.

"It's too late, but I'll let you have one more magic fingers and then it's time for bed."

"All right," Darren said, smiling and sitting up as their father handed him a dime. Polly never understood how her brother could forget about things so quickly. She closed her book and went into the bathroom to change into her pajamas and brush her teeth. When she emerged her father was lying next to Darren, who was under the covers.

She crawled into her bed and clicked the light off above it. Polly always slept with her mother when they stayed in motels. She turned to the wall and brought the stiff covers over her head to shut out the remaining light. It felt strange having the bed to herself. She wondered if her mom missed them, or if she had called that old boyfriend. He was probably driving her around in some convertible or Rolls-Royce.

Carmen's father left one day too, and moved into an apartment. Carmen stayed with her mom. Polly thought she would want to be with her mom too, but she couldn't imagine living with just one of them. They were stupid, she thought. It was only a game show. She had tried to keep from crying, but her efforts failed and her eyes were wet. She dug her head into the pillow and forced herself to cough so that Darren and her dad wouldn't hear.

Polly woke up to a low hum, and looked over to see her brother squirming under the covers of the shuddering bed. She couldn't place the uneasiness she felt until she spotted her father packing the suitcase, shoving her mother's things in the bag with the same hastiness that he packed his own.

"Are we still going to the wild animal park, Dad?" Polly asked.

"What do you mean, still going?"

"I thought we might go visit Mom."

"So far your mother's had all the fun on this trip. I think we should get something out of it."

"Yeah," Darren yelled from under the covers.

"Get up, you two, it'll take an hour to get to the park," her father said.

Polly got up slowly. She neatly folded her clothes and put them into her small duffel bag, wondering how her mom felt waking up in a strange house without them. She followed her father out into the parking lot, where the heat had already begun to rise off the asphalt, baking the pleasant cool of the motel room off her skin.

While her father put the suitcases in the trunk, Polly moved her books to the front seat.

"Oww, shit," she yelled, her bare legs sticking to the hot vinyl seats, scalded before she could tear them away. She placed her books under her thighs and waited for her dad to get in.

As they drove, the air struck Polly's face like her mother's hair dryer, getting hotter as they moved away from the water. Soon the city disappeared and they could have been anywhere. Polly wondered why at seventy miles per hour the scenery seemed to pass so slowly. Her book said California was the Golden State, but what she saw of it looked a dull brown. She could see the sign for the park from miles away, jutting into the sky, though she was uncertain whether it was real or a mirage. When they reached the entrance gate her father paid, and was given a brochure and a park map.

"Can I see it, Dad?" Polly asked. He handed her the map. "So the animals come up to your car sometimes."

"Will we see tigers?" her brother asked.

"Everything, I hope. It says to keep the windows rolled up three quarters of the way. We better do it." Polly rolled up her window as her father pulled away from the gate slowly, following the road signs.

"It's just like the drive-thru at McDonald's," her brother said.

"Yeah," Polly replied, smiling. "The food's still moving."

"Very funny, Polly," her father said. "Guess where we're eating after this?"

His comment cheered Polly up a little. She was beginning to think that if they started talking, she might be able to get an answer about when they were going to see her mother again.

"Look, Dad, no honking the horn." Polly pointed to the large sign they were nearing on the right that read "Honk Only in Emergencies."

"Well, this oughta be a peaceful drive. No traffic, no driving above fifteen miles per hour, and no honking. I think I'm going to like this." He looked at her and smiled. Polly smiled back, encouraged.

"I wonder if anyone's ever been attacked or eaten," her brother said excitedly.

"Well, it says here you're not supposed to get out of the car, so if you do I guess it's your own fault if you get attacked," Polly said.

"Can we ask the lady when we leave?"

"She's not gonna tell us if people have been hurt. We'll never come back."

"I will," her brother replied.

"Look at the flamingo," her father said, pointing past the dry weeds to the small lake beyond.

"Where's the camera?" Polly asked.

"In your mother's purse," her father said.

"Oh," Polly said, looking out the window at the flamingo, surprised that something wild could be such an attractive color and not get attacked. She thought of her mother, and how she had walked away without waving goodbye. Polly hoped she was all right, and that she would come back.

They passed the pond and drove up a small hill. From the top they got a short view of the barren valley they had just driven beyond. The only animals in sight were the birds in the water. She figured most of the other animals were hidden in the shade of caves and trees, away from the heat. The radio said it would be 105, and Polly could tell the late morning temperature had reached the nineties. She rolled down her window all the way, figuring that by the time an animal reached the car she would see it coming.

"God, it's hot," she said, looking down at the map. "The giraffes are coming up along the next stretch."

"I hope we can see them. This is boring," Darren said.

They drove several miles, finally coming upon two giraffes feeding on a cluster of trees. They watched for a few minutes, and Polly hoped one of the giraffes would approach the car, as in the brochure, but they only seemed interested in the trees. Her father drove for another fifteen minutes, passing several more giraffes and a distant elephant without stopping.

"There's something in the road up there," her father said, slowing. "Rhinoceros." They stopped about ten feet in front of it and waited for it to cross. When it reached the other side her father pulled up to it and turned off the motor. Polly rolled up her window most of the way. The large animal stared at them, its one horn jutting up from between its eyes.

"I wish we had the camera," she said.

"Tell your mom that," her father said.

"Dad?" Polly said, looking out at the rhino. She found it hard to believe such a humble creature could turn angry and charge at cars or humans, as the brochure warned. "Dad?" she repeated, hesitating. "Are you and Mom getting a divorce?"

"No," he said, stretching the word into a question. "Your mother needed a little break from all of us."

"Why?" her brother asked, pulling his eyes away from the rhino to look at their father.

"Sometimes people need a break. Maybe she wanted to see her cousin without us interfering."

"She's never taken a break before," Darren said sadly, turning his gaze back to the rhino.

"Exactly why she needs one now. So, we had enough staring at this rhino?" her father asked.

"Yeah," Darren said. "He's boring. I want to see lions."

"I think he's waiting for us to do something, just like we're waiting for him," Polly said. "It's too hot to do anything."

"All right, we're going." Her father turned the key, listening for the ignition to catch. He stopped and tried it again. The car always took several tries before it started, but it was so hot Polly was nervous. Her father waited a few moments, and tried again.

"Is it overheated, Dad?" she asked.

"We haven't been driving fast enough for it to overheat. I should have kept it in neutral," her father said, his voice rising. "Damn it."

He tried again.

"Goddamn it. American cars don't run. I never should have listened to your mother and bought American. Shit. I didn't want to come on this goddamn trip." Polly looked back at her brother, who was holding his fingers over his ears.

"The worst time to come down here, in this heat." Her father hit the cracked dashboard with his fist, and Polly turned to the window to see the rhino had moved a few steps away from the car. She looked over at Darren cowering toward the door. His eyes had tears forming in them, which fell to his cheeks as he turned his face quickly away from her gaze. She watched her father try and fail to start the engine several times. She hadn't seen a car pass since they stopped.

"Why don't you honk, Dad, this is an emergency."

"I'm waiting for someone to pass," he said abruptly. They sat several minutes before her father began to honk. He made several long honks and several short honks, interspersed with curses. Polly looked back at the rhinoceros, which did not seem bothered by the noise.

"I guess our horn's not very loud," Polly said.

"There's no one around this goddamn place. What if there was a real emergency, for Christ's sake? Wait, wait. I see a car now."

Polly turned around and saw a car coming down the hill in the distance. Her father honked and put his arm out the window to wave it over. The car pulled up to them and a woman on the passenger side rolled down her window.

"You guys having some trouble?" she asked.

"Yeah, the car died and we're gonna need a tow," her father said.

"We'll go on ahead and let them know you're stuck. You all right otherwise?"

"Yeah, yeah. Thanks. It's hot out here, but we've got some water."

"Okay. We'll send someone right back."

"Thanks."

Polly watched them drive off, envious of the small head she saw bobbing up and down in the backseat.

"Won't be long now, guys," her father said, making an effort to sound cheerful.

"Guess we should've gone to Disneyland, huh, Dad?" Polly said.

"Yeah. I'm never coming to one of these places again. I'll watch *Wild Kingdom*."

Polly looked back at her brother, who was sitting dry-eyed, looking glum.

"How you doing back there?" her father said, looking at Darren through the rearview mirror.

"Fine."

"I'll get you some water," Polly said pouring each of them some warm water out of the pitcher that had been sitting in the front seat since the day before. Her father looked at his watch every five minutes, getting more restless with each glance. Ten minutes stretched to a half hour, and then some.

"I can't believe this," he said. "We've been sitting here an hour. Damn it, damn it," he shouted. Polly had never seen her father cry, but she thought he was close to tears. He opened the door.

"Dad, don't get out of the car, Dad. You're not supposed to get out of the car. Let's just keep honking, or stop some more people."

"We've been waiting almost an hour, Polly. That guy didn't bring anyone back."

"Dad."

"Don't worry, these animals just look threatening. Really they're just afraid."

Polly watched her father walk down the middle of the road toward the entrance gate, past the rhino, which stared, unmoving. Darren began moaning in back, the high-pitched wail of a lost cub.

"It's okay, Darren, we'll be all right."

"No we won't. Neither of them is coming back. We're bastards now." Darren's cries got louder. "I wanna go home."

"Come sit up front with me."

"Nooo," he cried. Polly crawled in back and put her arm around him. He turned and hid his face in her shoulder. After a few minutes his muffled cries got weaker. She didn't know how long they waited, whether it had been longer or shorter than the last wait. She just knew that it hadn't cooled down, that no animals had bothered them, that she wanted to rip the torn upholstery off the seat in front of her. The afternoon sun made her woozy, discombobulated. She had heard that in the desert you become delirious, you see things. Everything was murky to her now, and time was irrelevant.

She heard the truck as it pulled up. Her father got out and talked with the driver outside. Their voices were muffled, monotonous.

"Get in the truck, kids," her dad said through the open window.

"I want to stay in the car," she protested languidly.

"Fine," her father said. "Is that okay?" he asked the tow truck driver.

"Sure, why not," the man replied. Polly watched him hitch their car to the back of his truck, raising the front end up so they were seated at a slight incline.

"That's the closest we're gonna get to a ride at Disneyland," she said to her brother, who had been mute since her father left. He sniffled and she worried he might start crying again. When she felt the car begin to move she crawled into the front, this time taking the driver's seat. She put one hand on the wheel, sliding her fingers into the grooves on the underside, and rested her other elbow on the door. She pretended she was in command of the car as they sailed smoothly through the park absent the uneven jerk of the brakes. Polly looked up at the blue skies as the back tires spun on the hot pavement, moving them across the landscape that from her angle looked golden. The ride was peaceful and she liked it, being in the car with just her brother.

After some time they slowed, pulling into a service station. They waited outside by the Coke dispenser while the men tried to fix the car, and Polly was envious of the Cokes for being cool inside the machine. Her father walked to the phone booth and made a call. He spoke for a few minutes and hung up. Soon after the pay phone rang and he answered it, staying inside and talking for a long time. When he came out she watched him walk over to the garage, to the men who were working on the car. After a while he walked back to the pay phone. She watched him as she would watch her hamster in its cage, interested only in its larger movements from one area to the next. After making a phone call her father walked over to them.

"They said they can't fix it today, but they can start it," he said. "We're going."

Polly and Darren followed their father to the car, sitting dead in the garage.

"Start it," her father said to one of the mechanics.

"You got it," the man said, fiddling with something under the hood while her father waited in the front seat.

"Go," the man said, and her father turned the ignition until it took. The engine revved loudly and her father gassed it repeatedly, thrusting his foot roughly against the pedal. The sound echoed loudly throughout the garage and gas fumes permeated the air, stinging her nostrils and causing her head to reel.

"Get in," her father said. She and her brother did as they were told. Her father got out and said a few words to the men, then got in and they were driving. They drove through the desert to a strange house near the beach, and her father kept the car running while he ran in and got her mother.

"Mom," Darren said.

"Mom," Polly echoed as her mother shut the door and reached out to give each of them a hug and a kiss.

"We broke down . . . in the desert," Polly said, the words coming slowly.

Her mom's mouth turned up into a half-smile. "I know," she whispered, as her father released the emergency brake with a jerk and pulled the car out of the driveway. They drove, windows open through the heat, only stopping to get gas, never turning off the engine. They drove and Polly pretended to sleep, waiting to get home, to get back to normal. With her eyes closed she listened only to the sounds of the engine, the wind, and the road, recalling what it felt like to be at the wheel, knowing that it would be a long time, a long, long time, before she would get there again.

WHITE FLIGHT

TIM VANECH

The call came at 12:38.

"Mr. Karis, gentlemen, I'm sorry to interrupt. It's your son, Robbie."

"Can I call him back?"

"He says it's an emergency. Line one."

I sat down in my chair and leaned back so that I would be out of the overhead projector's line of fire. From my seat, I could see the investors' expressions lit up by the projector as they turned toward me.

"Hey, Robbie. What's wrong?"

"Dad, this changes everything. That's it. It's over."

"What's going on?"

"Fuck this whole thing. Fuck this school."

Robbie's voice cracked. An investor on the board of the construction company was squirming in his seat, trying to make eye contact with one of his partners. I couldn't help feeling annoyed by my son's interruption of such an important pitch.

"Dad, I know you're in a meeting. But there's been a shooting here."

I leaned forward and put my elbows on my knees. I looked straight down into the black carpet.

"I think they killed some kids. They just shot them. Just shot them, Dad." His voice broke off and he choked back crying.

"Robbie, are you hurt? Robbie?"

"No."

"Are you in a safe place?"

"No, I'm in fucking school."

"Stay put. I'll be right over. I'll find you."

"Hurry, Dad."

"I'm on my way. Don't worry. Don't move. Stay with the teachers."

I looked at the digital display on the phone. The call had lasted forty-seven seconds.

Not a white face in the crowd of frenzied teenagers. Through the glare on my windshield, I watched a young Asian couple—the boy pulled the girl close to him as a group of screaming black girls ran toward them. A bunch of black boys followed the girls. The guys walked faster, but they still walked. I hit the lock button.

I stiffened when I heard the thud. I was afraid to turn around. In my rearview mirror, I saw a black kid with a red bandanna around his head. He looked directly into the rearview. We made eye contact. A smile flashed across his face as he cocked his head to one side, showing me his gold tooth and then his palms as if to say that he could not help punching my car. I reached for the window button, then thought better of it.

The kid was staring me down, nodding his head, his tongue locked to his bottom lip. He waved his shirt aside to show me the gun tucked into the waist of his jeans. I froze and looked straight down. The last time I'd seen a gun I had also been threatened with it—only that gun had been a rifle. It had been cradled by a kid, a white boy about the same age as this black kid. I had been marching in Alabama behind Martin Luther King. "Go home and cut your hair, Yankee fucker," from the shade of the brim of a Harvester cap. I had looked down then, too. You had to. It was all you could do in that kind of situation. They couldn't see you anyway. The hate was so deep it made a young man smile at a hippie protesting, at a rich white guy in a fancy luxury car. Now the kid laughed, turned on his heel, and swaggered away to join his friends, his jeans billowing as he went. Then a knock on my window caused me to lunge forward against my seat belt.

"Sir, you're going to have to move your vehicle."

"What?"

"Your car. You can't come in here." It occurred to me that there were no other cars around.

"What the hell are you talking about? I'm here to pick up my kid."

The cop looked at the kids swarming all over the cement court-yard behind him. "Sir, you're only asking for trouble by going in there. Make it quick. We need to clear the area."

The officer drew his nightstick and walked toward the blacks approaching the Asian couple. I pulled into the parking lot, and immediately my son emerged from a side door. He ran to the car with his head down. He pulled on the handle, but the door was still locked. I saw his face as he looked in at me, his eyes pleading that the door be unlocked, that the door swing open. I hit the button, and he jumped in.

More police cars arrived, followed by two ambulances. A heli-copter flew back and forth. A news van rushed into the parking lot as we left. Robbie pointed at the car in front of us at the red light. We watched the car accelerate through it.

"That was Johnny Ranieri and his sister. She was in the courtyard when it happened."

Robbie was looking straight ahead, speaking in a scratchy mono-tone. I put my hand on his neck, fearful that my son had just seen a murder—fearful of how much he had actually seen. Feeling my other hand tighten around the leather of the steering wheel, I wished I didn't volunteer my time on the advisory board of the Providence Public Education Fund. I couldn't just pull Robbie out of public school. I bristled at the thought that I'd kept him in Providence Latin to keep him tough. I didn't want him to be one of those drugged-out preppies who would cave under the pressure if life ever challenged them. Robbie was tough, perhaps too tough.

"Dad, this bullshit's over."

"Let's talk."

"Are you shitting me? A kid just got his head blown off. His *homey* was dancing around 'cause he got shot in the foot by a bunch of Asians. There's blood all over the pavement. These fucking Mong or Vietnamese or Cambodians or whatever . . . they just shot into the crowd. I'm reading Marx, and then boom, there goes the bloody revolution. I was under my desk, Dad. Me and the teacher were the only ones. Everyone else ran to the fucking window. They were *pushing* each other to get the best view. Dad, it's not like when Dean went here. It's not fistfights or stabbings anymore. I feel like I'm in *Boyz 'N the Hood* or fucking *Platoon* or something. I'm waiting for the fucking grenades. It's not fair." Robbie flipped on the radio, loud, and again tried not to cry.

He was right. It wasn't fair. There was nothing fair about the fact that he had to deal with the world he did day after day. Here was the old argument. Robbie was at me to go to private school. If he was desensitized enough to make an articulate plea for private school so soon after the shooting, it spoke a truth I was not prepared to hear. The announcement on the radio cut into the music.

"You are listening to WBUR News. Our top story today: a shooting in the courtyard joining Providence Latin and Central High Schools leaves at least one dead and several injured. Exact details are still unavailable as officials try to bring order to the scene. Eyewitnesses report that an Asian gang fired into a crowd of mostly African-American youths as racial tension mounted. . . ."

I turned off the radio and tried to ignore Robbie's look. I wasn't ready to hear it, not while I was driving, not while I was sitting so close to my son.

We reached our neighborhood. The old trees bowed over the road. It was hard to believe we'd driven only thirty blocks. The car phone rang, and I hit the speaker button. My wife's voice shrieked throughout the car.

"There's been a shooting at P.L. I'm going over there."

"Karyn, Robbie is with me. We're about two blocks from home."

She regained control of her voice as she realized that Robbie could hear her. "You're okay, Robbie?"

"Yeah, Mom," he said. "Just another day at school."

Robbie was gloating about the dramatic support that the shooting had provided for his arsenal in our ongoing debate. And I shook my head, then almost laughed at myself. Robbie had nicknamed me "the Head-shaker." He said that I was always rejecting his plans, limiting his freedom. But every weekend there was another friend's beach house or ski condominium to visit. I'd shake my head when he'd joke about going to Spenser, a private school. He'd say, "You know, Dad, you're right. Why would I want to go to a place that had the best baseball coach in the state, photography classes and dark-rooms, and beautiful girls?" I'd just shake my head and say, "And no Julios, no Angels, just Ashleys—mostly Laura." The slap and tickle would end with Robbie saying, "The Abominable Head-Shaker has struck again, goddamn it." This time I really had struck again, and I'd almost gotten him killed.

I turned onto our street and saw the Biffs and Chips standing on our front steps, some of them wearing baseball caps backward. Why did they have to wear them backward? And they were always wearing them inside the house. If the caps weren't on their heads, they were fastened to their belts—in case they should need to cover up a recently noticed bald spot left over from the stitches of a lacrosse injury, in case a group ribbing erupted over a bad haircut. But no laughs here. They looked solemn, silent. I realized that they had left their school early to welcome the public school soldier home from battle. When I was their age, we had left school early to see my older brother's best friend come back from Vietnam. Jimmy O'Toole had come back with a Vietnamese wife, with a little girl, and a limp, having left his knee in the thick of some smoky jungle. His leg had dragged along our gravel driveway with his toe nearly pointing straight behind him, and the sun had shone on his long hair, greasier than I remembered it.

"Well, Robbie, looks like the Hat-Backer Committee has convened on the stoop." I ignored a look from Robbie.

I shook hands with each of the future frat boys as I walked up the stairs, and each one looked me in the eye and called me Mr. Karis. Their respect might have been heartfelt. That their eyes did not accuse me for sending Robbie to public school made me feel like a criminal. Maybe they hadn't even reasoned that far—not even thought to place blame. Or maybe they thought that I couldn't afford to send Robbie to private school.

I went inside to find my wife, regretful that she had not been outside for our boy's arrival. Maybe she hadn't been there because she didn't like Robbie's friends. She thought they were spoiled brats, immature and superficial. She came from a military family with a stern father. Her parents desperately hid any fault or emotion from their children. I knew Karyn wouldn't give ground, and I wondered if boys like Robbie's friends had tormented her growing up in suburban New Jersey, and if that could actually hold sway in her life as an adult, or mine. I left Robbie surrounded by his friends, already breaking into laughter and biffing one another, seemingly released from the gravity of the day.

My wife wasn't in the kitchen or the basement. I found her in our bedroom looking at baby pictures of our sons. She was putting the pictures back into a photo album: pictures of Dean hugging Robbie on Robbie's fifth birthday, hugging him in the mechanical way that young children do when they imitate the actions of adults. Robbie had chocolate icing smeared on his cheeks from the cake, and Dean was kissing a chocolate-covered cheek as Robbie looked blankly into the camera. I wished that Robbie were there to see his mother. I sat down behind my wife and wrapped my arms around her. I put my lips to her shoulder, and she gently laid her head against mine. We stayed together like that for a while.

Later that afternoon my assistant called to check on Robbie and to fill me in on what had happened after I left the office. She told me that the investors were impressed that I would leave a final round meeting to take care of my son. They hadn't met money managers who still kept their kids in Providence's public high schools. When Robbie had called me about the shooting, it had helped me secure my largest account.

Then came more phone calls. Karyn and I fielded calls from the parents of Robbie's friends, while he hung out with the plaid Hat-Backers.

"Jesus, Steve, how are you all?"

"Well, we're all holding together pretty well, considering."

"You and Karyn must have had some anxious moments there for a while."

"Karyn more than me. Robbie called me right away."

"So what the hell happened over there?"

"I don't know. I guess one of those Asian gangs shot into a crowd of black kids."

"Any reason?"

"Some kind of retaliation for a fight a couple of nights ago."

"God, Steve, I can't imagine how we'd react. I don't know how you and Karyn do it."

He meant, "I don't know *why* you and Karyn do it." After all, none of our friends had stuck with the public school system. The Andersons had moved to the suburbs as soon as their oldest daughter finished elementary school. They had planned on sending her to the public middle school's gifted program along with our youngest son, Darren. But the city had begun busing special ed kids to the school, and the Andersons had feared for their daughter's safety.

The Rosenbergs had decided to put their twin boys, who were Robbie's age, into private school when there was a bomb scare at Central High School. The firemen would not search the lockers at school for the bomb, because nothing in their contracts said they had to. The principal, a man who had worked with me on the Public Education Fund board, was forced to search every locker in the school himself, until he found the fake bomb. There had been a threat attached, warning the principal to reinstate Rafael Ramirez, who had been expelled for carrying a gun in school. He'd said he needed it to protect himself.

My wife was cooking chicken piccata. It was Robbie's favorite dish, a meal she usually cooked in celebration of good report cards or well-pitched games. This night I let my boys continue playing ping-pong. I started putting out the plates. As I folded napkins, I thought about whether or not Robbie should see a psychiatrist. I was hesitant to mention it to Karyn, since I had just recently pushed the three of us into going to a counseling session together.

Over the past couple of years it seemed that there had been nothing but arguments between my wife and my middle son. Karyn spent several hours a week as a volunteer in the public school system as a tutor and an educational advocate, and even as an unofficial foster parent for throw-away kids who needed a place to stay for a couple of nights. At least two days a week I would come home to find a black kid or a young immigrant from the Dominican Republic pouring a tall glass of Tropicana before sitting down to a drilling in English grammar from my wife. Almost in response, Robbie had embraced the private school social scene and his prep school friends, who wanted him to transfer to Spenser to join them. Robbie didn't even look at his mother when he spoke to us at the dinner table, because she was unsympathetic and downright scornful of his foolish dreams.

My wife has diabetes. Sometimes I think it makes her feel overly vulnerable. Being a victim, knowing she has to be strong, seems to put her on her guard. Her contempt for Robbie was so strong at times that I half thought the disease was affecting her behavior toward him. Each day I came home to hear my wife's vitriol about our lazy son and the wonderful progress she'd made with Francisco or Camilla. While Karyn worked for these small successes with eager immigrants, Robbie did the absolute minimum for good grades, and we paid for tutors when he complained about bad teachers. In fact, Karyn *did* everything to keep him from self-destructing. She would type his reports when he dropped them on her at eleven o'clock the night before they were due. She screamed at him for being inconsiderate, but she typed them because they were good and thoughtful and would never have been turned in if not for her. She washed and folded his clothes and cleaned his room. She ironed things that didn't need ironing, and Robbie told her so. Karyn would look down toward the ironing board and hunch her shoulders as Robbie looked at me wide-eyed and shook his head as if she were crazy. Then he'd bite his nails and stay up late listening to Pink Floyd and sleep as late as we'd let him. Karyn drove him to school so he wouldn't have to ride public transportation, and so he would go, and wrote him notes when he was a few minutes late because it was the most important year for college, even though he didn't care. He wanted to self-destruct and she wouldn't let him—he hated her for it all because he sensed that she was the strength behind him. Her actions were never louder than her angry words for Robbie, and he spoke about not going to college because he didn't see the point, and he never missed a Spenser party because he saw the point—to feel good, to drink, to be with a girl, and to be wanted.

A few nights before the shooting, Karyn and I had caught our drunken son returning two hours past his curfew with a girl who was cleaning dirt from her knees in the kitchen. My wife took that evening as evidence of Robbie's falling apart. I used the event as a way to convince her that Robbie needed help and that the three of us had to try a counseling session.

Things became more confusing to me after our visit to the psychiatrist. When we got into it in front of the shrink, I was no longer the referee between Karyn and Robbie. I was one of the fighters—an unprepared one—taking shots from my wife with my back against the ropes. Suddenly I seemed to be as guilty as my son, and, in the shrink's presence, it dawned on me that my wife had contempt for me, as well. Perhaps Robbie's recent behavior reminded her of distasteful and untrue rumors about me when I was an academic, doubts about my character that had never been articulated, and that I had never suspected. A student of mine in the late seventies had told half the academic community that we'd been intimate. She used to call my wife and tell her about our "affair." I didn't even recognize the girl from my lectures. A few years after that, when Darren was born prematurely with an undeveloped lung, Karyn felt that I had gone away from her emotionally—she said "abandoned" in front of the psychiatrist—that I'd retreated into my new career as a business-man when she needed me most. She couldn't understand that. But I couldn't pay the bills on an academic salary. I wasn't abandoning her or the life of the mind. I was learning about reality—about bills and debt and the pressure of owing, things she really didn't have to worry about.

Based on the initial meeting with the three of us, the psychia-trist suggested that only my wife and I return. I got the impression that Robbie's behavior was within normal parameters and that per-haps mine and Karyn's was not. She was raging against the way our world was changing, and she was striking at me through Robbie for giving up teaching. She was pissed as hell that everyone had given up. She hadn't.

"Hey, Dad. Guess what?"

"What, Darren?"

"Guess!"

"You finished your homework?"

"No, Dad."

"You walked the dogs?"

"Dad."

"Tell me, Darr."

"I beat Robbie at ping-pong."

Robbie walked into the kitchen. "I let him win." He reached over Karyn's shoulder and picked a cucumber from the salad she was making. We said nothing.

Darren looked over at Robbie and then back at me. "He did not."

"He did not *what* . . . ," I prompted. "Be more specific."

Darren rolled his eyes. "Robbie did not let me win. I killed him twenty-one-seven, and he tried his hardest." He had a logical mind for a ten-year-old. He plopped himself into the chair at his setting and waited to be served. Robbie looked over at his little brother without making eye contact with me. He said, "Hey, scumbag, you forgot to wash your grubby little hands."

"C'mon now, Robbie," I said.

"C'mon now *what*, Dad?"

"C'mon now, Robbie, don't take your frustration out on your little brother."

He replied bitterly, "Frustration?"

"Yes, Robbie."

This time there was less of an edge to his voice. "Frustration?"

"Okay, Rob, what would you call it?" His condescension was beginning to grate on me.

"I don't know, Dad. You were the English teacher. Just sounds a little weak, that's all." He seemed to be backing away from the argument, so I let it drop. We were silent for a while. Robbie and Darren went to wash their hands and exchanged obscenities that floated, muffled yet audible, into the kitchen. The boys came back to the table and sat down. Karyn placed the salad bowl on the table. She turned back toward the stove to make sure it was off. Just as the tension began to ebb, she said icily, "Robert, did you thank your father for picking you up at school today?"

Robbie jumped to his feet. The back of his chair hit the refrigerator behind him. "What?" he yelled. "What did you say?" He stood next to his mother with clenched fists. Stunned, I watched him take a step toward her. She turned and faced him. He said, "Did you say, 'Thank him for a ride'? Thank him?" She looked up at him without stepping back. He was at least six inches taller than she was. He stepped back, turned, and punched the refrigerator. His last report card fell to the floor with a couple of magnets. Darren sat at the table and looked straight ahead. Karyn continued staring at Robbie, stroking the back of Darren's head, who was still seated at the table. Suddenly, she said softly, "Pick up the paper and put it back on the refrigerator." Karyn bit her lip.

Robbie exploded.

"Fuck that!" He picked up the report card and put it close to her face. "That's not just any piece of paper. It's my report card, Mother. Oh," he said, pretending to read it, "and it is damn good, isn't it? Look at all those A's. You must be so proud of your son getting those grades in a 'multicultural melting pot,' like Providence Latin. Oh, wait, it's more of a 'tossed salad,' isn't that what they call it nowadays? Each culture a separate flavor unto itself, yet robust and flavorful when combined—when served together." His smile was saccharin-sweet. "All bullshit, that's what it is."

"I'm not proud of you at all, right now. You're acting like a coward."

Robbie ran to the kitchen window. It was pitch black outside. He threw his hands against his ears. His eyes were shut tightly. I stood up next to Karyn, and Darren got up and leaned against my wife. Then Robbie spun around, facing all of us. I said, "Robbie, do we always have to do this before dinner? Can't we just eat in peace?" I turned to my wife. "Karyn, can't you just leave it alone sometimes? Can't you both just not take each other's bait?" My wife looked at me for a few moments, and Robbie punched the wall. It was incomprehensible. This woman woke up in the middle of the night screaming Robbie's name. She worried about him getting in car accidents. She couldn't sleep when he went out after their fights, because she thought he'd drink and smoke pot, or worse.

Darren began to cry. He tugged on my shirt and said, "C'mon. Let's just eat. We don't need fighting."

I stroked his head softly and lied, "Darren, we're not fighting. We just need to talk things over." I turned back to Karyn. Robbie was looking straight at her, still furious over her calling him a coward. Furious at her being his mother. I stood between them. We all stood there. We stood there for a few seconds until I suggested that we sit down to dinner and discuss what had happened and what we should do about it.

"Dad, you want to sit down to dinner, now? Just looking at the both of you is making me sick."

"Robbie, you'd better watch yourself. I've been very understanding so far. Don't make me lose my temper."

"I'm a fucking coward, right?"

"No."

"You sit in an office with a view of the statehouse. Your whole office is a bunch of guys with fat white asses. All their fat little shithead kids go to private school and grow up to be just like their fathers, just like the other guys in the office, just like you, Dad. Except you and Mom are so different. You're liberals—harmony between races and classes, right? If I went to a private school, maybe I could believe the things you do. Maybe then I wouldn't have to feel guilty about becoming a fucking racist."

Robbie was pointing his finger at us. Spit came from his mouth as he talked, his voice becoming more and more hoarse. His hands were shaking when he tried to wipe them on his jeans. He reached down and picked up a glass of milk from the table. The glass shook until it reached his mouth. He guzzled about half a glass. He wore a milk mustache from his drink.

"Do you like driving your Legend knowing that your sons pay the price for your conscience? Huh, Dad?"

"Do you really think that I want you to suffer, Robbie? Don't think that these fights don't become family problems—that they don't hurt the family."

"Dad, don't lie to yourself. We're not going through P.L. together. You didn't see what I saw today. The blood I saw was real—all over the courtyard where I hang out and eat lunch. The ricochet could have been mine. The bullets from the kid I look at the wrong way, fuck that, the bullet from the kid I look at, will be mine. A present from you, Dad. The ignorance of these kids is mine to deal with. All mine. You can't have any."

Darren was almost hyperventilating. Karyn got him a glass of water. For the first time, Karyn's voice was sympathetic. "Please, Robbie, please," and she pointed to Darren. But Robbie was too far gone.

"Fuck that, Mom. Hey, Darren, all this is ahead of you next year. Next year, you goin' into the hood, boy. Mom and Dad gonna keep those values and you gonna pay for them. You goin' to th' hoood, booooyyy. To the wolves."

Robbie didn't see my hand coming. He looked surprised, and then he fed off the slap I had given him.

"Dad, hit me again. C'mon, make you feel good? Love those hippie values—nonviolence, King, make love—not war." His cheek became redder. A welt from my wedding band was raised on the side of his face. "It's your generation that fucked us over. Integration equals violence. Free love equals fucked-up black kids without fathers. AIDS owes a lot to free love, Pops. You fucked us with your free love. You fucked us. . . ."

"Robbie, calm down. You're out of control." I was out of control. I couldn't believe I'd hit him. I needed time, time to think what to do for my son, for the family.

"You're damn right I'm out of control. I'm out of my fucking head."

"Listen, Son, we'll take a couple of days off from school . . ."

"We? What the fuck is this 'we' shit?"

"Robbie, we're going to see you through this."

"I'm not going back to that school."

"Listen, we'll see what other possibilities there are. In the meantime . . ."

My wife said, "Stephen, we've talked about this. Are you forgetting that we're against private school? It's only one of the most important things we agreed on when we decided to have kids. At least be honest with him, Stephen. Don't give him false hopes of going to private school or boarding school. He's staying at Providence Latin."

"Listen, Karyn, your son just saw a kid get shot today. You might want to show a little compassion."

"Lies and false hopes are not compassion."

She glared at Robbie. It was the same glare that her father, the army general, had given to her in her sophomore year of college after she had disregarded his advice about what classes to take, only he hadn't spoken to her for six months. She glared at Robbie while speaking to me. "No, Stephen, no compassion until he shows some to the family. Not until he stops behaving like a beast."

"Karyn."

"Oh, yeah, Mom? Well, guess where I learned to be a beast—at school with the other beasts."

"Oh, poor Robbie," she said with mock sympathy, her sarcasm biting at the tension that spread tighter and tighter like invisible wires pulled taut throughout the room.

Now that she had shown emotion, Robbie sensed weakness. I watched him stiffen like a tiger about to pounce. Suddenly he seemed to change his mind. Maybe he finally saw Darren through his rage—all red-faced and teary-eyed. Robbie stretched his neck and looked almost calm, so his response shocked me.

"Ma, what the fuck do you know about any of this? You grew up in the woods of New Jersey. You can't help me. Go teach Julio to read. You could die right now for all I care. I wish you would drop dead right here, right now. Maybe the diabetes could really kick in and finish you off."

Karyn's face went white and she grasped the back of a chair to steady herself.

I had him against the wall. Tears were in his eyes. I pushed my hand to his neck and his head banged against the windowpane behind him. He tried to shield himself from my blow with his hands, and I swung again harder. Then he pushed me back. For a second, I saw him as a man. Robbie didn't try once to hit me. My hands hit his head, grasped at his elbows, shoulders, and I cracked the glass, frantically trying to force him close, to pull him in to me when he was pushing me away. Darren screamed in the background as I went back at Robbie. I heard Karyn say, "No, Stephen. Please. Stop," and then I remember most clearly what she said next: "It's not worth it." Those words stuck in my mind like a bayonet, stung me, as I tried to hold him. But he wouldn't be held. I tried to put together words.

"Karyn, it is worth it. It's worth more than anything. Helping Angel or Julio is easier than this. He's your son, for God's sake. Look at him. He's your son, and he hates you. You're shrinking from the challenge. You're the coward, because you can't speak with him. Look at him, for God's sake. Really look. Boys grow into men. They disappoint you, but they are going to be men who have their own ideas, ideas that aren't ours—that couldn't be ours. Now I'm ready to do anything, to pay anything, to keep it all together, since what we've done has failed." My knees went, and I slid to the floor.

"Sending our children to public school was not a social experiment. You used to know that. You make me sick."

Tears streaked Robbie's swollen red face, too. He was crying so hard that he could barely speak. "I'm out of here." Darren ran over to Robbie and put his arms around him, begging him to stay. I got to my knees sobbing and watched Robbie's hand gently smooth Darren's hair. He bent to kiss his little brother on the cheek and guided him toward Karyn. Robbie did not move in her direction. She had regained her glare.

"How dare you pull this family apart?"

"Fuck off, Mom. I'm not staying here."

I could barely breathe. "Please, Robbie, don't go. Just stay. We'll work it out. We can get through this."

Darren ran to the bathroom gagging. I reached for Robbie's legs as he started for the front hallway. I heard Karyn say, "Let him go, Stephen." But I had him. I pulled Robbie down to the floor and tried to hold him, hoping the anger would pass, that all would be forgiven, all would be calm and fine. But his face was burning hot, with a power and anger I couldn't stop, and my wife still stared him down as he got up, put on his coat, and walked out the front door into the cold February air.

ASYLUM

PATRICK YACHIMSKI

Marty lets me go on his rounds with him this morning. It is a sight to see. Frail as he is, he struts boldly down the middle of the corridors, people parting on either side of him, while I follow meekly behind. The way he carries himself, you might think he was some kind of doctor, or at least someone important. But he's not. He's just a patient here, like the rest of us. Wherever he spots a sufficient group of people, together, milling about in one place, he gathers them around, waving them in with his hands and arms, nodding his head up and down.

"Listen," he says to them. "Life is not so bad. It could be worse. It could rain every day, for one thing. Think about that," he says. "How pleasant would that be? California could break off and fall into the ocean. The sun could overheat and burn up the planet. You might wake up one morning and not remember your name or anything about yourself. Worse yet, you might wake up one morning and your heart could stop. Then where would you be? It could happen to you, me, any of us. Any of these things. All of these things."

Life is not so bad. It could be worse. Marty really and truly believes this, and he parades around in this manner, giving his stump speech, handing out his business cards left and right. For some time afterward, you see them all over the place, people shuffling around with a card of his in their hand, staring down at it for hours on end, trying to make some sense out of it.

This speech he gives, it is the same one every time, word for word. Some people, when they hear it, will just shake their heads a bit, turn, and walk away. Others will open their eyes wide, wider than you'd think eyes could be opened, and stare. I can see where they are coming from. We are not on the West Coast here, and Cali-

fornia falling into the ocean or not makes not the least bit of difference to these people. Waking up in the morning and forgetting their
names and where they are—here—would be a blessing in disguise
for some of them. To live and to forget. Or, to live and to try to
forget. Truth be told, a fair number of people here are in this state
already. The rest of them, those that still remember, if they had the
choice of succeeding at one thing in their otherwise unremarkable
lives, just one thing, would have it be this.

I'm not sure if anyone around here, besides myself, believes in
Marty or takes him seriously. But he preaches to them all the same,
and he doesn't stop preaching to them. And it is the same people he
preaches to every week, here, and they keep coming back to listen.
You'd think Marty was running for some kind of office, the cam-
paigning he does. But he has to do these things, you know. Someone
has to. Someone has to bring some kind of hope to these people,
get them to cross their fingers and hope against hope.

I live on the top floor.

I am not the only one. The only one to live on the top floor, that
is. There are others. My room is along a corridor that runs the entire length of the floor. Along this corridor are other rooms, too.
My room, along with some of the other rooms, stands on one side
of the corridor. The rest of the rooms are on the other side of the
corridor. Each room has its own door that enters into the corridor.
Apart from the fact that different people live in each of these rooms,
the rooms are identical in every respect. It can be confusing for a
while, it really can. You walk into a certain room, thinking it should
be yours, but it isn't. You can walk into some embarrassing scenes
in this manner. But, before long, you get a good idea which room is
yours, and you stay away from the rest.

I don't know too many of the people that live in these rooms. I
do know Marty, though.

I have only been here for a week or so, you see. I do not remember
first arriving here, and I do not intend to leave—nor, I suppose, do
they intend to let me leave—until I can remember it. Figure it all

out. That, along with a few other things that need to be taken care of. When I first came to and opened my eyes here a few days back, I thought that this might be some kind of holy place. Everyone was dressed in white, their immaculate robes streaming to the floor and trailing behind them wherever they went. The robes covered even their feet, and they moved so slowly and so smoothly that it seemed they were more likely floating than walking.

These robes are not quite robes at all, but are, instead, gowns of some type. They are thin like sheets and open from the back. They reach down to knee level. But, Marty says, be that as it may, men such as ourselves can take no pride in wearing gowns. We wear robes. We call them robes.

I wear one of these robes. Marty wears one, too.

We have slippers, too. We wear slippers.

The floors and walls of the corridors and all of the rooms here are painted spotless white. Along each of these corridors are a number of rooms. Some of the rooms are on one side of the corridor. The rest of the rooms are on the other side. At the end of each corridor is a tall window, extending from floor to ceiling, nearly across the entire width of the corridor. These windows let in nothing but the purest sunlight, interrupted only by the bodies that pass back and again, floating across the corridors in front of them.

One such window stands at the end of the corridor on my floor. I live on the top floor.

Some of the people here fiddle with their hair and with the ties of their robes. And they tend to look at you in a queer sort of way. Also, they have this habit of talking to people when no people are around. I thought this might be some kind of holy place.

There is Marty, though. He's not exactly holy, but he is full of wisdom. He knows some things. This is how I meet Marty. It happens like this.

I have this routine. I wake up every morning. After, or before I wake up, I open my eyes. I get out of bed. I stand up and walk across the room, toward the door that leads into the corridor. It is not a long walk, from the bed to the door. Five paces.

These details, all of them, they are important. You will see.

I open my door and step out into the hallway, always leading with my left foot. Seven paces and I reach the center of the hallway, where, each morning, I pretend like I am shaking hands with someone. Then I nod to that person. Friendly sort of nod. If it is a lady, I take off my hat and bow, bending at the waist. That done, I thrust my hands behind my back, pivot on my heels, and march in step, left foot first, then the right, down the corridor.

One hundred and twenty paces. After one hundred and twenty paces you have to stop, else you will walk right into the window. The window reaches from floor to ceiling and nearly stretches across the entire width of the corridor. It lets in nothing but the purest sunlight. There are steel bars across the window, on the outside of the glass, steel bars that run vertically, parallel to one another, and are three inches in diameter. This is probably a good idea. It contributes to the safety of those of us on the inside. From where we are, here, on the top floor, it can be a long way to the ground. I wonder, though, whether they might not want to have the bars across the inside of the window. It is the safety of the glass I am having in mind. You know.

This one morning, Marty is standing at the window. Only I don't yet know him, so, to me, he's not yet Marty. He's just some other guy. That's all he is. Some other guy. The first thing I notice is that he has no hair and no teeth. He is not short and he is not tall, but he has no hair and no teeth. No eyebrows, too. I notice all of these things. It's hard not to. He is facing toward the window, and his palms are pressed up to the glass, level with and on either side of his head.

One hundred and twenty paces, and I am right there next to him. I am standing there for a time or so, and I begin to think that he has not even noticed me. But he does. He notices me. He turns, not just his head, but his entire neck and shoulders, and glances over at me. His eyes, they are staring right at me, and they are as black as I don't know what. There isn't even any white in them anywhere. They are just black.

I don't know. I must look like I've been through all hell or some-thing, because this guy, he starts right up talking to me. And it's not just any casual conversation, either. He means business, this guy.

"Listen," he says to me. "Life is not so bad. It could be worse. It could rain every day, for one thing. Think about that," he says. "How pleasant would that be? California could break off and fall into the ocean. The sun could overheat and burn up the planet. You might wake up one morning and not remember your name or any-thing about yourself. Worse yet, you might wake up one morning and your heart could stop. Then where would you be? It could hap-pen to you, me, any of us. Any of these things. All of these things."

Life is not so bad. It could be worse. This guy, I can see, really and truly believes this. He waits for an answer, for a response from me. What can I tell him? They say I'm crazy and they keep me locked up in this place. How, how can it possibly get any worse than that?

I say, he waits for an answer, then, finally seeing that none is forthcoming, he reaches down and into one of the folds of his robe, pulling something out of it. He has his hand on what appears to be a business card, and he offers it over to me. He stretches his arm out across the distance between us, and, I swear, his arm is so pale and thin and hairless that it looks like even the slightest breeze would snap it clean off.

"Say, friend," he says. "Why don't you take this?"

I reach out my hand and take the card, being careful not to acci-dentally brush the scabbed fingers that are draped around it. I take the card into the flat of my palm, and look down at it. It has, writ-ten across it, in bold, black letters, MARTY. Nothing else. It must be some kind of joke. I try to hand it back to him.

"No, please. Keep that. I have plenty more," Marty says.

I do not particularly care to keep the card, but I am hoping that, if I do, Marty will take that arm and shove it back beneath his robe, or wherever it came from. Anywhere, so long as I won't have to stare at it. I crumple the card into a ball and thrust my arm straight down along my side.

"If you ever have any problems," Marty says, "don't hesitate to give me a call. We can arrange a time. Set up an appointment."

After this, this one time, Marty and I become fast friends. Things happen like that, without you ever thinking about it. It has even gotten to the point that I don't mind so much looking at his arm anymore.

Marty is not all I have here. There is more than Marty.

There is this nurse who has been coming around these past few days, since I've been here. Changing my sheets. Those sorts of things. She has brown eyes and reddish hair that flows from beneath her nurse's cap and down to her shoulders.

There are important rules for these nurses to remember, being in a place like this, various things that I have heard and picked up on, things that these nurses whisper to one another. Marty, he tells me some of these things, too.

These nurses, they can speak freely with any of the patients here, but they are not supposed to ask us any personal questions—namely, any questions that have to do in a significant way with our past, present, or future. The weather is always a favorite topic. It's a beautiful day out there. Are you ready for your thioridazine? Participation in chess, board games, and other such activities is strongly encouraged. No strip poker, though, I imagine. Nurses are never to tell their last names to any of the patients—though first names are definitely fair play—and they are never, never under any circumstances, to tell us their phone numbers, no matter how much we may beg for them. I suppose this is necessary. From the looks of things, they keep the real problems someplace else, but you can never be too careful. Things have been known to happen, here and elsewhere.

There are other rules, of course, but these are the important ones, the ones that all of the nurses are supposed to know and adhere to.

There is this nurse who has been coming around these past few days. Changing my sheets. Those sorts of things. She has brown eyes and reddish hair that flows from beneath her nurse's cap and down to her shoulders.

She is nice enough.

I sometimes wonder what it would be like to do something to her.

Marty confides in me, tells me things he wouldn't dare tell other people. When he says these things, he leans right over and puts his mouth an inch or so away from my ear, so that no one but myself can hear what it is that he is saying. For my part, I listen. He has become something of a teacher for me, a guru. He is full of wisdom. He says some things.

"Tell me, friend," he says. "If you had to describe yourself in one word or less, how would you do it? What would you say?"

I don't know how you would describe yourself in less than one word. I don't know. I suppose it must be possible, for some people. For some people, anything is possible. There just isn't anything there worth mentioning. Nothing.

"Do you know what I would say?" he asks. He is leaning close to my ear and whispering, as he likes to do. "Do you know how I would describe myself?"

I don't. I swear, I don't. Evidently, this is some kind of lesson he has prepared for me. A riddle. If it had animals in it, it would be a fable.

"A cactus," he hisses. "I am like a cactus."

We are standing at the window as all of this takes place. Marty draws apart from me and goes back to staring through the window. I wait for him to go on, to tell me what this is supposed to signify, to represent. He is full of wisdom. His eyes, his little black eyes, are starting to tear up, and he is reaching some kind of emotional state.

I wait for him to say something else, something more, but he doesn't. He doesn't have anything to say. The man is full of wisdom.

When I say I would like to do things to her. You know what I mean. Nothing serious, I hope. Nothing that would either hurt her or disgrace me. A slight touch, maybe. A glance in passing. Nothing serious.

I decide to follow her one day. Trail her. She passes by me in the corridor, and I turn quietly and follow behind. I keep a safe distance, sure. I wouldn't want to give myself away. Fifty paces or so. She is pushing a wheeled metal cart in front of her, with a basin of water and some other things on it. She has this way of swinging from side to side with her hips and the backs of her thighs when she walks. If she knew that those things went like that, she would try to stop them, I imagine, or at least do something about it.

She stops suddenly before this one door. She gathers the basin and some other things off of the cart and enters the room. She has her hands full, so she has to turn to a side and push through the door with one of her hips. I keep my distance. A few minutes later, she steps out of the room, places the basin back upon the cart, and begins to move on. She stops again a few doors later, and the same process is repeated. Her entering, me waiting. On we go, up and down corridors, in and out of doors. On one of these occasions, the nurse takes a good deal longer inside one of the rooms than I would like to allow. I pull up against the wall, breathing heavily, only a few feet away.

I wait fifteen minutes or so, but nothing happens. No one enters and no one exits. If they did, I would spot them. Eventually, I move over to the door, and nudge it open, just a touch, just enough for me to squeeze one eye through and see what's going on. The basin is on an otherwise empty table that stands against the wall and near the door. I crack the door open a bit farther. There is a poor old woman, with white faded hair and even more faded eyes and skin, lying in a bed. My nurse is beside her. From behind, sunlight streams through the windows and into the picture, brightening things a bit. As I watch, my nurse leans over the bed, and, ever so slowly and carefully, helps this woman to sit up, to move forward. She does this by reaching around and supporting this woman's back and shoulders with one arm. With her other arm, she sweeps a plastic cup to the woman's lips, and allows the woman to sip from it. After a few seconds, she pulls the cup back and away, allowing the woman to swallow and breathe. She then moves the cup closer again.

After this process has been repeated a few times, after the woman has finished drinking whatever it is that's in that cup, the nurse helps the woman to lie back down, as gently and as slowly as before.

When the woman is back in place on the bed, my nurse draws her arm away from beneath the woman's body. She turns her hand over and smoothes that woman's white, crinkled hair, hair that dangles in strands along her forehead.

Me, I watch this picture. This woman and my nurse, the sunlight wrapping itself around the two of them.

Some of the people here, you have to watch out for them. Marty warns me about these people, tries to steer me away from them. But still, a place like this, you get to see some things. Hear some stories.

There is this one guy who smashed both toilets in his sister's house with his bare feet, then threatened to do the same to his brother-in-law, his sister's husband. Another guy, he sprawled himself over a crosswalk at some intersection somewhere, and traffic was at a standstill for forty-five minutes. Things like this you hear about, the things that people do. Why did these people do these things? Why do any of us do the things we do? Who can say? And these are not even some of the worst stories.

Then there is this other guy. He used to be a musician, and he talks like it. He has a phonograph player and an entire record collection in his room. He can't remember much about what went on back then and on the outside. But I imagine he is reminded of it by his records. One time, out of the blue, he comes right up to Marty and starts talking to him, for no reason at all, like they are old friends. This is according to what Marty says.

"Myself, I've been here eleven years," this guy says, this musician. "Eleven years. It's not so bad, though. Why, look at Brahms. Did you know it took him twenty-one years to write his First Symphony? It really did. He began working on it in 1855, and it was not completed until 1876, when it was premiered."

Marty just stands there, opening and closing his eyes. He hopes that on one of the occasions when he closes his eyes and keeps them closed for a few seconds, when he opens them this guy will be gone. But this guy, he just doesn't know when to quit.

"Twenty-one years is a long time. Brahms knows about that," this guy says, as if Brahms were living right here among us, around the corner and down the hall. "I've only been here half that time. Once I've been here twenty-one years, then I'll have earned the right to place myself on a level with Brahms. You, too. Until then, I don't want to hear any more complaints."

Just like that. And the thing was, Marty hadn't even been complaining, really. Imagine that!

So Marty gives this guy one of his cards and sends him on his way.

It's people like this who are dangerous, Marty tells me. These are the people you need to stay away from.

This musician guy, and the guy who smashed toilets, and the guy who sprawled himself over an intersection. Eventually, like me, they ended up here.

Eventually, like me and like these other people, Marty ended up here, too.

Apart from the fact that he does not like to be called Martin, and the fact that he was already here when I got here, I can't say that I know much of anything about Marty.

I do not tell Marty about my nurse, but he gets to meet her once. The two of us are standing at the end of the corridor, by that window. Marty is explaining some things to me, some things he thinks I ought to know. What nurses, what doctors to go to when you have problems. What kind of medicines will do the right kinds of things for you. These sorts of things. This is what Marty is telling me. I begin to hear footsteps approaching from behind, growing larger as they make their way down the corridor. Closer, closer they come, and then they stop.

"Excuse me," this voice says. A woman's voice, vaguely familiar.

Marty spins around to look. I keep my face to the window. I can see him out of the corner of my eye. Marty just looks at whomever this woman is, just stares at her and waits for her to go on.

"I was wondering," this voice says, "if the two of you would like me to bring some chairs up here for you."

"Chairs?" Marty's voice.

"Yes, you know," this woman's voice says. "The two of you spend so much time standing at this window, I thought you might like some chairs."

Marty looks over at me, tries to whisper into my ear.

This voice continues to plead her case. "I could have them put right here at the end of the hallway for you, exactly where you are standing. Right in front of the window. After all, sitting would be more comfortable than standing, wouldn't it?"

The voice stops, and then there is a slight tapping on my shoulder. I wheel around, and oh God, there she is, my little angel, my nurse, staring directly into my eyes. She appears to be a bit nervous. Her eyes are glassy, and her forehead and her cheekbones are covered with a thin film of perspiration, untraceable except from this close distance. I wonder if she might be a new recruit, might have just begun working here recently.

We get new nurses here all the time, Marty tells me. There seems to be a high turnover rate. Most of them stay for only a few months or so, and then move on to something else. Something more promising, I imagine. And it is always the friendliest and most helpful nurses that move on, he says. The new nurses all arrive in the same fresh state: shy and eager-eyed, willing to help; those that leave, they leave a little different from the way they were when they came in. It's not that we're necessarily that bad here. But still.

I've only been here a few days, but I can see it in their eyes, some of these nurses. They have gone through all the training and they have heard stories, sure. They have this set image in their minds of places like this and they think they know what to expect. But what they end up seeing is that this place and the people in it are different from what anyone could imagine. We come in all forms, they see, in all shapes and sizes. We are young and old here, some of us strong and athletic, others of us not so much so. Some of us are intelligent and educated, while others of us, as anyone can see, really don't know the first thing. There's only one thing that all of us have in common here, and that's this: we're all a little crazy, or so they say. I prefer to say we're unlucky. We are all, for one reason or another, down on our luck, and we are waiting for our luck to turn around.

And why shouldn't our luck turn around?

This nurse, she might be one of these new recruits. I can tell by her eyes and the expression on her face. She is still standing here in front of me, staring at me.

"Sir," she says to me. "Are you all right? Do you feel okay?"

I don't say anything. Nobody says anything.

"Your friend over here. How is he? Is he going to be all right?"

Me, she means, and she is speaking to Marty. She points a finger at me and turns her face away from mine and over to his as she says this.

"Who? Him?" Marty asks. Now he points at me. The two of them, they stand there with their arms raised and outstretched, pointing at me, my nurse staring at Marty and Marty, in turn, staring at me.

I don't stare at anyone. I let my gaze shift around, trying to take everything in.

My nurse looks at me for a second or two, then turns to Marty again. Marty just shrugs a bit.

"Oh, he'll be fine," he says. "He's always like that."

My nurse turns back to look at me. I smile softly at her, as a sort of apology.

"But what's wrong with him?" she asks. "Why is he like this?"

This nurse is definitely a new recruit. Most nurses, I would think, would know better than to ask patients here for diagnoses on their peers. What the hell do we know? Marty is not supposed to know what's wrong with me. He's full of wisdom, sure, but he can't even tell what's wrong with himself, never mind me. I wonder, if I ask nicely, if this nurse will give me her last name and phone number. She doesn't seem to know any better.

Marty just shrugs again, and now he is smiling, along with me. Marty has no teeth. He has no hair, either, and no eyebrows. These antics, this clowning around, do not seem to satisfy my nurse, or reassure her, but she lets the matter drop, and appears to try to clear it from her mind. After all, she will be used to me before long, will come to expect—as Marty has come to expect, even appreciate—this type of behavior from me.

"So how about it?" she finally asks.

"Sorry? What? How about what?" Marty says.

"How about some chairs?"

Marty has forgotten about the entire proposition, has been distracted by one thing or another. He glances over at me, but I have no particular opinion on the matter.

"Listen," he says to my nurse. "Life is not so bad. It could be worse. It could rain every day, for one thing. Think about that," he says. "How pleasant would that be? California could break off and fall into the ocean. The sun could overheat and burn up the planet. You might wake up one morning and not remember your name or anything about yourself. Worse yet, you might wake up one morning and your heart could stop. Then where would you be? It could happen to you, me, any of us. Any of these things. All of these things."

Marty goes on and on. He reaches into a fold of his robe and pulls out one of his cards, one of his MARTY cards. He pauses, looks up, looks around for someone to give it to. This nurse just isn't there anymore. Her footsteps have long since echoed down the corridor, and she is nowhere in sight. Marty looks down at his card, stares at it for a while, then slips it quietly back into the fold. The thing is, though, he is all wound up now. He is just hitting his stride. He turns to me.

"Listen, friend," he says. "Life is not so bad. It could be worse."

Marty, sometimes, worries about me, and tries to cheer me up. It helps to have someone like that looking after you. All the same, though, I usually don't pay much attention to him when he starts talking like he talks when he worries about me.

"What are you always so glum about?" he asks from time to time. "You're always just standing around, brooding. And you never have anything pleasant to say, to me or to anyone else. Never a good morning, or a how do you do? — in fact, you never have anything to say at all."

It is not usual for Marty to be so upset. He doesn't usually make many pointed statements. When he does, you just have to stand for it and deal with it. All the same, though, I usually don't pay much attention to him when he starts talking like he talks when he worries about me.

This one time I have to pay attention. And it is not Marty who makes me notice. It is this other guy, the musician guy. Marty is doing his rounds, and I have accompanied him again. Marty is doing all the talking, as always, but today he has delegated some authority to me. He lets me hand out one of his cards to whoever is around. We are walking down one corridor, and there is this guy standing there. I go over to him with a card.

"Not him," Marty says to me, but it is already too late.

I have attracted this guy's attention, and he is staring at me oddly.

"You don't look so hot," this guy says to me.

What can I say to this?

"Beethoven once said to an acquaintance of his that whoever knows and understands his symphonies can never be unhappy again."

I'm not listening, really. Really, I'm not. Marty has even snatched me by the arm and is trying to drag me away. I can feel his bony fingers try to circle around my forearm. They are long, his fingers. But this guy goes right on, oblivious to all of this.

"I generally regard this as an accurate rule of thumb. I know myself, for instance, that whenever I am faced with any disappointment or ill feelings, I retire to my room. There, I select a Beethoven recording from my collection and place it on the turntable of the phonograph player. Almost immediately after I place the needle on the rotating record and adjust the volume knob, I can feel Beethoven's music begin to seep into me. Before long—before the end of an opening movement, say—my troubles, whatever they may be, have disappeared completely."

He wants me to stop by his room and listen to some Beethoven sometime. I really must, he says. Or, at the very least, I really ought to. But, of course, I won't stop by. I don't know much of anything about Beethoven, I'll admit that. But whatever it is that's wrong with me, I don't think Beethoven will do the trick.

This guy goes on and on, talking excitedly about this or that, pointing at Marty, then at himself. He pretends, at one instant, to be holding and playing a violin, swooning and weeping into it in order to emphasize his words. Then he picks up a trombone, puts it to his mouth, and begins to pump the slide back and forth in front of him. He kicks into a beat and begins to parade down the hallway, past me and out of earshot.

Marty, muttering a few curses under his breath, has wandered off in the opposite direction. His business cards flutter from his robe, one by one, leaving a trail behind him. Some of them land faceup, others of them scattered and facedown.

This musician guy gets me thinking. He may have a point, and Marty, too. I am not doing so well, I am afraid. I haven't been for some time, actually. I never smile, for instance. In addition to this, I am not in good physical shape. I don't eat well, and I stand in such a way that I have acquired a permanent stoop. Plus, every time I look in a mirror, my eyes are bulging out of my head in what I'm sure must be an unhealthy way.

I can't remember what I am doing, exactly, but my nurse passes by again. She is not pushing or carrying anything this time, but is merely walking along, her hands and arms empty and hanging limp along her sides. I stop whatever it is that I am doing and glance over at her. She does not notice me.

She walks along the corridor and I follow on behind. She turns a corner onto another corridor. I turn as well. She turns again. Each time she turns, I am right there with her.

She seems to pick up speed, and the distance between us suddenly grows larger. I run after her as quickly as I can without drawing attention to myself, picking my robe up with both hands and raising it above my knees, so that it will not distract my progress.

I am gaining on her. There she is passing by two men with walkers. She stops, talks with them a bit, gives one of them a friendly pat and squeeze on the shoulder. This helps me to make up some time. After pausing briefly, she continues on, nodding hellos and greetings to whoever passes by. I am gaining on her. She is not so far away now. Just as I think I can reach out and grab her, she turns, eluding me, and heads into a door on the left side of the corridor, closing it behind her. I stop in my tracks, looking up at the door.

It's now or never for me. Should I knock first, or just enter? I choose not to knock, and just open the door an inch or so and slide my body through sideways. I am thin as a rail. I can hear murmured voices not far from me. I take a slight corner and glance around it. There is this guy lying in a bed, a patient. His head is sticking out from under the sheets, but he is so wasted away that there is nothing else there. The sheets don't rise up where his body should be. It is just this head lying there.

Sitting on the edge of the bed is my nurse. She has this book in her hand, and she is reading to him. I don't know what it is that she is reading. I don't know so much about that sort of thing. But it is soothing, I can see, by the expression on this guy's face. His eyes are closed, his lips are mumbling, but every muscle and contour seems relaxed. She stops every now and again and glances down at him, smiling, then picks up again where she left off.

I don't know. I must make some kind of sound, do something to attract their attention. Because, of a sudden, both my nurse and this guy snap their heads around at me. The nurse leaps up from where she is sitting, and begins to walk from the bed and toward me.

"Hey," this guy says. "Hey."

"What's this all about?" my nurse asks. "Can I help you? What do you want here?"

I am not so bad on my feet, even these days. I burst through the door, and I don't stop, even when I am safely back in my room. I dive onto my bed, clawing at the covers, my legs still churning and kicking and running.

Things go on like this, day to day, the same thing over and again. Nothing ever changes, and, worse, nothing ever happens. There is me, there is Marty, there is my nurse. There are times, sometimes, when you feel like you might be making some progress. When you feel like you might, you just might be getting a little better, or might be learning something about yourself. Take this one time, for instance. I am standing at the window, and Marty is standing there with me.

"Say, friend," he says, "tell me what you see on the other side of that window."

I have never thought, or cared to think, exactly, about what lies on the other side of this window. I raise one arm, slowly, as if to scratch my head, then drop it back abruptly to my side. I glance down at the floor.

"You don't know, do you?" Marty says to me. "You are always staring at this window, but your gaze never gets farther than the glass. You need to look farther than the glass. Windows were made to be looked through, not to be looked at. Look through the other side. Tell me what you see."

From where I stand, looking through this window, I can gaze out across the landscape, toward where it reaches and meets with the horizon. This is a hill country, this, and the pines cover it. The trees roll over and through with the hills. The crests of these trees, they are huddled so closely together that, from here, they seem like a blanket: green on a sunny day like today, the sun burning down on and illuminating them such that it is a wonder they do not catch fire; blue, I imagine, in the snowy and muddled throes of winter; black, black as can be, in the gloaming; blacker still, they must be, as night falls.

It is not such a bad view.

The steel bars do not get in the way as much as you would think they might.

There is a world of activity that is carried forth beneath these trees, I imagine. A world that cannot be seen from here. The boughs and limbs of these trees are so mixed together, jostling with one another for position, that even the slimmest touch of light has the utmost difficulty in trying to pass through. But there is light enough. Light enough for the birds who chirp and nest in the midst and realm of those trees. Sparrows, jays, finches, owls even. Light enough, too, I imagine, for the squirrels and raccoons—possibly bear and deer—who make their homes amongst the maze of trunks, beneath the impregnable canopy of those trees.

Beneath the pines, all the way beneath them, the ground is covered with needles. Pine needles. Thirty, forty years' worth.

Untouched by any rain or wind, because rains never reach and breezes never blow where those needles lie, piling over one another, scorched and dry, year after year. These pines, in every direction I can see and as far as I can see. Suddenly I saw all of this. And I saw that it was good.

It is not such a bad view.

Marty has moved over and snaked his arm across my shoulders.

"So tell me, friend. What do you see out there?"

Another world. Another world.

And then sometimes.

I am having this dream. Marty is not in my dream. I don't bother anyone, in my dream. I just sneak from my room quietly, get up from my bed and walk to the door. Seven paces to the center of the hallway, then handshake, pivot, and march. One. Two. Three. Four. Five. Six. All the way to one hundred and twenty, and I am right up against that window, my nose almost touching the glass. The lights in the corridor have been turned off for the night. Everything is black, inside and outside.

I hear footsteps approaching behind me, in my dream. It is my nurse. She is carrying a chair in front of her. A big maroon leather armchair, something you would see in a fancy office or club somewhere, and something that looks too heavy to carry. She places the chair down beside me, facing the window, in this, my dream.

Of a sudden, in my dream, and with no warning whatsoever, I begin to stare about frantically in all directions. I begin to wave my arms up and down and stutter with my feet. My mouth opens and closes, and I am shouting the loudest voiceless screams that, I swear, have ever been heard. My nurse rushes over to me, in the most motherly and comforting manner you could imagine, and wraps her arms around me. She glances behind her, along the corridor, looking for someone to send for help.

I carry on in the same fashion. I begin to cry, and I mean really cry. Tears are streaming down my face from my eyes and nose, and are running under my chin, disappearing beneath the neck folds of my robe. If I keep this up, the front chest of my robe will be soaked through before long.

What can I do? I begin to shake violently, uncontrollably, in my dream. My knees give way and I sink to the floor, my nurse sinking with me. We are huddled in the corner of the corridor, our foreheads pressing against the cool, damp glass of the window. I am crying harder and harder, and this nurse begins to cry, too.

And then I am awake. I am soaking wet. That is the first thing I notice. Whether it is from tears, from sweat, from urine, or from what, I can't tell. I am crying out. It is early in the morning, and I can hear footsteps outside in the corridor, rapidly approaching my door. Always, those footsteps. The door opens, and the footsteps come over to my bed and stop, looking down at me, trying to see if I am all right. I pretend to be asleep, though I still cry out. There is a tapping on my shoulder. The tapping becomes firmer, becomes a nudging, then a shaking.

I flip my eyes open. It is my nurse. I spin around in the bed and grab onto her wrist with both of my hands. I grab hard, and I can feel my fingernails where they are edging into her skin, drawing blood. I give her a crooked, jagged smile, the best I can give.

She screams, tears her arm away. Literally tears it away. And runs from the room.

There is this mirror in the washroom on the top floor. I look into it from time to time, not because I have any particular interest in the reflection I find therein, but because each time I look in, I want to compare that reflection to the ones that I have seen on previous occasions. Just for the sake of comparison. I look into the mirror this morning, and, dear God, I don't like what I see. Where did this thing come from, this thing that seems to be staring back at me? Dear God.

I move my hair around a bit, to see if that will change anything. I try on a new set of smiles. I half close my eyes, seeing how that looks. Nothing seems to work. I'm stuck with this. I wonder if things look this bad on the inside of me.

Marty's words ring in my head. I try to look through the glass, to see what lies on the other side.

Calmly, and without making a sound, I raise one arm. I make a fist with my hand, and plunge it deep into the mirror, sending the glass in bits and shards across the floor. Some of the fallen pieces, a half-dozen or so, have landed in my arms and on my shoulders. I gather them into my hand. None of them is bigger than a nickel. Broken bits. I arrange them so that they all lie in my palm, an inch or so away from each other. It is an interesting thing, to look into bits like these. There is an eye in one of them. A nose over here. This one of them has the bottom half of a smile. All of me is in there somewhere, disjointed rather than connected in some sort of way, each part staring back up at me. Broken bits.

I turn my palm over and let these bits fall down onto the floor with the others. I bend at the waist, let my arms hang, but my arms do not reach quite as far as I would like them to, down to the floor.

I sigh, and sink down on my hands and knees. The tiles are white and cool and surprisingly soft, save for the places, here and there, where the bits of glass have fallen onto them. I spread my arms out and lower myself forward, turn my head to a side and press my cheek down against the tiles. I close my eyes and feel, just feel, and it is comforting.

After a few moments or so, I push myself up from the tiles, back onto my hands and knees. I sweep my arm across the floor, trying to gather the pieces together into some kind of pile. I start to pick up the pieces, one by one, looking at each of them and trying to make some sense out of them. Each of them has broken in such a way, or has a particular picture to show. I take one between my fingers and hold it close to my eyes, look at it in the light. A second or two, then I add it to the pile, move along to the others.

Yes. These pieces. Yes. Every last one of them counts. And surely, they will all be of some help to me, in one way or another.

ANIMAL STORIES

JASON BROWN

When I first heard about my mother's brain tumor, I got in my car and drove like a lunatic. I am known for erratic bursts of self-destructiveness punctuated by unpredictable lapses in concentration, which make operating a motor vehicle extremely dangerous —I get this from my mother. Any man's mother is a source of grief until she dies.

At the hospital she asks, "What is this thing?" pushing all the buttons on the remote control at once and pointing it at her nose. "It's a hat," she explains, giggling and placing it on the top of her flat, bald head. In the next bed, Sharon, the woman who overdosed on drugs, rolls her eyes. "Life is not my style," Mom says, taking the remote down and handing it to me.

I press play, but just as *The Nesting Habits of the Semipulvinated Plover* comes on the screen, the doctor arrives and stands in front of us; he's come to ask how much my mother has forgotten since yesterday.

By the time this happens, it is too late for me. I already have several chins, and if I were to die tomorrow, only about four people would notice and none of them, except my mother, would be a woman. I'm like a nut magnet—the people I *do* know couldn't tell you what day of the week it is, and the people who want to know me look like they just escaped from somewhere. But I'm a happy man, even though this may be hard to believe given my circumstances. I lost a job (which I disliked anyway), I don't have much money (never will), and older people say I don't know anything (they're right). I once had a girlfriend who said she would marry me if I would agree to change who I am, which is like agreeing to buy a used car that just needs a new engine. Lots of strange things have happened that

I don't understand. If I ever have any money, I'll hire someone to explain them to me.

When people ask what I'm doing now, I say I'm not doing much. I have interests. In 1984 I became interested in nature. You can't blame most people for not thinking, because they work instead, but now that I don't have a job and there is a tumor in my mother's head eating her memories, it's time to think about what's important in life. Lately I've been spending a lot of time shedding things, like jobs and cars and old clothes—trying to think. It's what the trees start to consider doing in late August—at least in this part of the world. It's when life starts to turn in on itself as if it were something that happens once.

"The tumor is fulminant," the doctor says. "We will have to perform the biopsy tonight, and then we will know the extent of its malignancy by morning." He tries to smile, turns around, his business done, and looks at the screen. "Ah," he says, "plovers."

"Not exactly," my mother says.

Sometime in 1977 God had told Mom: watch out for doctors, they just want to touch you. It was not until April of last year that my father, a doctor, noticed that my mother had started losing little things. Once she came into his kitchen, sat down at the table next to him and my stepmother, and said, "David, who is this woman?"

This happened shortly before she lost her boyfriend while on vacation in Nova Scotia while he was taking a nap. She left the bed and breakfast, drove to the nearest airport, boarded a commuter flight, and ended up in London.

"Listen," she said over the phone to me from London, "what do you think about your father and me getting divorced? I think he's seeing another woman."

"You divorced him over ten years ago," I said cautiously. "He's married again. I don't think about it." There was a silence, and then I asked, "Mom, what are you doing in London?"

"I'm happy, Jamie . . . I don't know," she said. "I think I want to meet the Queen."

* * *

My mother believed in God from the 7th of February 1976 to the 10th of September 1977. That winter we had the biggest snowstorm in twenty years, and that spring all the cows in town died of a mysterious disease. Mom used to wander the streets at night, leaving notes from God in people's mailboxes about what was important in life. "Gloves," one would say. "Fresh Milk," said another. "Heat."

This is what happened. We were living in a town outside of Buffalo, New York, called Waterville, which was so free of water during the summer that people went to visit relatives in the next town just to bathe. The town was probably named Waterville because whoever lived there thought constantly about water.

During that summer of 1977 we were sad for each other—it was new to us then. My father moved out and my girlfriend Alice moved in with us. Another friend—Tom, who didn't care what happened to himself because he was overweight—moved in also. Mom spent the summer teaching us how to drink gin. We sat around the kitchen table drinking slowly, not saying much, kind of sinking into a smaller life. We drank until what happened would not be remembered the next day.

"When the doctor comes in again, tell him I'm not going to do this biopsy thing," my mother says to me as if she is talking about a dance step.

"We have to find out," I say.

"I don't want to know," she says, "and besides, I don't have time."

Ever since Mom got to the hospital she's been thinking about what's important, and so she's decided to write a book on how animals remember. In 1979 she changed her name to Meadow Star and developed an amateur preoccupation with the lives of animals. Mom loves animals because they can't remember in the same way we do.

"The dog is an exception," she explains. "It learns from people."

Sharon, who is sprouting little clear tubes filled with liquid, reads to us from *People* magazine. "James Caan married a slut," she says. "What bullshit."

Mom pushes the button on the remote control (which I had showed her how to use) to activate one of the tapes I brought from her house: *The Threatened Pygmy Shrews* from the hills of Great Britain. Apparently, industrial fallout in the rain acts as a narcotic for the animals, causing them to become disoriented and irresponsible. Some of them wander into roads and are killed by cars, some just fail to camouflage themselves adequately and are caught by dogs or other predators. The video shows a pale hand wrapped around the neck of a black-eyed, gray rodent. Another hand moves in to indicate parts of the animal's face. The chemical has been isolated as Cr 34#; it is made outside of Suffolk.

Lately, I've been trying to forget things. Through her book on animals, Mom has tried to teach me little tricks about forgetting, such as trying to think about something else. But most of the time it is useless—like trying not to get wet while you're swimming. For all the energy we spend trying to remember and record our lives, all we really seem to want is to forget. To have forgotten and not know one has forgotten, Mom tells me, is the happiness of animals.

One of the biggest mistakes I ever made was trying to think about who I was by remembering the things I had done. I have consistently been much better at being other people, living out scenarios that I read about in books. My mother was the one who always said that being myself was the most important thing I could do. This was before 1977, of course, after which she became a person none of the family could recognize. But my mother's family cannot be trusted: they are all in the business of killing themselves. Sometimes when people in her family die, they actually have fatal diseases, but it is usually something so intangible as to arouse suspicion, like an attitude or a tendency to think too much about the past. Sometimes it's more subtle: buying land fifty yards away from a nuclear power plant, for example, or eating food with an enormous amount of red dye #2.

"Do we have to keep watching this shit about rudiments?" Sharon moans.

"That's ruminants," my mother replies. "No, we don't have to watch this." She presses the fast-forward button, eager to use her new knowledge. She stops on *Animal Impostors*. A carnivore that looks like a tulip waits for insects to land on its petals before the flower snaps shut and rumbles around for a moment, masticating the captive down its gullet until opening up again, innocently smiling bright yellow.

The angler fish looks like a rock that hasn't moved in centuries, but when something edible floats by, it strikes at 4/1,600 of a second.

"That's a fish?" Sharon says in disbelief.

The coiler snake: first it looks dangerous, then it looks dead. The snake rattles its tail like a rattlesnake, but when its predator, the cat, still won't go away, it rolls over and emits a horrible smell.

The Tasmanian devil, thick set, apparently ill-tempered marsupial that was once plentiful in the time of English explorers, is now rarely seen by tourists. The television camera approaches the devils at ground level. After an initial display of fear, one of the devils rushes the camera, screeching and waving its front paws in the air.

"Where's the bathroom?" my mother asks, getting up out of bed.

"You were just there twenty minutes ago," Sharon says.

"Well, will you tell me which direction I took twenty minutes ago?"

"You go down that way and turn left." Sharon says, pointing with her finger.

"Are you sure?" my mother asks.

"I promise," says Sharon.

I can understand my mother's reluctance to enter these halls without directions, so I walk with her. The hospital is a place where people lose themselves—sometimes part by part, sometimes all at once. Even the people who come out alive, maybe carrying someone else's liver or skin, look like people who have been robbed. We wander down the corridors, past humming contraptions with beeping lights, afraid that around each corner might lurk a cluster of diseases waiting to bore under our skin. There is a paralysis in the air at a hospital. As if the air is hiding some awful secret.

* * *

If you knew me, then you would know that nothing is less like me than the things I've done. If you met me in line at the grocery store, you might think I have been to college and that I at least *could* have received good grades. But my past is pocked by sores, such as an inability to spell my own name. My grade-school teachers declared that I had a condition, but the symptoms varied so much that they were never able to make a diagnosis. I had a kind of roaming retardation in degenerative form. One week I stuttered uncontrollably, the next I could not tie my shoelaces. I visited speech therapy, physical therapy, and a class entitled Living Skills that taught the importance of being clean.

I was born with serious intent and not without means, but somewhere along the line I failed to acquire an adequate degree of clarity. Many potential geniuses lie like broken cars waiting for one missing part. By 1982 I had stopped being in a hurry to improve my life. Shortly afterward I stopped caring so much.

During the summer of 1977 my girlfriend, Alice, who had an IQ measured at 165, said that I reminded her of Procrustes—the Greek god who either stretched or sliced off the legs of his lovers to fit his bed. She was the one who had to have sex three times a day to stay within commuting distance of her sanity. My mother must have known about all the sex in the house—activity we seemed to need like air. For my mother, cooking was as much an act of desperation as our sex. After a while we had to forbid her to use the pots and pans for fear that she would destroy the house. Tom, who had worked in a restaurant, took over the cooking for us that summer. It was just the four of us sitting around the table, mostly eating salad and drinking gin, listening to my mother talk about what a wonderful man she was leaving.

My father was a man of inaction; it is the most valuable thing I learned from him. He also taught me not to worry about what I am not. "You can either be you or someone else," he said. "In the end it really doesn't matter." I can't understand why he said things like that. I don't think thinking ran in his family the way it did in my mother's, though it might have. We never heard much about his family except that they came from a Pennsylvanian mining town where they were all miners or miners' wives. My father was a person with something inside him, an idea that had been ready to burst forth. He used to come over that summer when he left the hospital and work in his garden out back until dark. My mother sat on the second floor, smoking cigarettes, drinking, and watching him bury his thoughts with the azaleas. There is nothing to replace the failure of our parents.

Whenever he encountered my mother that summer while transporting a potted plant to the backyard, my father looked at her as if she were a nice piece of jewelry he had just dropped into the ocean. She was unrecognizable with her hair dyed red and with one of her new orange or purple blouses bought from Goodwill. She was usually a little drunk.

During that summer we moved as little as possible; people outside were dying of heatstroke. By about August we had more or less decamped to the cellar during the daytime, where we remained, slightly refrigerated, until the fall. Occasionally my father joined us in the cellar for a drink, and he would talk about politics with my mother as if they were two people who hadn't been introduced. My mother wasn't sure who was president. She blames the tumor on that summer, which makes sense now. She often remarked how wonderful it was to have all these new friends. Sometimes she looked at me as if I were someone else's son.

Tumors may grow because people can't forget, as Mom says in her book. A psychic friend of the family once said that my mother's soul is older than the rocks in China, which means she has a lot to forget. To me, tumors seem like illusions—they come from nowhere and steal everything. When desperate they will eat anything that we pretend to know.

Mom pauses the VCR and reaches for a drink that the nurse left for her. "What is this?" she asks, looking at me.

"It's a glass," says Sharon.

"I know, but what's in it?" she asks.

The three-toed sloth of Colombia: a living bug carpet—home to beetles, ticks, fleas, and a steady companion, a moth that lays its eggs in the sloth's dung. After hatching, the next generation of moths will fly, seek out sloths, and begin the cycle anew. The sloth catches its prey by curling into a form resembling a shrub where insects might choose to live.

The doctor comes in again to threaten my mother with a total loss of self-awareness followed by a painful sinking into idiocy and death, unless she undergoes the biopsy and allows him to operate. He has seen it happen to other people—they lose themselves. It is worse than death, he says. She covers her face with a *National Geographic* until he leaves.

Following the doctor, two people—a man and a woman, both dressed in black pants, black shoes, black shirts, and with hair dyed black, setting off ghostly pale faces—sidle up to Sharon and shove a paper bag under her pillow.

"Sharon's drug dealers," Mom whispers to me.

The man fingers the tube leading into my mother's arm and comments that her body is worth about four hundred dollars in narcotics. Sharon starts slipping little pills into her mouth.

Unlike the nuthatch and the blue tit, the tree creeper can only move in one direction, which is a serious competitive disadvantage.

Mom can't remember any of this now, but on the 27th of August 1977 my father cut his flowers down with the push mower, after which he never returned to the house again. He didn't see her again until last year, when she burst into his kitchen and demanded to know the identity of his new wife.

The night my father cut down the flowers my mother told me that my father was a cruel man, which is something I have never been able to see. But I learned too late that you should never trust what your parents say about each other. I think I know now that he was just demonstrating how much he could hurt himself, just for us. That was probably the most important lesson he ever taught me— that in a few seconds you could destroy days' worth of work and walk away as if nothing happened, ever. As if you just stepped off a ship from another planet, everything was completely new and nothing had a name.

The things my father taught me about life have made him an unhappy man. The day before he cut down his garden, he looked up and said, "Jamie, it doesn't matter how you feel about things." Then, my hands full of potted azaleas, he said, "Do you want to end up like your mother?"

"No," I said.

"Then don't listen to what she tells you."

We stayed inside, drew the shades, and let ourselves grow like fungi —faster than the grass outside. The only thing that could have helped us would have been a team of highly qualified parapsychologists. That summer, if you had walked by our house, nestled between two colonials on Woodford Road, and stood for a while looking at the peeling paint, the shutters hanging askew, and the five-foot-tall blades of grass, then you might have guessed that the people inside were experiencing some kind of sadness that was being taken very seriously. Or that there were no people at all, that the place had been abandoned for some reason. It wouldn't have been hard, though, to imagine that the three people inside were lying under the sadness of the shadows as if under a giant quilt. If you were a neighbor across the street you might have looked out your window after sundown and seen a small light at the very back of the house and asked the rest of your family if they could imagine what we could possibly be doing under that dirty light. What could possibly have happened to those people?

When my mother and I talk now it is about things like politics or migratory birds that anybody could read about in a book. This is another mistake people make about knowing each other too well— they end up talking about nothing.

The doctor comes in and says, again, that he must do the biopsy or my mother must leave the hospital for the time being.

I looked past him at the images on the screen. The only sad animals I have ever known are the ones in cages or the ones who have spent too much time with people. Animals seem to get better at surviving, but this is not the case with people. We look back and collect antiques. We go to our mothers' closets when we are young, haul out grandparents' clothes from the Jazz Age, and pretend we are Gatsbys. We pretend we are *anything* else. We don't eat, we grow thin and solemn, we think about our lives.

Animals seem to have a way of seeing what's necessary and acting on that. When unexpected things happen to them, such as encounters with human scientists, they look momentarily disoriented before they are at it once again—whether it be pecking through bark for worms, or, in the case of the hermit crab, skittering across the ocean floor in search of an abandoned shell suitable for a new home. Animals seem to know that whatever we lose is returned to us in time.

Normally, I'm an avid carnivore, but whenever I think of that summer when my mother started believing in reincarnation and we couldn't eat chicken, I stick to vegetables and breads—sometimes fish—things that never had legs anyway. I think Tom and Alice spent the whole summer eating mostly celery in order to lose weight. Every day there was less of them.

That summer it felt like we were exchanging secrets, pouring them into each other's glasses and drinking them down. For instance, imagine four ways to kill yourself: Tom's mother had tried and failed to succeed at each one of them. She had a small job in the state prison system having something to do with paper; the only reason her position had not been eliminated by the state budget cuts was that only about three people knew she existed.

Once in a while we went to Goodwill to buy shorts, playing cards, or funny hats. Usually we left laughing, dressed in stripes or checkered and dotted patterns, and sauntered out to the Toyota as walking collages of other people's lives.

But our sadness that summer tasted like licorice, and my mother taught us to savor it. It was, she assured us, our only real friend, and we believed her. Sadness is not learned; it happens to us and seems unavoidable. We learn what to do with it, though. She could not have known that she was teaching us only one kind of sadness—the kind that didn't go away but whirred through our dreams like bedroom fans.

"Jamie," my mother says, dismantling the back of the remote control as if it is a mystery she is trying to get to the bottom of, "how did you do on that biology test?"

"I haven't taken a test since 1983," I tell her.

"Oh," she says, feigning comprehension. "That must have been a long time ago."

"It was," I tell her.

The doctor comes in again, his arms crossed. She tells him that she will be packing in a few minutes, and he leaves without saying a word. The end of the videotape contains short blips on different animals. A buffet: *The dark reputation of the cormorant—also known as sea raven, shag, fish hog. Copulation occurs quickly. The pair mate frequently, insuring the eggs are fertilized.* The camera shows a shoreline covered with hysterical black birds.

"As if that's what they're thinking," Sharon says, hands up in the air, looking at me.

When not breeding or feeding, cormorants are often preening. A black, long-billed bird is shown plucking feathers from its side.

Mom pulls her suitcase from underneath the bed, unplugs the lamp provided by the hospital, and crams it into the lingerie compartment. She pulls her clothes out from the drawers and drops them on Sharon's lap. Sharon picks through each one, throwing the rejects onto the guest chair.

The creatures of Madagascar: the lemur, baki-baki, the malagasy giant jumping rat, and the gastric brooding frog whose young grow in the mother's stomach for several weeks until she belches them out during optimal environmental conditions. *The dozing mouse—not a real mouse, but a close relative. The wild bear . . . followed by flies . . . like people, they are sometimes unpredictable.*

My mother sits next to me in the car: bald, smocked, and medicated. I'm not sure she knows where I am taking her, but she seems thankful to leave the hospital even though soon, the doctor told me, the pain will bring her back again. By that time it will probably be too late.

In the silence I start to think that the good kind of sadness is like a shooting star, which rises from within us, crosses our vision, and then sinks again. This may mean that I am hiding certain things, and I'm sure this is true. But why should that matter? I have come to love the things I do not know about my past. They are like possibilities for the future, which, to any person, is just as important to survival as food.

In a way our sadness was a kind of courage that summer, because we were able to admit our disappointment with every last thing, even if at some level we understood that our disappointment was a kind of crime. What doesn't pass out of our lives, even if it is good, ends up killing us. Finally there is something that won't pass, like a disease or a tumor, that takes us out of life.

I stop in front of the house from 1977. Almost all the paint has peeled off, all the shutters are gone, several windows are broken—it looks like an old man in captivity. I'm almost certain that my mother can't remember the dreams behind buying this house, even though she still, year after year, refuses to move out.

I now remember waking up from a nap in that house on an August afternoon in 1977 and hearing my friend Tom's voice. When I went into his room to see what was happening, I ran into my mother, standing, completely naked, arms spread out, next to his bed. We were all so frozen that I thought it would take an ice pick to free us of that situation. But all it took was Alice's hand on my back for us to scatter like terrified fish into the darkest corners of what even then was a building in collapse.

"Do you remember our trip to Vienna?" she asks, turning to me with a smile. I know that neither of us has been to Vienna. "We went to the opera, didn't we?" she says. I nod. *"The Magic Flute?"*

"It was in German and I couldn't understand a thing," I add.

"But that didn't matter."

"No, it didn't," I say. My mother is in the flowering of her life: her own past has been replaced by the most pleasant memories from other people's lives. Now I have the urge to reach over and touch the side of her face before she gets out of the car, because I know she is dying. But she has darted out of the passenger's seat with her suitcase and run across the street, her bald head glowing under the streetlamp. A few seconds after she disappears into the darkness of the front room, a small, dirty light appears at the back of the house.

This is about my entire life, about everything that I remember. It seems that what we know makes us sad, and what we don't know is who we are. In the end it's all about little possibilities that vanish, like snow. My story is about what happens to sadness after it grows weary and forgets itself. There is only one sadness to speak of, and it has no name. It passes between us like air.

CONTRIBUTORS' NOTES

MARIE ARGERIS (b. 1969) was raised in Burlingame, California, and attended the University of California, Davis. She lives in New York City and works in television.

I wrote "Waiting Game" under a deadline as part of a workshop. Elements of the story came from memory: my mother did try out for a game show, and our car did break down in a wild animal park. I knew I wanted to pinpoint that time in childhood when you are waiting, not to grow up exactly, because that is too nebulous, but to be able to make your own choices and do things the way your parents would not. I called my parents for some help, hoping they would provide me with the details I had forgotten. They humored me. No story.

During one evening of sitting blankly in front of the computer, the first sentence came to me and set up the conflict that pits the three optimists, who preserve the hope that a game show could actually make things better, against a pessimist, or maybe realist, who is confronted with the very adult pressure of their expectations and his own inability to control their situation. I met the deadline.

HOWIE AXELROD (b. 1973) was awarded a Michael C. Rockefeller Memorial Fellowship in 1995, with which he spent a year in Bologna working on a novel. He lives in Tempe, Arizona, where he attends the MFA program at Arizona State University.

Like a lot of stories, "Like a Crossing Guard" began with the end. The scene of the challenge, where Sean knocks the cereal out of Richie's hand, happened to me the summer after my sophomore year in college. I had gotten a job working for a community service group, and during the orientation my roommate and I started to become friends. I was from white suburbia, he from the black inner city, and though we began by stealing glances at each other, we did slowly begin to talk, to hang a shirt or two on the line for the other to see. But, just as I was beginning to feel we were opening up to each other, the scene with the Rice Krispies occurred.

I didn't begin the story until over a year later, when I was in a writing course with Jill McCorkle. I knew that I wanted to write about that confrontation, but I wasn't quite sure how to get there. I didn't want to set the story at a community service group's orientation, and I didn't want myself to be the main character, if only—so my thinking went at the time—because that would make the story less "creative." But alas, Richie is many parts me. Or, more accurately, the type of kid as a teenager I often romanticized myself as being: a street-smart orphan, misunderstood, fighting against the world. The real teenage me came from a loving home, wasn't getting in trouble with the law, and didn't even go to the public high school. But I did, like most teenagers, feel very alone at times, cynical about and distrustful of the people around me; and along with that, I had an underlying need to reach out, which was, as for Richie, hard for me to do. So, though Richie's voice initially seemed a gift from the Muse and a testament to my "creativity," I eventually came to recognize it as a voice of my own, a voice I had tried on several times, at least in my head, as a possible persona.

With the revision process, I began to see more deeply into the characters. Now it is Sean I am most intrigued by—his walls, so much higher than Richie's, and his hidden kingdom inside. At heart, for me, that's what the story is about: the desire we all have, or at least had as children and may have lost portions of along the way, to find goodness in other people; and the need we all have, often despite ourselves, to reach out toward that goodness.

JASON BROWN (b. 1969) grew up in Portland, Maine, and was a teaching fellow in the MFA program at Cornell University. His stories have appeared in the *Georgia Review,* the *Mississippi Review, Triquarterly, DoubleTake,* and the 1996 edition of *The Best American Short Stories.* He was awarded a Wallace Stegner fellowship in 1996, and now lives in northern California.

"The Dog Lover" wrote itself over a period of years. All but the idea of conflict between generations evolved unconsciously. I tried to mine deeper into this dream each time I returned to revise the story, and was often surprised by what I found. Some of the narrator's struggles have been real for me, and some were fictionalized. When I went to work on the story, the boundary between these two worlds dissolved. I had a sense when I became this narrator that I wanted to say everything about life—he feels such an enormous void inside himself, and he hopes to fill it with these words.

I wrote "Animal Stories" when I was twenty-two, the summer before I finished college. My mother had gone into the hospital for an operation and had come out again in good shape, but my relationship with her was bad enough that I had not gone to visit her. The guilt drove this story on.

I was so confused at this time in my life that I could barely make a sandwich, and I certainly could not have written a traditional story. In the afternoons after work, I would sneak over to my father's house and watch animal documentaries on one of the educational channels. I thought they were the funniest things on earth. Everything seemed absurd to me at the time. This was not just a passing growing pain, though it was a pain, and it was, thankfully, passing.

I wrote the story one line at a time and set the order later. I would sit for hours at my job renting canoes and think of one line. On rainy days I might come up with a couple of paragraphs. It took me three months, trying to pull together the fragments around me. When it was over I had the feeling, at least for a while, that my life made sense.

JUDY BUDNITZ (b. 1973) is a native of Atlanta, Georgia. Her stories have appeared in the *Paris Review* and *Story*. Also a visual artist and cartoonist, her work has been published in various newspapers and other publications. In 1995, she was a recipient of a Rona Jaffe Foundation award, and she is presently a fellow in NYU's creative writing program.

I wrote "Park Bench" when I was a senior in college. In the fall I took a play-writing class where one of our first assignments was to write a three-minute play. For the exercise I wrote a scene portraying a speeded-up relationship between a man and a woman.

It was a very confusing play. So I decided to convert it into a story. As I worked at it, the story became something more than a relationship set on fast forward. It became a story about memory, and the funny tricks it can play with time and the past.

The story is also an apt reflection of my own mood at the time. I was writing a senior thesis, and time seemed to be passing terribly quickly. Everything was busy and hectic and crazy, and I felt as if I were in one of those time-lapse films where trees grow and cities spring up in seconds. Yet, even in the midst of it I knew that in a few years I'd probably think back on my senior year as a wonderful time. And I do.

AARON COHEN (b. 1971) has studied creative writing at the Iowa Writers' Workshop and the University of Florida. His stories have appeared in *Quarterly West*. He lives in Gainesville, Florida.

The story of how this story came to be has nothing to do with my or my father's experience in Vietnam. Of course, I never served in Vietnam. And my father, although he *was* drafted, didn't *go* go. He was one of those smart dudes with wild hair and horn-rimmed glasses who sat at a desk stateside, with a slide rule and a pocket protector.

The story instead has all to do with rivalry. One dank, dragging Iowa afternoon, my writer friend Mr. U (we will call him), a colleague and my ping-pong nemesis, received word that he had been awarded a big-ass literary prize. Well, big-ass as far as we infantile and inexperienced writers are concerned. That night, after finding out this sickeningly sweet news, I stood in the heavy shadow and enchantment of his good, and at that time inconceivable, fortune. Floored, exhilarated, with doors of possibility swinging, I thrashed about in my dirty sheets, desperately seeking sleep and retribution (to put it kindly).

Suddenly there came a buzzing sound. I was actually half asleep when this obnoxious rickety thing with rotor blades started flying across my brain, wobbling and grazing rooftops as it went. Finally, in a state of undiluted delirium, I started writing about it.

A week later, I got in my '77 hail-dimpled two-tone Olds and headed for Mr. U's cabin. I delivered the envelope and went for a walk. When I came back, he said, "You've done it. Now cut twenty pages and send it out." I called my dad to tell him I might have written a good story, and without so much as a congratulations he asked if I'd done my research.

For the first time in my life I listened to Dad and set up camp in the governmental stacks at the library. I must have rifled through hip-high mounds of military flight manuals and river explorers' diaries. I was looking for particulars. I even ended up going to the Big Brown Muddy to find out if "my boy Ryan" could really make it all the way down without getting slammed down and torn up if not outright killed.

Two years later, Mr. U is now doing quite well for himself; he's got a wife and kid and is living in the mountains writing an honest novel, and I'm crossing my fingers that he'll win lots more of these big-ass awards so I can keep riding in his wake.

In the meantime, I challenge Mr. U to a simple game of ping-pong.

LUCY HOCHMAN's (b. 1970) stories have appeared in *Caliban,* the *Iowa Review,* the *North American Review,* and *On the Edge: New Women's Fiction Anthology (Chick-Litz).* She has taught writing at Brown University and at Duke University. She lives in Durham, North Carolina.

I decided to start writing and write forward until I came to the end. I'd never done that before. Usually I write a bunch of sentences, put them next to each other, and then write in the space between.

At the time, people in my life seemed interchangeable, the weight placed on any moment seemed arbitrary, the meaning of an interaction seemed dependent on my personal level of desperation more than any omniscient-esque value. Also the song "Getting to Know

You" was on a TV commercial for some luxury car. I mean, a car I could never own.

Also, I was thinking about a person who actually committed to his thoughts, who held them equally, and behaved according to them limited by time and physics rather than by propriety. Also the old thing about how a name/word/arbitrary language structure physically limits a form of reality. Like a person, a culture, all that.

Mostly, I suppose, psychologically, the story comes down to one take on how I hang out at my house with my dog. Sure, it is as reasonable a way to live as any other, regardless of my consistent, utter frustration with my inability to believe in anything, let alone any*one,* regardless of how totally articulate, empathetic, educated, way-cute, and plum (plumb?) stuffed with desire I am. Actually, I could say that about all my stories. Same old, etc. However, luckily, I plan to learn and grow. The goal, as I've been telling my students lately, is not to die.

CRESTON LEA (b. 1971) was formerly the fiction editor of the *Iowa Review* and is a graduate of the Iowa Writers' Workshop. He lives in Vermont.

About a year before I wrote "Indian Summer Sunday," my best friend from childhood days died where he was living out in California. I went back home from where I was living in upstate New York to eulogize him at the memorial service in our hometown, Lyme, New Hampshire. The church was filled with all the different people who live in that little town now: those whose families have been there forever, as well as those who have recently come, in droves, from more southern places. See! — I'm pretty territorial for someone who has left the territory.

The year passed and I was walking around the train tracks by my apartment in Iowa City, where I had just moved, missing my dead friend and thinking about where I'm from and how that place has, in my short lifetime, been transformed from a farm town to the richest place per capita in the state of New Hampshire. I was thinking about the changes being forced on upper New England, about morality, about old colonial Congregational churches with horsesheds in the churchyards, about apple orchards and migrant workers, about addiction, about some chickens my brother used to chase around with a Wiffle ball bat. I went back to my apartment with all this stuff on the brain and wrote this story.

DAN O'BRIEN (b. 1973) was a contributor in fiction at the 1994 Bread Loaf Writers' Conference. Also a playwright and actor, his plays have been produced and performed in Vermont and Maryland. He presently lives in Ireland as a Thomas J. Watson fellow, studying Irish history, culture, and mythology.

"Borges" came to me one night quite clumsily, comically even, when I fell on the ice and struck my head against the pavement. It was one of those wintry evenings when one has the luxury of walking about in the dark while entertaining several tragic and dramatically gloomy topics at once, when suddenly I slipped on a patch of seamless Vermont ice and found myself stretched out prostrate on the cold pavement, looking up into a starry sky. It was as if someone were saying to me, quite forcefully, "No, not down. Look up!" (Perhaps it was the voice of that whimsical but inept Author who writes my life?)

Jorge Luis Borges, like the icy pavement, like my kindred passions for poetry and morbid self-pity, has always given me something of a terrific headache. Labyrinths, cosmic conundrums, onions of consciousness, philosophy masquerading as detective narrative masquerading as historical truth: a mess of solipsism and poetry, a certainty in uncertain truth that seems to confirm all my worst fears (which is consolation enough, perhaps, to have your fears confirmed), but fails to confirm my worst and most dire hopes. Even Borges, despite his better judgment, must have been a man who found hope. So, masquerading as Borges, I went looking for hope in the labyrinth of Coney Island.

So it is a story in the act of composing itself, trying desperately to bring together many apparently disparate themes or emotions or memories. I was confronted at the end (the story's end, but perhaps yet another beginning for the protagonist) by what every writer dreads: a tangible, physical truth, a truism, perhaps the very definition of cliché. But what more just way could exist for a great writer, a monolithic introvert, to find a moment's happiness or elation? I invite anyone to dispute that life can, sometimes, be something of a roller coaster.

In the end, however, I reserve the right to quote Borges himself in offering two responses to this story: "How priggish, perhaps"; and more important—what is the story about?—"I don't know, really." Every word in the story leads only to that final question mark.

ZZ PACKER (b. 1973) is a native of Louisville, Kentucky, and attended Yale University, where she was awarded the Wallace, Bergen and Willets Award in Fiction. She later earned a masters in writing at the Johns Hopkins University in Baltimore, where she now lives and teaches public school. Her stories have appeared in *DoubleTake, New Stone Circle,* and *Seventeen.*

If good, crafted writing is the constipated effort of thinking and writing and rewriting, then I regret to admit that the first draft of this was a bit more like diarrhea. It may not be accidental that I wrote this story—set in a cramped and crowded apartment in cramped and crowded Tokyo—only when I was proximally and culturally removed from the expatriate life. I found myself feeling just as isolated in my wretchedly small efficiency apartment in Baltimore as I had in "lonely-but-never-alone" Tokyo, and this similarity may have brought on the explosive completion of the first draft, from start to finish, in under four hours.

I am incredibly jealous of writers who set out to write a particular story in mind, Freitag triangles mapped out and such. As far as the content and themes in "Geese" are concerned, I can say only one thing: After hearing so many writers analyze their fiction with lines such as "This is a story about *choices,*" or the double-whammy, "This is a *postmodern* story about *anger,*" I cannot bring myself to do it here on this page. If I haven't already ruined the story in its telling, then I dare not risk ruining it in analysis.

BENJAMIN PESKOE (b. 1972) is a native of Louisville, Kentucky, and attended Harvard University. He lives in rural Michigan.

"Flamingo" was originally part of a short story cycle which traced the fortunes of Cathy, her husband, and her kids over a number of years. In "Flamingo" I was interested in the questions it posed: what would it be like to be just out of a treatment center and to go home to an empty house with your children taken from you? I began this story because I didn't know the answers to these questions rather than because I did. I went through three drafts before I began to see that the story was really about guilt and anger, and what is gained by hanging on to them, and how hard it can sometimes be to let them go. For Cathy it is so difficult that she finally fashions it into a choice, as her mother might say, of whether or not she'll "just keep on breathing!"

DAWN KARIMA PETTIGREW (b. 1970) received her MFA in creative writing from the Ohio State University, where she now teaches. She is a regular contributor to *News from Indian Country*. "Manna Walking" is part of a forthcoming collection of fiction and poetry titled *Manna in Gallup*. She lives in Columbus, Ohio.

"I love the Lord because He hears my prayers and answers them. Because He bends down and listens, I will pray as long as I breathe." While reading these words in Psalm 116, I was moved by God's faithfulness to me and to my family. I wanted to celebrate God's goodness in prose.

Drawing on my Cherokee, Creek, and Chickasaw heritage, I created a resourceful and very human heroine, who must depend on Him in difficult circumstances. God dramatically delivers Manna from danger, but He also cares enough to provide her with cool water sprinklers to revive her in the desert. This story is meant to bless readers with the knowledge that God cares about all of us and loves us, always. That knowledge makes me, like Manna, want to pray as often as I breathe.

ADAM PLANTINGA (b. 1973) earned a degree in English from Marquette University in 1995. He lives in Houston, Texas, where he works with street kids in the StreetWise Houston program.

I got the idea for this story from the song "Jimmy Sharman's Boxers" by Midnight Oil. It's a haunting song, one that tells a story. I tried to write that story. I would like to thank Professor C. J. Hribal and his creative writing class for their help and advice with this story.

TIM VANECH (b. 1973) works as an investment executive in Boston, Massachusetts, and as a teaching assistant at Harvard University. His work has appeared in *DoubleTake*.

I began this story after my sophomore year in college. I had transferred from the University of Pennsylvania after my freshman year, and I had sat out the first semester of sophomore year, living at home, painting houses, and scribbling the beginnings of short stories and novels that never got finished. The academics of my first semester at Harvard combined with playing baseball served as distractions from reflection and writing, so I enrolled in a creative writing class for the following summer. One of our first assignments was to produce a page of first-person, voice-driven writing. "White Flight" evolved from this assignment.

In preparation for the assignment, I had thought about my early childhood in a neighborhood with drug dealers, drunks, pimps, and prostitutes. I had gone to high school in a tough area—the shooting in my story is not fictional—and had begun college in a tougher area. At Penn I worked with high school student leaders to seal off crack houses and condemned property, and I found that optimism had died in me. An unhappy year at college, which had followed a tumultuous high school career, was capped off with having a gun pulled on me for the change I was about to put in a Coke machine, as well as having everything that I owned, and my mother's car, stolen from a parking garage in Philadelphia. Flooding the previous night had prevented us from leaving after we had packed to head home.

I was piecing these bits of my past together more than a year later, perhaps looking for a voice with perspective or authority or the power of explanation, when I simply began writing in the father's voice. My own father had recently called me to talk about something that had happened weeks earlier. My younger brother had been thrown down a flight of stairs at school by some members of a gang for no apparent reason. Why my father would call me was beyond my understanding, and that first writing assignment of the summer of 1993, in which I tried to write about the incident in the stairwell using the voice of a father, was how I tried to learn why he was looking to me. That search, assisted at different times by Maxine Rodburg, William Alfred, and Susan Ketchin, led to "White Flight," my first tentative steps in fiction.

PATRICK YACHIMSKI (b. 1974) is a native of Boston and recent graduate of Harvard University. His work has appeared in *Double-Take*.

As I wrote "Asylum," I turned again and again to two short stories: Raymond Carver's "Where I'm Calling From" and Denis Johnson's "Beverly Home," two stories which go far beyond capturing the landscape of a particular convalescent or recuperative place. For me, the main attractions of these stories are the people who inhabit them. These are stories by, of, or about people who are at the cusp, or on the far side of well-being, trying to find their way back to healthier ground.

For some time before I wrote "Asylum," and for some time after, I was part of a group of students trying to make a homeless shelter work successfully. While the story does not draw in any explicit way from what I saw or heard or learned during the time I spent at that shelter, the story does, I hope, speak of some of the human vulnerability present there, in an "asylum," or in almost any other place.

Library of Congress Cataloging-in-Publication Data
25 and under, fiction / edited by Susan Ketchin and Neil Giordano :
introduction by Robert Coles.
    p.   cm.
"A DoubleTake book."
1. Short stories, American. 2. Youths' writings, American. 3. Young
adults — United States — Social life and customs — Fiction.
I. Ketchin, Susan. II. Giordano, Neil.
PS648.S5A147   1997
813'.0108. — dc20
ISBN 0-393-04120-4
ISBN 0-393-31610-6 (pbk.)